W9-AHO-158

ABOUT THE AUTHOR

After stints working in South Asia, Sam Smit is now based in Cornwall, where he helps develop Eden Projects around the world. *The Serendipity Foundation* is his debut novel.

His musical project and other miscellany can be found at www.allthenumerals.com.

Sam Smit

The Serendipity Foundation

unbound

This edition first published in 2016

Unbound
6th Floor Mutual House, 70 Conduit Street, London W1S 2GF
www.unbound.co.uk

Text Design by Ellipsis Digital Limited, Glasgow

A CIP record for this book is available from the British Library

ISBN 978-1-78352-270-5 (trade hbk)
ISBN 978-1-78352-272-9 (ebook)
ISBN978-1-78352-271-2 (limited edition)

Printed in Great Britain by Clays Ltd, St Ives Plc

1 3 5 7 9 8 6 4 2

To Mum and Dad,
This, I suppose, is my thank you letter

Dear Reader,

The book you are holding came about in a rather different way to most others. It was funded directly by readers through a new website: Unbound. Unbound is the creation of three writers. We started the company because we believed there had to be a better deal for both writers and readers. On the Unbound website, authors share the ideas for the books they want to write directly with readers. If enough of you support the book by pledging for it in advance, we produce a beautifully bound special subscribers' edition and distribute a regular edition and e-book wherever books are sold, in shops and online.

This new way of publishing is actually a very old idea (Samuel Johnson funded his dictionary this way). We're just using the internet to build each writer a network of patrons. At the back of this book, you'll find the names of all the people who made it happen.

Publishing in this way means readers are no longer just passive consumers of the books they buy, and authors are free to write the books they really want. They get a much fairer return too – half the profits their books generate, rather than a tiny percentage of the cover price.

If you're not yet a subscriber, we hope that you'll want to join our publishing revolution and have your name listed in one of our books in the future. To get you started, here is a £5 discount on your first pledge. Just visit unbound.com, make your pledge and type **SERENDIPITY** in the promo code box when you check out.

Thank you for your support,

Dan, Justin and John
Founders

The Serendipity Foundation

Sins against hope are the only sins beyond forgiveness and redemption.

Carlos Quijano

For all the large-scale political solutions which have been proposed to salve ethnic conflict, there are few more effective ways to promote tolerance between suspicious neighbours than to force them to eat supper together.

Alain de Botton

PROLOGUE

Two Negotiations

The Crest Voyager Hostage Crisis

4 years earlier
The boardroom of GoldBlue Oil, City of London

'This will be the hardest conversation you've ever had. Remember, no matter what they say, it's not your responsibility. You won't be killing the hostages. They will be.'

Richard looked away from the negotiator, up at the grainy photographs of his five employees. The pixilation robbed them of their present tense, as if destined for tomorrow's papers: obituary portraits for those caught up in tragedy.

'So, is everybody happy with how we're going to play this?' The negotiator paced at the head of the boardroom table. His ex-military realism consoled GoldBlue's executives, convincing them that five lives would be a sad but necessary sacrifice for the protection of principles. It was easier to romanticise martyrdom when you weren't the martyr.

Opposite Richard was the new Foreign Minister, Michael Reyburn, with an adviser on either side, ushering their fledgling minister away from voicing the concerns written over his face. Richard imagined him better suited to a post in Youth and Sports. His anxiety was foregrounded against a panorama of the City from the thirty-third floor. Such scale quickly showed up those who weren't comfortable with it.

Richard scanned the table. His eight board members looked

more enthralled than nervous, having relinquished their moral responsibility to him.

The phone rang. The negotiator looked around the table and nodded, before one of his team picked up the phone and placed it on loudspeaker.

'Hello.'

'Who is this?'

'I'm the lead negotiator for GoldBlue Oil. My name is—'

'Give me the CEO. Put on Richard Pounder.' The male voice had a light Nigerian accent. It was deep and deliberate, betraying no signs of tension. Ted Monroe, the chairman, nodded to Richard.

'This is Richard Pounder.'

'Good, good. Richard. I like your voice. Powerful. Authoritative. You practise with your negotiator? Give first impression that you won't be bullied?'

Richard looked at the negotiator, who shook his head, silently mouthing to him to stay silent. Deep laughter came through the speakers.

'It's OK, Richard. No need to look at the negotiator each time I ask a question. Tell me, who else is in the room with you?'

Richard instinctively looked up. The negotiator pointed to his team, Monroe, and two other directors, bypassing the panicked Reyburn.

'There's me, a three-man negotiating team, and three of my board members.' He was met by a few seconds of silence.

'Richard, you need to be honest with me. Put the minister on.'

'What minister?'

'You think I'm an idiot, Richard? You're a big British company and I've got five British hostages. Put the minister on.'

The ministerial advisers shook their heads at Richard before glaring at Reyburn. The negotiator had warned them that they would have to be strong and stick to what they had agreed on. Government anonymity was high up the list.

'In front of me, I have five men. They're on their knees. They are yours. And there are two other men with guns. They are mine. I will count to three by which time the minister will say hello, or we shoot them. One . . .'

The advisers urgently gesticulated with Reyburn, jotting notes on pads.

'I promise you, there really is no minister here with us,' said Richard.

'Two . . .'

The advisers stared intently at Reyburn, who closed his eyes and covered his face with his right hand. They heard the intake of breath from the speaker. 'Th . . .'

'I'm here. This is the Foreign Secretary Michael Reyburn.'

His advisers shook their heads. The negotiator turned his back and stroked his hair. The others watched transfixed.

'Welcome, Minister. I commend your humanity. The others in the room will call it weakness. Tell me, Richard, are you angry at your minister?'

Richard looked at the negotiator, who mouthed, 'Take control,' with a clenched fist. Richard nodded and took a deep breath.

'Enough of these games. You arranged this call because you wanted to negotiate. So let's focus on that. You've asked GoldBlue to abandon drilling on our rigs in the Niger Delta. I think we all know that's imposs—' Laughter interrupted him mid-sentence.

'Richard, Richard. When did I say we wanted to negotiate?'

Ashen faces turned towards the negotiator, who paused out of concern rather than strategy.

'Let me guess . . . you were waiting for us to come back with something a little more . . . reasonable?' came the voice.

The negotiator nodded his head tentatively.

'You seem to know a lot about how we'd react,' said Richard. 'You know it's impossible for me to pull my company out of an area that has billions invested in it overnight.'

'Come, Richard. You have your rules of the game. Your procedures. Stories you tell yourself. But the stories I tell myself cannot live alongside yours. I see our children die from pollution from your rigs, from starvation by your theft, from murder through your collusion with power. For me, unreasonable is asking for what you think is reasonable.'

The room was silent. Richard no longer looked at the negotiator.

'Imagine you are me. Is it unreasonable to try to rid yourself of the cancer that is killing everything around you?'

Richard sank his head into his hands. With his eyes closed, the voice reverberated throughout his body.

'Tell me,' the voice said, becoming louder and impatient. 'I repeat, am I being unreasonable? As one human being to another, tell me.'

'I . . . I . . .' As Richard stumbled, the negotiator strode urgently to the intercom system and switched off the microphone.

'Mr Pounder . . . Richard. Look at me. I know this is hard. I do. But remember what we talked about. *You* aren't negotiating with him. Don't let him engage you like this. Take a step back and start—'

'Your negotiator telling you to take charge, Richard? Here's something for you to discuss. Unless you tell me it's your company that's unreasonable, I'll shoot them right now. I need to hear you take responsibility. You have one minute.'

Richard took in the room. The once familiar corporate art, the plasma screens and whiteboards, coffee cups and assorted biscuits offered no comfort now.

'They're words . . . they're just fucking words,' said Richard to no one in particular, the mic still muted. 'You can't risk the lives of five men for a few meaningless words.'

'But they're not just words, are they?' said Monroe calmly, as if unaware of the timeframe. 'They would be words undermining our reason for being.' He had a confrontational drawl, contrasting sharply with his small, ageing frame. 'Start allowing the story of what we are to become complicated . . . it all falls down. The company has its own ethics, Richard, which overrides our own. We are not the problem. Humanity is, and we're a necessary product of it.'

'What the fuck are you talking about?' shouted Richard.

A seething silence descended.

'Thirty seconds,' came the voice.

Monroe leaned forward and took a sip of water. 'These words mean nothing. I don't hear a deal here. Meanwhile they'll know we're chicken-shit. You really think they're serious? They're going to kill the hostages, just like that? They're the same as all these other motherfuckers who ring in thinking the world gives a shit about them, and we offer them a few hundred thousand and ride off into the sunset. This is the first play of a long game, and we stay strong. Gimme a show of hands. Who's with me on this?'

They looked to their stricken board members. All, tentatively, raised their hands.

'And you, Minister?'

Reyburn, his hands visibly shaking, stared at the table, unable to square their consensus with his own instincts. 'Surely we need to view this as a way to buy more time,' he said. 'How can we be debating something so trivial, based on your hunch that they're bluffing?'

Several board members shuffled uncomfortably in their seats; the others tried to avoid making eye contact.

'May I clarify,' one of Reyburn's advisers said nervously, 'that the government is not party to this negotiation, and our presence cannot be used as an endorsement of any decision taken here.'

Monroe nodded.

'Ten seconds.'

No one said anything, not wishing to undermine the fragile resolve of the group – one many would later deny sharing.

The negotiator turned the microphone back on.

'So, Richard. It's down to you and me now. The others don't care. Tell me you are the problem. I need to hear it now.'

Richard could feel the eyes of the room upon him. 'It doesn't have to be like this. We can work this out. Just give us a bit more time.'

'We're not bluffing, Richard. We're not fucking bluffing. You can stop this.'

Richard covered his face with his hands, unable to think. 'Please, you don't need to do this.'

'Is there anybody there willing to stand up for these men?' came the voice angrily. All eyes were on Reyburn, who in that brief moment shrank in surrender to the deafening silence.

'Very well,' shouted the man. 'You've made your decision, now live with the consequences.'

Five shots rang out. The phone went dead.

The Kidnap of Police Commissioner El Sayed

January this year
A ramshackle first-floor room off a secluded street in Old Cairo

Thin beams of light streamed through the shutters. A ceiling fan struggled in the thick humid air. Black and white portraits hung from the wall: sinister clues to an impenetrable puzzle.

'Come, sit.' The kidnapper motioned her rifle to a small wooden seat. Opposite sat a silent second figure, similarly dressed in black, with a balaclava hiding their face.

'You know why you're here, don't you?' said the one with the gun.

He shrugged ironic innocence. Her voice sounded young. Fourteen? Fifteen? The silent one seemed older.

'Come on, why have we kidnapped you?'

'You think your grievance against me is special?' He smiled and shook his head dismissively. 'You think I remember everything that happens, everyone who gets hurt along the way? Tell me who you want released or how much money you want. I can do that for you. But you think you'll make me . . . regretful?' He sat back defiantly. 'Do what you've got to do.'

The gunwoman laughed, perched on a cabinet near the window. 'We're here because the community needs us to be.'

El Sayed snorted contemptuously. 'And what community

might that be? And who put you in charge to save it? If it wasn't me, others more ruthless would take my place. You think being the law is all black and white? Look at you, saving your community with a gun.'

'I am the law!' impersonated the gunwoman.

The other figure sat back and crossed her legs. The eyes seemed to smile at El Sayed.

'Are you anything else apart from the law, Mr Commissioner?'

El Sayed narrowed his eyes. 'What are you talking about?'

'I mean, do you also see yourself as a father, as a husband?'

He glared. 'You touch my son and I'll kill you.'

'Relax, Mr Commissioner. Your family is safe. Did you think about what we asked you?'

El Sayed wiped the sweat from his forehead and moustache.

'And?'

'And what? Let's stop playing. What do you want?'

'It will help us both if you take our request seriously.'

They locked eyes. He grunted, before staring aimlessly at the ceiling. The two kidnappers exchanged a glance.

'Your son,' she said, starting to pace behind El Sayed. 'I asked if you thought of yourself as a husband or father, and you responded by only defending your son.' She left the sentence hanging. 'You love him very much, yet spend no time with him.'

El Sayed's tone softened. 'How would you know?'

She continued pacing. 'You used to play football with him every week. He looked up to you. Then you stopped coming to his school matches.'

'Who the hell are you?'

'That's irrelevant.'

There was silence. El Sayed heard each footstep as a subtle

judgement on his parenting. 'Life isn't about kicking a football around in a park,' he said. 'Life is violent. It's war. What I do, I do for him.'

'How happy that must make him.' She stopped and stared at him.

'I don't have the time to do everything.' He breathed out heavily and rubbed his face. 'This is ridiculous. Justifying missing a football match when I'm dealing with the fate of the country.'

'Maybe the fate of every country rests on fathers watching their sons' football matches.'

'The terrorist philosopher speaks. Do you have any idea how the real world works?'

'And how is that real world working for everybody? How many problems has it solved recently?' She continued pacing, slowly, deliberately, patiently disarming El Sayed's defences, letting him move the conversation on when he was ready.

'And what would you have done with the real world, then? Suspend it? Ignore it? Turn it upside down?'

'Of course,' she said, exchanging glances with her accomplice, before taking the seat opposite El Sayed. 'Why else would you be here?'

With the commissioner missing for a week, many had presumed, and hoped for, the worst. He was a man who inspired no empathy. He had betrayed the community that had raised him: arbitrary arrests, selective justice – a home-grown example of how power corrupted.

A week after his disappearance, the ransom appeared. It was childish, vague, an open invitation to seal his fate.

> To secure the release of Police Commissioner El Sayed, the main market street must be closed, without the help of

state authorities, for an under-16s football match. Kick off 5pm, tomorrow.

The neighbourhood was incredulous. It seemed insulting that while their sons lay in jail, El Sayed could be freed so flippantly. Why didn't the kidnappers ask for their loved ones' release instead? Something tangible. Something just.

The following morning, the teahouses were ripe with arguments about the rights and wrongs of inaction. Street-side vendors gossiped about how various factions would force the street to stay open. Why should they save a man who had caused such pain?

Some spoke of how the ransom was a challenge to the community to show they were better than those who ruled. But were these people not aware of the realities around them? The brutality, the corruption – the idea of uniting to save a hated man struck many as offensively romantic.

In the early afternoon plain-clothed policemen mingled among the crowds, whispering veiled threats: promises of future crackdowns if the neighbourhood left their boss and protector to his fate. Warnings were made about the safety of wives and sons. But this only strengthened the resolve of those who finally felt armed with the advantage.

At 4pm traffic gridlocked the main street: taxis and bikes fought for every inch in between street vendors and those unloading goods. Elderly men stared from cafés. Traders collected on pavements. They talked excitedly about the inevitable conclusion, ignoring the seed of guilt growing in their hearts. Policemen loitered by the junction, weighing the repercussions of closing down the street against the ransom's instructions.

At 4.30 a woman and boy held hands as they walked along the pavement. The boy wore an oversized replica of the national team kit and carried a football under his free arm. Pedestrians stepped back and fell silent as they passed. The two stopped halfway down, the eyes of the street upon them. The woman kissed the boy lightly on the head before entering a teashop, leaving him alone. His shining eyes nervously skirted those in the shop before he looked down and stared at his trainers.

The twelve-year-old son of El Sayed stood vulnerable and alone before them.

They tried loading the wrongs of his father on to him. They tried placing his imminent loss into the perspective of the many who had lost their fathers before him. They tried looking away, their silent collusion justifying that this was the way things must be.

And yet El Sayed's son remained, name on the back of his shirt, football in hand, ready to save his father. His presence reflected and amplified their lingering guilt. In his innocence he seemed unaware of why the crowd was behaving this way.

An elderly man stood up from his seat. 'It should not be like this.' He stepped out on to the street and placed his arm around the boy's shoulders. Others stood and followed.

Wishing for a bad ending was different to taking part in it.

Scuffles and threats met the swelling numbers who directed traffic away from the street. For years the neighbourhood had been intimidated; but in the minutes that followed, people ignored their fear and found themselves blocking taxis and helping to unload trucks parked on the street.

Makeshift goalposts were erected. Teenage boys appeared, swarming around El Sayed's son, arguing only about the picking of teams. An irresistible momentum now took over. Cars that had been purposefully abandoned were pushed clear. Immovable trucks were integrated into the pitch.

Confused by the ridiculousness of the situation, the opponents of saving El Sayed were reduced to petulant remarks; stopping proceedings would have meant violently dispersing a group of young footballers who were an assortment of cousins, brothers and nephews.

The crowd retreated to the pavements. A man appointed himself as referee and selected two captains to shake hands. The whistle blew.

PART ONE

The Hostages

Liam

Thursday, April 9th
London School of Economics lecture theatre

'So, what's your favourite kidnap?'

'My favourite?' Liam emphasised the second word disdainfully. 'Kidnaps aren't the type of thing you're supposed to have favourites of.'

'Come on,' said the male journalist on the second row. 'You've spent eighteen months writing a book on them. There must be one that does it for you.'

Liam looked across at Dr Mosley, the professor chairing the event, attempting to convey that this was not the sort of question he thought appropriate at his book launch. Dr Mosley seemed eager to hear Liam's response.

'Why? What's yours?' Liam asked the young journalist. He folded his arms, and let his face rest in his trademark dissatisfied expression.

Book launches for other authors consisted of fans and well-wishers; his were opportunities for his detractors to socialise together, where journalists goaded him into controversial soundbites. It was an unspoken agreement: they gave Liam publicity in return for painting him as the pantomime villain.

'That's easy,' said the journalist. 'John Paul Getty. Classic kidnapping mistake: take a hostage the family don't want back. His billionaire grandfather only agreed to pay the ransom if it was tax deductible.' Cautious laughter filled the half-full LSE lecture theatre.

'I'm surprised your favourite part wasn't when the kidnappers cut off his ear and mailed it to the police during a postal strike.' Liam's thin smile failed to turn the jibe into banter.

The journalist shrugged with a grin. 'Just thought it'd be nice to balance the serious tone with something a little more accessible.'

Liam's smile now flirted with a grimace; he had built the book's premise around a list of failed abductions, before intellectualising it with the history of kidnappings: warring tribes, empire building, the slave trade, bride stealing, fundamentalism and rendition. Its title, which lay projected on to the back of the stage, reflected its contrived basis: *Kidnap: A Tale of Alternative Taxation in a World of Inequality*.

'I'll take your invaluable suggestion on board,' Liam said as he took a sip of water, and placed the glass back on the table that lay between his and Dr Mosley's seats.

'Yes . . . well . . .' Dr Mosley flustered over her notes. 'One thing I found particularly interesting in the book was the divide between purely money-driven kidnappings, and political kidnappings: selfish greed versus a strategy to force a better world. You seemed to have a pretty damning opinion of the latter.'

'That's because none of them has ever been successful.'

Dr Mosley smiled politely and fiddled with the cord of her glasses behind her ear. 'Success is relative, though. Maybe some *you* deem fruitless, others view as having achieved some of their aims.'

'Can you name me one?' He instantly regretted continuing with the dismissive tone he had adopted with the journalist.

Dr Mosley puffed out her cheeks to the audience, raising a few charitable smiles. 'What about the Iranian hostage crisis? It worked for Khomeini in rallying personal support and propaganda against the west.'

Liam purposefully nodded encouragement, as an apology. 'Maybe. But the crisis led to Iran becoming a pariah in the international community, so that when Iraq attacked, it received no support. A million Iranians died in the following war. For me, that isn't success.'

Dr Mosley nodded, deep in thought.

'Any other ideas of a successful political kidnap?' said Dr Mosley, scanning the audience below. There were maybe 150 people scattered around the ground-floor seating; the upper tiers remained empty. Journalists and academics monopolised the front row, with the public and students at the back. Dr Mosley pointed to a woman in her forties, halfway down.

'What about the Crest Voyager crisis? I know they asked for the oil company to leave Nigeria altogether, but I think part of their motive was to show the world how heartless capitalism is. And on that point, many people think they were successful.'

'I'm sorry – you think that by murdering five innocent people, the kidnappers showed that *other* people were heartless?' Liam shook his head.

'I'm . . . I'm not saying that they looked any better,' said the woman. 'But desperate people don't have the luxury of an alternative.'

'You're saying the needless killing of five people was their only alternative? How about not killing five people? Given the choice, would you kill five innocent people, or would you choose not to?'

'I'm not sure that's exactly what she was trying to say,' Dr Mosley tried to interject.

'No it wasn't, but it's where her logic ends up.' Liam had worked himself up into the intellectual self-righteousness the press had come for. 'Liberal opinion is filled with people making excuses for evil done by the poor. There are plenty of people in similar situations who choose not to take five hostages and kill them in cold blood. Maybe you should focus on those trying to improve their lives ethically rather than become an apologist for an act of terrorism.'

The theatre went quiet, except for the eager tapping of laptop keys as journalists recorded their lead quote. Dr Mosley shuffled some papers and made notes to try to look preoccupied as she thought of a way to change the subject.

'So . . . I was wondering, considering what you just said, do you think there's any cause, or situation, that could ever justify a kidnapping?'

Liam sat back in his seat and gave himself a few seconds to calm down. 'No. A worthy cause will always do itself more harm.'

'So there's no point in trying? The desperate should give up as history's not on their side?'

'Look, don't get me wrong, there're a lot of evil people in the world, and the least they deserve is to be abducted and locked in a room for what they've done. I'm not being squeamish. I'm being practical. You kill an oilrig worker, the oil company puts more guns and security on their rigs. You successfully trade prisoners – don't be surprised if your enemy kills those they capture next time instead of jailing them. You take a rich man's money – don't be surprised if he pays for someone to hunt you down. Kidnaps put the have-nots against the haves. The haves like revenge and control the resources to realise it.'

'So there's absolutely no circumstance where you think it could work?' probed Dr Mosley.

Liam was tempted to reply immediately in the negative, before catching himself on the intake of breath, and elaborating on the thought that had just entered his mind.

'A successful kidnap, I suppose, has the same quality as a successful con. A great con leaves both the con artist and the victim feeling like they've had a good deal. In the same way, a successful kidnap would require the ransom to ask for something those being ransomed would *want* to give . . . a demand they would demand from themselves—'

Liam broke off, staring at the back of the lecture theatre. 'But I am yet to come across a case of this happening.'

Michael Reyburn

Friday, April 10th
10 Downing Street, London

Demands. Ultimatums. You have to do this or we'll have to do that. *Have to.*

Michael could tell a situation was grave when groups talked of being *forced* to do something they didn't want to. Bankers, religious extremists, union leaders: self-selected mediums for the coercive powers of money, God and the zeitgeist. Who the hell did they think they were? They were left with *no choice but to do this*, even though the demands they forced on Michael had only been decided upon after hours of procrastination.

Then there were the arbitrary timeframes. *You have two weeks to change this*; *your army has one month to leave*; or the one that haunted him the most: *you have one minute to admit responsibility for*. He respected the power of a deadline, but the lack of realism tended to create a sense of inertia rather than urgency.

Most of all he disliked the confrontation. Not because he was the type of man who reacted better to a request when it ended in *please* (although he was), but because it made him feel like the enemy. He would happily champion many of the ultimatums (with a few tweaks in vocabulary): raising wages, ending military occupations, redressing the injustices of global capitalism. They were in his manifesto.

He just wished they could do things together in partnership, rather than at metaphorical and, occasionally, literal gunpoint. Demands created conflict, opposition where none existed before. He accepted that not having done them yet implied he might need a gentle push, but government proved to be a blunter instrument than he had dared imagine. He, too, was frustrated. But he was an ally, not an adversary.

But ransoms transformed issues into principles. They gave those in power an out: never mind the murder of innocents, because we do not negotiate with terrorists. Forget helping the needy, because you can't afford the precedent. Forget right and wrong, empathy, humanity. The principle of non-negotiation trumped all else.

Michael had made a list of all the demands he had faced while in government, and the majority read like a utopian manifesto. Maybe extreme measures were all that were left to people when faced with a system that lacked any empathy. He didn't know any more.

'Yes, Prime Minister, that's correct. You *have to* push through this banking legislation in *one month*, or my union *will be forced* to strike.'

He had grown to despise them all.

Michael stared out the window towards the hum of tourists gathered by the security gate.

'Prime Minister.'

Michael turned around, slightly dazed, and struggled a smile at his press officer Charlie, who was eating breakfast out of a bag saturated with grease.

'Everything all right?'

Michael shrugged. 'Nothing I can't handle as indecisively as always.'

'Heard the bankers are making threats over your reform suggestions.'

'I'll force their talent elsewhere apparently, and we can't have them destroying someone else's economy when they could be destroying ours. I'm betraying my lack of business acumen.' Michael took a seat opposite Charlie.

Charlie smiled as he wiped some rogue puff pastry from his two-day stubble. 'And the unions are serious? They'll strike unless you submit the reforms to parliament?'

Michael pursed his lips, flicking a pen around his thumb using index and middle fingers.

'The unions know you can't agree, right? You'll look like you're being held to ransom.' Four years on from Crest Voyager, Charlie still felt bad for using the word around Michael, like using the word *dead* around the bereaved.

Michael forced a smile.

'Look . . .' Charlie said warmly, 'unless we become a little more proactive, the press will deal with it for you.'

Michael nodded absently and turned back towards the window. 'Good luck to them.'

Liam

Friday, April 10th
Newsdesk of the Daily Voice, *London*

'Enjoyed the book. Many editors would be a little pissed if they didn't get a preview of a book one of their staff wrote.'

'Pleased you enjoyed it,' Liam said without pleasure, taking a seat next to his press editor Jane Barrett, who remained staring at her computer screen as she spoke.

'Wilcox across the road called. Requested I ask you if you think he's a terrorist sympathiser.'

'Probably.'

'My hunch too. But apparently he wasn't just making small talk.' Liam stared back, motionless. Barrett pulled her eyes away from the screen for the first time and towards the jumble of papers on her desk. 'That became apparent when one of my interns brought me a copy of, well, any of today's news-papers.' Barrett placed a couple of them close to Liam. 'YOU'RE A TERRORIST SYMPATHISER,' POWELL TELLS SINGLE MOTHER, read a headline.

'It's strange. Whenever Crest Voyager is bought up, you transform yourself from a man people dislike but respect, to a man people simply dislike.'

Liam lost himself for a moment as he read the various accounts of him accusing a woman – who turned out to be a forty-two-year-old nurse and mother – of sympathising with evil. 'And what would you recommend?'

'For starters, I'd urge you never to write a book about it; but if you did I'd ban you from holding a book launch, giving interviews, or opening your mouth generally in any direction.'

Liam sat back in his seat.

'Liam,' Barrett said, taking off her glasses and pushing her hair behind her ears. 'You've been here a long time at the *Daily Voice*, and as our readership has become more liberal, you've taken it upon yourself to even things out. You're our token hawk. But you've got to avoid labelling single-mother nurses who volunteer their weekends to help the disabled as terrorist sympathisers; especially when their views match those of your editor.' Barrett raised her eyebrows. 'It might work for your book sales, but it doesn't work here.'

When he'd started at the paper, nearly two decades earlier, he'd been conspicuous for being more liberal than the paper's editorial – breaking stories highlighting the destructive nature of multinationals on their environments, the collusion between energy companies and states, and human rights abuses committed in the name of democracy. His style built a reputation, but few friendships along the way. Barrett, then a fellow journalist, made a deliberate effort to be a friendly face. From then on, everyone saw them bound to each other: maybe not as friends, but perhaps as mentor and protégée. As the next decade passed, and he embarked on his journey from activist to right-wing commentator, Barrett became his editor; it drove a confused loyalty.

'So what? You want me to apologise to this woman for disagreeing with her?'

'It's a shame, as a writer, you don't recognise the problem lies not in the disagreement, but how you frame the argument. As the realist I'm paid to be, I know you'll view an order to apologise as compromising your integrity. So let's start with you trying for a few weeks to avoid criticising others. And in the meantime you might want to look into a few rumours I've been hearing from our stringer in Cairo.'

Liam looked blankly at Barrett. 'What's happened in Cairo?'

Barrett smiled mischievously. 'It seems there's a group undermining the whole thesis of your book.'

The Kidnap of Head Teacher Salma Mirza

When Miss Mirza didn't arrive at school on Monday morning, her staff were immediately concerned. When she hadn't called by break time, her assistant visited Miss Mirza's house to no response. This was a school she had almost single-handedly saved through a decade of onslaughts from local government, property developers and extremists. The school remained in a permanent state of dilapidation; she had joked that so many plasters had been stuck on it that the structure was 80 per cent gauze. In a community that had become increasingly transient and crowded, she was a figure everyone knew and respected.

The police were called in on Tuesday. The recent release of Commissioner El Sayed had led to an uneasy truce between the community and the local police force. But no leads were forthcoming. The police widened the net to Greater Cairo, but by the end of the week worst-case scenarios dominated people's thoughts. Parents and ex-pupils reflected on how they had taken her leadership for granted.

On Sunday morning, early risers found the following message on posters stuck on walls around the neighbourhood.

We have Head Teacher Mirza. To secure her safe return,

60,000 EGP must be raised by Tuesday afternoon. The maximum donation is 200 EGP, and will be collected in buckets at the school reception. All donors must leave their names and amount donated in the provided books. Cheating will end badly.

It seemed safe to presume this was the work of Commissioner El Sayed's kidnappers. Yet he himself proved useless to the investigation, claiming his captors had neither spoken to him, nor shown their faces, and no, he hadn't any idea if Miss Mirza's life was in danger.

At 8am on Monday morning, Commissioner El Sayed joined the donation queue outside the school.

Richard

Tuesday, April 14th
GoldBlue Oil offices, London

Richard pressed his face against the glass wall of his office, craning for a view of the pedestrians 30 floors below. Early in his career he had believed there was a correlation between the level of your office and the power you had to change the world; now he would only vouch for the improvement of the view.

After guiding a small mining company from villain to ethical stock market hero, headhunters offered him the opportunity to recreate his success on a global stage. A couple of high-profile accidents had left marine driller GoldBlue Oil looking to rebrand, and they needed a young, progressive CEO to make the transition credible, and they were prepared to pay for it: a brand-new mission statement, wedded to a commitment to explore a new energy future was what it took to make him jump. At his inaugural speech to the shareholders, he held out a vision of the future where the name of the company stood proud for the gold of the sun and the blue of the ocean waves.

Now, 16 years on, he was preparing for the big goodbye. He had seen it coming for a long time, and yet as he prepared for the inevitable showdown, all he could think about were the reasons he hadn't quit: the power, the respect, the being somebody. He had never been in denial. From the start he shook hands with dictators and fought regulation. Oil, the lifeblood of the age, couldn't choose whose land it lay under. But he was convinced one day he would build a company that had no need for such glad-handing.

As the honeymoon period wore off, it became clear the board loved the brand, not the substance. Renewable energy initiatives were greeted with great fanfare, but then offered every assistance short of actual help. The present was profitable; the future would have to wait.

And then five of his employees were kidnapped from the Crest Voyager.

The vanity of power ill prepares you for the reality of grieving widows and fatherless children – the pain of being found wanting when it really mattered. He spent restless nights creating stories that would absolve him from blame, wishing for anonymity in a dizzying cast of thousands.

And then there was his board, resolute in the defence of its convictions: a commodity, like any other, that has a price. While they sat in the shadows, Richard became the face of corporate heartlessness.

On his office wall hung, as it had done for a decade, a poster of a Teddy Roosevelt quotation:

> It is not the critic who counts; not the man who points out how the strong man stumbles, or where the doer of deeds could have done them better. The credit belongs to the man who is actually in the arena, whose face is marred by dust and sweat and blood; who strives valiantly; who errs, who comes short again and again, because there is no effort without error and shortcoming . . . who at the best

> knows in the end the triumph of high achievement, and who at the worst, if he fails, at least fails while daring greatly, so that his place shall never be with those cold and timid souls who neither know victory nor defeat.

Its display was tactical. Adversaries arriving for meetings would scan the words and be on the back foot before the conversation had even started. But there were side effects: Richard came to believe the primacy of simply being in the arena. Bad decisions could be excused purely by having made them; opponents were dismissed as naïve non-combatants.

This led to an initial bout of self-righteousness in the wake of Crest Voyager. The media scrambled to hold him responsible; his photo framed next to grainy images of the deceased. He was portrayed as a cold pragmatist, unilaterally weighing the odds. He steeled himself to it – people preferred blaming a celebrity rather than a system. But this time it was more personal. In the *Daily Voice*, the journalist Liam Powell traced Richard's descent from a young progressive CEO to one who sacrificed employees in order to retain his ability to pollute. The article was a hatchet job, but this time it was accompanied by memories of the distraught families he had tried to console.

The victims had joined him in the arena – one increasingly crowded with ghosts whose existence he had previously ignored.

In desperation, he tried to find comfort in minor acts of rebellion.

It began with lifestyle changes that would have confused those close to him, had such people existed. He became vegetarian, cycled his bike, recycled his waste, and cold cycled his laundry. He even volunteered to join a team cleaning the wings of seabirds after an oil spill on the east coast. But none of these acts soothed the festering contempt he felt for himself.

He started signing online petitions for good causes. One night, in his inbox was a request to sign a petition against GoldBlue. It was a strange moment, as if the ether had placed a direct challenge to make a long-awaited stand. He scrolled up and down, rereading the case against him. The text was emotive and embellished, but the argument of GoldBlue's continued breach of environmental regulations held true. The barometer of millions of other signatories increased before him, as did the financial pledges to continue the legal fight against GoldBlue. He stared at the screen, unsure if the petition signalled a watershed moment in his life, or an act that would be instantly lost in the digital universe. He entered a fake name, only to be told the correlating email did not exist. After a couple of deep breaths, he entered his name, email address and card details, with a £25 donation.

And then things began to spiral. He gave a larger donation to an environmental pressure group a couple of weeks later. Soon after, he received a call asking if this was *the* Richard Pounder. He hesitantly agreed. The caller introduced herself as Fiona Kittle, the head of the pressure group. He mumbled an excuse that even GoldBlue's detractors deserved the resources to hold them accountable. Fiona made no attempt to probe his intentions further. Twenty minutes later, after a conversation that surprised Richard for its warmth, he agreed to meet Fiona for dinner.

At face value, there was nothing inappropriate about such a meeting: GoldBlue still coveted environmental credentials, and she indisputably held them. But he could feel the recklessness within him. They met at an Italian restaurant chain in the West End. She stood up as he arrived and hugged him like an old friend. She was in her early fifties, had lightly greying brown hair, a twinkle in her eyes, and wore a skirt and jacket that broke the scruffy environmentalist stereotype Richard refused to let go of. She exuded confidence.

'Richard, we're on the same team,' she said as she sipped from her third glass of red. 'You want what I want. My role is to make your job easier by putting your board under a little pressure.' Usually he felt apprehensive when spoken to about being part of a team, but he felt a kinship with Fiona. 'It's ridiculous the way you were treated after Crest Voyager. I was very disappointed with the coverage,' she said as they finished coffee, cementing the goodwill.

They saw each other every couple of weeks, and exchanged the odd email or text in between. At no point did their relationship hint at anything beyond platonic. She represented a rare chink of sympathy, matching each of Richard's anecdotes of thwarted ambition with one of her own. They plotted ways to change the system, without ever asking anything from each other. She invited him to dinner parties, introducing him to a range of people he had previously viewed with suspicion: fellow activists, scientists, government advisers and entrepreneurs. Richard felt their reserve melt away as Fiona championed him – she vouched for his good intentions. In front of him lay a world filled with people who understood the pressures he faced, where he felt he could slowly learn to forgive himself.

So when, on a Wednesday three years and eight months after Crest Voyager, he received a request from Fiona, he had no idea what to do.

'Richard. We've been working on a report about how energy companies have been blocking the development of renewables: sitting on patents and companies they've acquired, cutting R and D, launching green brand campaigns while inflating the quantity of reserves that won't be pumped for decades. You've told me so many stories about how your board blocked the funding they promised you. This is the opportunity to put them under pressure. But . . . well, we're going to need some hard evidence.'

He felt sad and disappointed as she spoke, foolish for being so blatantly played. Or had he been? Was this not the natural conclusion of their conversations? The public airing of hypocrisies he had suffered so long alone.

His instincts told him it was a bad idea.

That week, Fiona invited him to an exhibition launch. She didn't mention the request. It was as if the evening were a showcase of everything he would be granted in return. The path to redemption glittered before him. At their next meeting he handed her a padded envelope. She nodded and drew no further attention to it.

Anxiety filled the following week; every phone call sent adrenalin rushing through his body. But the tension eased as the weeks passed. He sat in the monthly board meeting, strangely exhilarated by the fact that they had no idea what was coming.

But soon after, Fiona rang. 'I'm sorry. Please believe me, Richard. I had no idea this would happen. I told them in strictest confidence. They knew this was absolutely confidential.'

'Told who, what?'

'The writers . . . of the report. They wouldn't include it unless the source was verified.'

'You told them it was me?'

'Richard, these are people I trust. They swear they spoke to nobody.'

'So what makes you think they did?'

There was a pause. 'I got a call.' Fiona breathed out heavily. 'They know, Richard. Your board knows.'

*

The emergency board meeting was about to start. He put on his jacket, and stared at the book that lay on his desk: *Kidnap: A Tale of Alternative Taxation in a World of Inequality*. The author had chosen a more conventional path to closure.

'How is everyone?' Richard said, as the board settled into their seats around the rectangular table. He was met with silence.

Monroe sat at the opposite end of the table, his stare bypassing the five executives sitting on either side. 'How's yours been, Richard?' There was menace in his slow delivery.

'Had better.'

'This meeting has only one agenda item, so let's get to it.' Monroe held up the report and dropped it theatrically on the table, all the time looking at Richard. 'What does our chief executive recommend?'

'We could deny the claims,' said Richard with a noncommittal shrug. 'Or we can try to turn this into a positive.'

Monroe smiled coldly. 'A positive, you say, Richard.'

'We could relaunch our commitment to a progressive agenda – with a programme and money up front. Our critics will be left with yesterday's news. We will own this story.'

Monroe took his time, wetting his lips as he prepared. 'My main concern right now, Richard, is that there's a rat in our organisation. Any idea who that might be?'

'There're 50 staff with access to our ledgers and budgets, and many others who cared about the technology we acquired. It'll take time.'

Monroe nodded. 'I don't understand how we left ourselves in such a position.'

'We made a song and dance of buying technology we claimed would change the world. Any reporter can go to these labs and see they're closed.'

'I don't remember pinning internal memos on the doors.' Monroe angrily continued, 'You seem to have avoided all criticism in this report. Instead it's the evil board blocking the dreams of our dear visionary chief executive.'

'I didn't read it like that, Ted. I think you're being a little paranoid.'

'Paranoid?' Monroe tried to regain his composure. 'I was named, as if I were the one who decided to kill all the funding.'

'Ted, come on. Everyone knows it's not the chief executive or chairman who makes these decisions. The company has its own ethics that overrides our own.'

Ted glared across the table as his memory located the quote, before his expression settled somewhere closer to regret.

'Of course I blame myself a little for how things turned out. You took the fallout from Crest Voyager and maybe we could've been more . . . supportive. Fine, but . . . none of us was prepared for this.'

'Prepared for what?' said Richard, daring Monroe to spell it out.

Monroe looked around the room, as if securing a consensus before speaking. 'After 16 years you've decided the company needs fresh blood at its head.'

'Have I now? You'll have to find another scapegoat this time.'

Monroe wasn't paying attention. 'You will resign, or you'll be fired for gross misconduct. Your call.'

Richard knew each second of silence bore testament to his guilt, but he had no inclination to plead his innocence. 'The veneer of choice where there is none.'

'You weren't seriously expecting a negotiation?'

They locked eyes across the table. Richard finally broke the gaze, surveyed the room and the cityscape one last time, then pushed his chair back and rose. 'Gentlemen.' He nodded to the room with all the dignity he could muster, and turned towards the door.

Liam

Wednesday, April 15th
London

Crowd-sourcing a ransom. Liam shook his head as he read the email from the paper's Cairo stringer. Five hundred donors – the money going on repairs to the school run by the hostage. Then there was the kidnap of a police commissioner who was released halfway through a football match. Both hostages claimed they knew nothing of their kidnappers.

But it hardly undermined the thesis of his book, as Barrett had claimed. Its ripples weren't rocking the geopolitical landscape. No other outlet was covering it, and unless he decided to pick it up, that would likely be the way it stayed.

He wasn't planning to undermine his book. It wasn't his type of story anyway.

He played back Barrett's words: *Whenever Crest Voyager is brought up, you transform yourself from a man people dislike but respect, to a man people simply dislike.* He suspected she meant *since* Crest Voyager happened, which would be a disservice: it had taken a decade to perfect his unique brand of misanthropy.

Writing these types of scathing, intellectual critiques of people and politics was hardly fulfilling the dreams he had as a young activist. But in a competitive world, he had a niche.

He appeared on *Question Time* as a guest whose answers mixed the profound with the vitriolic, to the point where those who agreed with his sentiments were loath to do so publicly.

Kidnap had been inspired after loosely covering the Crest Voyager disaster four years earlier. It had been without any redeeming features. Everyone had failed and five people were left dead. Out of it came two things for Liam: first he had written a lazy character assassination of the CEO. Barrett would later describe it as representing everything the younger Liam would have stood against. The second sowed the seed of an idea about the inevitable futility of all such actions, which germinated into a solid top-ten non-fiction hardback.

The newsroom was glass-walled and open-plan. In most cases, the journalists marked their territories with computers to the front and pictures to the sides. Liam's was cordoned off with high filing trays.

Over the last few years he had cut down to three days and two comment pieces a week. Younger journalists viewed him as a grumpy enigma, his bestseller reputation receiving grudging respect. For his peers, his misanthropy was singled out for banter, largely to disguise the varying levels of jealousy they felt towards his notoriety.

'Barrett wants to see you,' said Ronston, peering over Liam's computer. 'Once more, looks like one of your books is upsetting a few people.' He tapped his pen on top of the computer with a joyless grin.

Liam looked up. 'As opposed to your books, which we never hear anything about.'

Ronston scowled at Liam. 'Not everybody wants to write the type of books you write.'

'Published ones?'

Ronston laughed sarcastically. 'Yeah, gotta learn how to offend working single mothers better. Get some quality publicity for myself.'

'I very much doubt you have the ability to offend anyone.' Liam shot Ronston a look, and he promptly retreated back to his desk.

Liam felt anxious, but he was determined not to show Ronston his concern. Half an hour passed before he made his way to Barrett's office in the corner of the newsroom: a glass enclosure, with half-drawn blinds.

'Liam,' Barrett said, without looking up. 'You know, I didn't even have to see or hear you to know it was you. It was as if your presence changed the chemical make-up of the room.'

'You wanted to see me?' he said, taking a seat.

'Not really. It falls under my duty of care responsibilities.'

'How conscientious.'

'Thank you. Look, Liam' – she sat back and finally made eye contact – 'I've received a couple of emails over the last 24 hours, which should've gone to your publisher. I'm an innocent bystander in all this; but they don't see it that way, and these aren't the type of people you correct.'

'Type of people?' Liam said, leaning forward.

'Your book seems to have pissed off a few people. Notably those whose operations you've recently damned as failures.'

'I'm sorry?' Liam rubbed his face. 'You're saying you've been contacted by terrorists who're upset I didn't rate their work?'

'Yemeni. And using the word terrorist isn't going to calm them down. We're talking one-hit wonders who've got a single entry note in history and your book's just pissed all over it.'

'And what do they want?' said Liam.

'Retractions.'

'Retractions? They're demanding I retract my opinion of how bad their previous demands were. Do they not get irony?'

'*Your irony is killing me* was my first thought as a response.'

Liam sat back and ran his hands through his unkempt brown hair. 'So what now? What is their threat if I refuse? Please tell me you're not actually expecting me to agree.'

'No direct threat yet. We're cooperating with the police as we speak. But somehow those bastards next door have got hold of the story, so we're going to have to address it somehow – I guess with some generic freedom of expression bullshit.' She shook her head. 'This is a book this paper had no involvement in and yet still your—' She caught herself from finishing. 'Anyway, continuing this feel-good theme, did you look into those kidnaps in Cairo?'

Liam nodded.

'And?'

The nod morphed into a shrug. 'Nothing much.'

Barrett raised an eyebrow.

'I'll keep an eye on it,' Liam said reassuringly.

Michael

Thursday, April 16th
London

Michael consoled himself that at least, unlike Crest Voyager, the current ultimatum he faced didn't risk fatalities. It could threaten the life of his government, but he had already planned a year-long programme of euthanasia for it leading up to the next general election, so he was mentally prepared for the sense of loss.

The current crisis was just another example of special interests drawing lines in the sand, to which he had neither the energy nor the hope of finding a satisfactory solution. His Chancellor, Duncan Verso, headed an Exchequer that had informally seceded from Number 10. In a climate of austerity and cuts, Verso had delivered a budget of polarising imbalance. Unions argued that their members were shouldering an unfair share of the burden, and they would be forced to act: to avoid strikes they demanded the government push through promised reforms on bank pay and credit regulation to show everyone was 'in it together'.

Financial lobbyists quickly smothered any wavering MPs. By the end of the week, party whips admitted they didn't have a majority for banking reforms, with sheepish citations of the dangers of union power and the importance of the City to the economy. Michael was left with two opposing sides unwilling to negotiate, a party he had no faith in, and a status quo that tempted him to jump ship and join the picket line. It didn't help that a book had recently been published that detailed his silence during the Crest Voyager negotiations. Sections of the press had pointed out that he hardly had the glowing credentials to broker the current stand-off.

Michael looked around his office. Its refurbishment had been supposed to be a grand personal statement when he came to power three years earlier. Down came the historic portraits. Out went the unreadable leather-bound volumes from the bookshelf. A photo of Martin Luther King hung from his wall to remind him that the right words preceded action. A tall bookcase stood against the wall to the right of the central window; it contained all his favourite books, in rough chronological order, from the age of three. On the wall to the left hung a whiteboard and full-length mirror.

The refurbishment seemed childish to him now.

'How's the speech going?' said Charlie as he sat down opposite Michael in his office.

'Not bad at all, considering,' said Michael, nodding in mock satisfaction. 'So far I have . . .' he coughed lightly. *'It is said that hidden among us, vested interests lie in wait.'* He looked up. 'What do you think?'

'Solid. I like an esoteric beginning,' said Charlie.

'Honestly, when we got into this, did you expect to be a sitting duck being shot at from all sides of the pond?'

'No. I was very much hoping we'd be the ones to get the guns and do the shooting.'

'I'll presume you mean that figuratively,' said Michael.

Charlie shrugged. 'We could maybe use the threat of force up our sleeves in light of these new opinion polls.'

'Don't worry about them. It's like the start of the football season. Never look at the table until ten games in.'

'We're three and a half years into your term.'

'You can't win the title in January.'

'I think we'd have been forced out by the foreign owners for wasting their incredibly hard-earned billions.'

'Let's just pretend we're one of those shit teams that somehow gets promoted into the Premier League for a season. Enjoy the exposure, the primetime TV slots, playing with the big boys. We'll treat every day like a cup final.'

'You're the leader of a state of 60 million people.'

'Big fan base. Maybe an oligarch will buy us out,' said Michael, resignation overtaking his humour.

'Michael, we have an approval rating of 23 per cent. I know nothing screams "we're doomed" like a big policy relaunch, but it's getting to that stage . . .'

'Did you know that the Nepalese king once held a referendum over whether to remain autocratic or become democratic. The population voted overwhelmingly in favour of never having to vote again.'

Charlie nodded. 'Are you even in the 23 per cent?'

'You'll never hear me admit to it. Political suicide.'

Richard

Wednesday, April 22nd
London

For the first week Richard felt as if he had been dumped. Admittedly the last time that happened was 15 years ago, by a woman he knew was his superior aesthetically, morally and intellectually; but the feelings of longing and defensiveness felt familiar. What he didn't recognise was the burning need for revenge – against Monroe, the board, Fiona and the smirking critics of his imagination.

His release should have come as a relief, but he missed the stage. He had spent the last decade directing others from a position of superiority. Unemployment did not sit easy with his temperament.

He was bored. He frequented his local deli for a late morning coffee to get out of his minimalist apartment. The deference he used to be shown had been exchanged for a half-hearted welcome. He was now merely another member of the audience.

It was evening. Richard was on his third glass of red wine, letting his luxury microwaveable meal breathe for a couple of minutes, when the phone rang.

'It's me,' said the voice.

'It's me who?' said Richard.

'It's me, Larry.'

'Larry, you need to ring more than once a year in order to have the privilege of voice recognition.'

'It goes to show you never listened to the audiobook I sent you.'

'Your what?' said Richard.

'Well, the devil's industry at least taught you how to lie properly.'

'Self-taught, actually.'

'Well, they can't say you didn't bring anything to the table. The CD that's probably lying on the side of your kitchen counter is my vocal investigation into the relationship between the tetragrammaton and haiku poetry.'

'Sounds accessible.'

'I'm a sell-out. Last year we had our annual chat and I told you I was going to do something outside my comfort zone. Using a 17-syllable three-line Japanese poem as a tool to analyse the 88 names of God ticked the box. As, I imagine, unemployment ticks box one of your bucket list.'

Larry was one of Richard's genuine friends. Richard had no idea why Larry stuck by him – he was normal enough to have alternatives. They were university roommates who excelled at economics together. Larry travelled the world and wrote a bad novel, before making a fortune in the dotcom boom, despite knowing little about it. His strategy was based on the fact that neither did the investors. He took great pleasure in taking advantage of businessmen whose luck had been misdiagnosed as talent.

'I've ticked it now. It's shit,' said Richard.

'Look, man, CEOs these days have chummy names like Bill, Steve and Larry. No one's called Richard any more.'

'There are a surprising number of successful Richards about.'

'You're missing my point,' said Larry.

'Which is?'

'I don't know . . . just that maybe it's time to leave it behind, change direction. Start focusing on what's above ground instead of what's below it. Really, who has oil actually made happy?'

'I'd argue about nine billion people and counting.'

'It was a rhetorical point. Anyway, I'm close to finishing building a boat: a 35-footer made of your finest sustainable timber. Why don't you come on over and help? We can sail around the world together.'

'I already own a boat.'

'I was alluding to the sense of journey. Do you really miss it that much?'

'What? The job?'

'Of course not. You hated the job. I mean the power.'

'I don't know,' said Richard.

'I don't know? Come on. Speak to me, man.'

Richard fell silent. 'I guess . . . look . . . I don't know what the fuck to do. You know I hated some of the things I did, but . . . it . . . it defined me . . . fuck . . .'

Larry gave Richard a space to be emotional, which he chose not to fill. 'What you miss is being the central figure, so why don't we just find you something more rewarding to be the centre of?'

'Like?'

'Well, a year or so back a mate of mine started giving his money away – good projects, healthcare, housing, that type of stuff.'

'Why don't I just tattoo "Please fucking forgive me" on my forehead?'

'Calm down. All I'm saying is that you can drive a project where you won't have to be the bad guy any more. Have a think about it. I'll book you a meeting with these guys who come up with ideas for what you can invest in. If you decide you don't want to go, skip it. But you're a man looking at his options, and this is just another option.'

Richard remained silent.

'I'll email you the details,' said Larry, and hung up.

'So do you know what type of thing you're after?' said the sharply dressed man who welcomed him into the room and introduced himself as Si. He seemed too young to give Richard advice. The room had two seats separated by a coffee table. Pictures of uncomfortable middle-aged men next to downcast black children hung on the wall. Larry had emailed the details of the meeting he had arranged with Giving It Back, a philanthropic consultancy firm. Richard was torn as to whether to go, but had been at a loss for alternatives.

'For example, are you looking for legacy? Like building a university in your name. Maybe you're looking for good PR, which can take the form of creating a foundation, dabbling in healthcare, education and so on. Then we have what I call the joyriders club, for those looking for a bit of excitement, an immediate feel-good factor. You get involved in recent disasters: famine, war, natural disaster. It combines adrenalin and adulation in a photogenic tour package.'

Richard stared straight back at Si. 'Is this the standard presentation, or tailor-made for a cynic?'

Si smiled. 'Why an *or*?'

Richard shrugged. 'So where in the world deserves my money?'

'Well . . . you could spend it here in the UK. People will see you giving back to society. It'll work well if you want to go into politics. However, most of our clients give their money overseas, as it appeals to the romantic, adventurous side of philanthropy: destitution and salvation, darkness and light. There's less bureaucracy in key areas. You basically take your pick: disease, food, education, water and sanitation. You want it, they've got it.'

'Sounds like catalogue shopping,' said Richard.

Si smiled. 'On the other hand, Asia's good: India, Bangladesh, Burma's opening up. Your money goes further. The only issue is their governments are less likely to let you do what you want, or let you take too much credit for it.'

'What if I wanted to do what they want?'

'Then you'd already have given your money to the Indian government.'

Richard smiled at the scoring point. He took a few moments. 'Let's just imagine I don't have billions, but I wanted to get into *Time* magazine. What would I need to do?'

'Er . . .' Si puffed out his cheeks. 'Well, most of our clients have a lower bar. You're basically looking at taking a whole cause and being its benefactor. You could pick something small with a feel-good factor. Make a documentary. Say. . .' – Si paused briefly – 'maybe you could fight for the rights of a dispossessed people, or clean up a damaged environment.'

Richard forced a brief smile to acknowledge the direction Si was heading. Donating to an area his company had destroyed would grab attention, but after Crest Voyager and his recent resignation, he had no intention of portraying his actions as redemptive.

'Well, thanks all the same.' He stood up and made to walk out the door.

'There's maybe another approach you could take,' said Si. Richard remained standing by the door. 'The world likes controversy. It's the story that gets you into *Time* not the actions.'

'Go on.'

'Look, you're the oil guy. No one cares if you pour your

money into the AIDS programmes. You're competing with others. I get you don't want to return to, er . . . familiar pastures. But what if your philanthropy undermined what you previously stood for, rather than just cleaning up after it? That would be a story.'

Richard returned a quizzical look.

'All right,' said Si, 'let me put it this way. I know you left the industry on bad terms, and I'm guessing you want revenge. So why not invest in ways that will put the spotlight on them?'

Richard pursed his lips, nodded, and opened the door.

'I'll send you my invoice for the session,' called Si as Richard walked away.

The Kidnap of Fathima Ahmed

No one noticed the day that Fathima Ahmed was kidnapped. The seventy-eight-year-old lived alone. Her family had moved away. Most of her friends were dead. There were no events from which her absence would be noted.

No one noticed the day after, either. Had they been asked, neighbours or traders to the market stalls she frequented might have realised they hadn't seen her. But no one did.

On day three, the neighbourhood remained equally unconcerned. Had she been lying dead in her apartment the smell wouldn't have hit the stairwell for at least a week.

The following four days passed as unremarkably as the first – noteworthy, perhaps, only because of the absence of any strange events such as had so bewitched the community of late.

The next day, a note was pasted on the walls.

> Our current hostage has been with us for seven days. To secure their release, all you have to do is work out who we have kidnapped.

Few wanted to make the direct enquiry: *I just called to check you hadn't been kidnapped.* Instead subtle calculations were made to absolve responsibility: if someone lived with someone else, worked somewhere else, or had closer friends or family, then surely someone else would check. The odd phone call was made to a parent who lived alone, or an employee who was absent through illness, but there was a presumption that everyone could be accounted for.

There was no news that evening.

The following morning, the neighbourhood awoke to a new note:

> And all it takes is a knock on a door.

Many started the day normally; someone else's conscience would scout the tenement. But as mid-morning arrived, people's thoughts drifted to the vulnerable who chanced occasionally into their lives: the elderly, the sick, the lonely. Lunch-break plans factored in visits to old acquaintances who rarely laid claim to the time of others.

In between childcare, mothers drew up plans of their building to establish where the vulnerable among them lived. Sorties went out and knocked on doors; those who answered were asked if they needed anything. The lonely found comfort in brief conversations. Responsibilities were allocated between strangers.

In the early evening, a downstairs neighbour knocked at the door of Fathima Ahmed. After five minutes of knocking and calling to no response, she called her husband who forced the door open. The apartment was tidy, but empty. On a small table by the only chair in the room was a message. It simply read: *Well Done*.

Miller and Jordie

Friday, April 24th
Somewhere in Uttar Pradesh, North India

Miller knocked on the door timidly, until he built up confidence and called Jordie's name. He heard a body turn in bed, a slight pause, before the words 'fucking bollocks' emerged in a pained Glaswegian drawl. An assortment of grunts, moans and expletives followed.

'You all right?' said Miller.

Something bumped into the wall. 'Coffee, a glass of water with sugar and salt, some complex carbohydrate. No ethnic shit.' The bathroom door slammed shut.

He got the breakfast takeaway and sat in the lobby to hide from the driver and translator who had been waiting outside for over an hour. At 9.27 Jordie's bulk shuffled from the stairwell door. Jordie's walk was a waddle: his six foot two frame endured 18 stone of meat hanging on for dear life, and he had developed the art of getting from A to B using diagonal switchbacks, like workmen moving a heavy wardrobe. He wore khaki combat trousers, shirt and sunhat. A faded green sleeveless jacket, armed with a range of secret pockets and zips, broke the beige.

He acknowledged Miller with a nod, as he followed him out the door, liquids and complex carbohydrates in tow.

'Fucking hell,' Jordie said as his eyes met sunlight. He cracked open a bottle of pills and shook a few into his hand without looking, chasing them down with Miller's makeshift rehydration fluids. He threw the bottle of pills at the driver, who fumbled them in his surprise, as Jordie pulled himself up into the front seat.

'There are poor people to save, gentlemen. Let's get cracking.'

Miller joined the translator in the back seat. From the safety of the vehicle, Miller viewed the condensed chaos of life on the margins: cycle and motor rickshaws, bikes, cows, dilapidated taxis and modern land cruisers weaved in between vendors and beggars. He eyed it all with suspicion, seeing malevolence not in people, but in the infinite unknowns that made up this environment.

He occasionally caught the eye of the destitute and would quickly return to his phone, calming the anxiety brought on by random intimacies. Alleviating poverty was his destiny in spite of his discomfort at interacting with its sufferers. He cursed his liberal upbringing. His briefcase was filled with questionnaires and surveys that would mediate his relationship with the Indians he had been sent to consult.

Within minutes, Jordie had fully reclined his seat, placed his hat over his face, and started to snore. He was the polar opposite of Miller: he could bathe in extreme poverty and not even acknowledge it.

The drive would take two and a half hours and meander through urban sprawl and bumpy back road. A Norwegian foundation had contracted their think tank to write a study on the potential benefits and obstacles to delivering a solar-based energy system to a village off the main electricity grid. It was the type of project Miller wrote excitedly about from afar.

Miller had recently attempted to add a metrosexual twist to his natural intelligentsia style, but this was undermined by his awkward mannerisms, which proved stubborn to change. Still, your daughter could do worse; she probably already has. Lulled by heat and motion, he closed his eyes and fell asleep.

He awoke as his head cracked against the window. The vehicle stopped.

'What the fuck?' said Jordie. The driver jumped out to look under the car; Srinath, the translator, joined him. Apart from a bicycle slowly coming towards them there was no sign of life. It was 11.30, 43 degrees, and they were late.

Jordie eased himself out, and shuffled forward to afford a view under the car. Miller exited to meet Jordie's diagnosis.

'We're buggered,' said Jordie as he heaved himself back into the air conditioning.

Miller surveyed his surroundings: the endless baked brown of ploughed fields that stretched to the horizon: overexposed, vast and unforgiving. His insignificance brought on an attack of nausea, and he rejoined Jordie in the vehicle.

'This is what the third world is about: delays, breakdowns, futility. It's romantic, no?' said Jordie, struggling to reach for a water bottle in the footwell. 'Fuck me, it's hot,' he said, wiping the sweat from his forehead, and looking down his darkening khaki shirt. 'I think my body's become allergic to poverty. My nipples are lactating, and no matter what you've heard, sweaty nipples undermine authority.' His wispy smooth grey hair was smeared moistly on to his forehead and nape: the effect was more comical than repulsive.

'Have we got a number for someone in the village?' asked Miller.

Jordie shook his head, unconcerned.

'OK, well, have they rung for help?' Miller said, pointing towards Srinath.

'Be my guest,' Jordie said, elaborately waving Miller outside.

Miller had a quick look at Jordie before he reluctantly opened the door and left their guilty sanctuary.

After 20 minutes, a couple of cyclists stopped by the vehicle. Workers, previously invisible in the fields, soon joined the committee of onlookers. Miller wanted neither to stay outside, nor to complete the image of two white men hiding in the car. He resolved to circumnavigate it slowly. When outside, a group of four young women looked at him, giggling. He had no idea whether out of desire or ridicule.

Jordie opened the window. 'Relax. They're looking at me. My body always gets them hot under the saris. Hey!' he said loudly, pointing to a boy holding a bicycle. He waved a 500-rupee note. 'Coca-Cola.' He pronounced each syllable deliberately. The boy looked confused. 'Money for you, Coca-Cola for me.' The bill could buy 25 Cokes. The boy took the note. 'Before I evaporate.' Jordie wound the window back up.

The driver's phone rang, and Srinath conveyed the news that help was at least a couple of hours away. They were already two hours late.

Miller anxiously devised contingencies. Rearrangement? Cancellation? Reimbursement? As Jordie said, things went wrong in the field: their clients would understand. He felt tired and dirty, dehydrated and deflated. He got back in the car. The audience remained. Jordie was asleep. He closed his eyes and wished it all away.

Miller awoke to Srinath knocking on the window. In front of them was a land cruiser with tinted windows; behind them was an open-bedded truck filled with goats, accompanied by a fresh brown sludge.

'Good news,' said Srinath. 'The truck is going to the village. We can jump in the back and driver will wait for repair and come pick us up.'

It was two. They could be there in an hour. It was far from perfect, but they had time to do what they needed to, and get back late. However, after his afternoon doze he no longer felt mentally prepared to brave a village consultation.

'And where's that one going?' said Jordie, gesturing to the land cruiser.

Srinath look confused. 'That one goes back to city.'

Jordie attempted a polite smile. 'Could you give us a minute please?'

Srinath nodded as Jordie closed the window.

'You want to rearrange and come back tomorrow?' said Miller.

They made eye contact through the rear-view mirror. Jordie shook his head. 'Do you?'

Miller did not. But this opinion seemed irrelevant: people had spent a large amount of money to get him here, and he had got in to the industry, in part, because he believed in selflessly helping others. But Jordie read his silence.

'Of course you fucking don't.'

Miller looked nervous. 'What are you suggesting?'

He saw a hint of uncertainty on Jordie's face, as if the idea pushed even his flippancy to its boundary.

'I suggest we go back to the hotel, get a beer and fill in the questionnaires over some nachos.' The red, moist face appeared serious.

'Jordie, that's . . . that's . . .'

'I'm not stopping you. But my head feels like it's been raped by a horse, the seat contains more of me than I do, and

I'm past giving a fuck. Let's not get too high and mighty about what we were going to do there. They're the passive Play-Doh we unleash our weary altruism upon. We can do that by the fucking pool.'

Jordie opened the door, and turned his body for dismount.

'Jordie . . . We'll never pull it off.'

'Miller,' he said, feet dangling out of the car. 'One poor village is exactly the same as the next. Our clients couldn't give a toss which one we give them.'

'But . . .'

'Miller. If we go there, they'll start asking for things from us they actually want. And we're not here to respond to their demands. We have one thing to give them, and our job is to make that exchange seem mutual rather than the ransom it really is. So as you can see, not going has many benefits.' He heaved himself out of the car, using the door and frame as supports, then headed to the land cruiser.

Miller panicked. The horizon shimmered in the heat. He sensed derision etched on the faces of those crowded around him, and imagined countless similar faces at his destination. His limbs felt weak.

'Miller?' Jordie shouted at him, beckoning him towards the land cruiser. 'There're two seats.'

A goat shat against its companion in the truck. A drip of sweat ran down Miller's forehead into his eye. He reached for his briefcase on the back seat.

After showering, Miller arrived poolside; the water was pale green with rotting leaves on its surface: an attraction for the mosquitos that loitered under their rusting paint-chipped table.

'A beer?' Jordie asked politely. 'So look . . . if anyone can fake a fucked-up village perfect for this project, you and I can.

We both know there's no chance of the project being implemented. And, you know . . .' He paused. 'I'll try not to put you in this position again.'

They exchanged a glance, then Miller drew the questionnaires from his briefcase.

Over the next three hours they created their model village: poor, ripe with vulnerabilities, and ready for change. Jordie detailed the icebreaker games they played to put the attendees at ease; Miller held group discussions with women to understand their struggles; Jordie held discussions with the men, somehow managing to release their insecurities; they mapped the village, with children helping to detail where energy was generated and collected; elders contributed their wisdom; questionnaires were answered en masse by enthusiastic beneficiaries. Unfortunately they found out that another NGO had already approached the elders and had started the first steps on a similar project. The report, therefore, was valuable, yet the village unsuitable. Their dedication to doing good in the world would need a new location.

They stared at the pile of questionnaires, drawings and field notes. Jordie dirtied his hands on the floor and made brown stains on the crisp pages. Miller creased and ripped them. Jordie took out the work camera and dipped it in the swimming pool: the pictures of the meeting now sadly erased. They sucked deeply on their beers, in silent complicity: two men whose fates were now bound together.

Richard

Monday, April 27th
London

In Richard's inbox was an email from Si.

Dear Richard,

Over the weekend a Norwegian foundation approached me who are looking for a partner to implement an urban solar energy project in Cairo. They hoped I might know someone with both knowledge of the industry and commitment (money!). They have a great track record and are considered to be very cool among many opinion formers. It struck me this may be somewhere you might like to dip your toe in the water?

It may seem small beer, but the plan is to pilot a neighbourhood, scale it up to a city and start showing the world it's a viable alternative.

They are looking for 200K up front for the pilot. You can take it from there.

Let me know what you think.

'Larry, it's Richard.'
'Sorry . . . Richard who?'
'Larry, it's me, Richard Pou—'

'I know, you idiot, I could recognise that narcissistic tone anywhere. So what's gone wrong?'

'What do you mean?'

'I mean the last time you called me you asked if I knew anything about the land rights of native Amazonian tribes.'

'And you did.'

'I'm your go-to man for any issue you see as left of centre that has the potential to screw something up for you.'

'Well relax, I was ringing to tell you that I listened to your haiku analysis of the tetragrrr . . .'

'Tetragrammaton. And no you didn't. Nobody rings up a friend to say, "I hated what you sent me." Even you.'

'Why do you think I hated it?'

'Because it's a haiku analysis of the tetragrammaton. It's a niche market.'

'Well . . . So what do you think about solar power?'

Larry laughed. 'Would you care to be a little more specific? I thought you knew this stuff. That's why you bought up loads of solar patents.'

'Yeah, well . . . understanding it was less important than owning it. I'm talking panels on roofs and walls in poor urban neighbourhoods. What do you think?'

'Your moral compass has lost none of its magnetism. Look, the principle is great, and you're smart enough to deal with the detail.'

'So?'

'Go and be the man you always said you wanted to be.'

Michael

Wednesday, April 29th
London

Michael looked at Luther King on the wall. Would his message have withstood the inquisition of the modern media, or would his dream have turned from slave and slave-owner breaking bread together to that of a lie-in and an evening with a DVD box set?

'I'm starting to feel a little misunderstood,' said Michael as Charlie entered.

'You're right up there with Genghis Khan and Morrissey,' replied Charlie.

Michael pulled a face. 'I get the impression Genghis wasn't one to get bogged down by due process.'

'You can question his policy decisions, but man, could that guy implement,' said Charlie, dumping a pile of paperwork on his desk. 'Get these signed, and I'll be back in an hour for Cabinet.' Charlie shut the door behind him.

Michael had delivered a speech the week before that called on the unions to step back from the brink and engage in meaningful dialogue. He agreed with his critics that he lacked leadership. Words were his weapons: once used against others, now against himself. He thought he'd be able to change things when in power, but once he got there he realised the system was broken. The few had too much power to be convinced to negotiate. The only hope was for a changing of the rules, or a changing of the game. He would happily join the revolution. Abdication sounded enticing. Right now he'd settle for a little time spent on a project that made him optimistic.

Michael glanced at the words scribbled in black marker on his whiteboard: an old technique that had helped him to power, but which he had since lost faith in. He looked at the paperwork on his desk, then back at the whiteboard, before he stood up and locked the door.

Michael had surged through the political ranks with a rare gift for delivering a speech. He didn't talk about the failures of others, or criticise policies that sought to improve systems that were terminally broken. Instead he invited the listener to imagine what great might look like, occasionally describing the heroic journey to its attainment with reference to the popular stories that had inspired him as he grew up.

In a famous party conference speech, he wowed the audience by using *Beauty and the Beast* as a parable to describe his strategy against tax evasion. On another occasion, he cited Sinbad as his inspiration in a talk about entrepreneurship. In a darker moment, he talked of *Animal Farm* as illustrative of the evils of the far right's anti-immigrant rhetoric.

His words provoked some ridicule, but for many others they proved refreshing. Here was a candidate who avoided empty political grandstanding. He was aware of the disconnect between the reality of people's struggles and the fairy tales he sometimes used to frame a solution; but nonetheless, his election motto read: 'Rayburn: Suspend Your Disbelief'.

In the General Election 52 per cent of the voters did.

He refused to hide behind soundbites. Three years on, he

had nowhere to hide even if he wanted to. Disbelief was suspended no more.

He circled the floor in front of the whiteboard, black marker in hand. He split the whiteboard into four columns, labelling them *Exposition*, *Rising Action*, *Climax*, *Resolution*: the four stages of storytelling since time began.

He listed his proposed policy's antagonists and protagonists. He drew arrows for tensions and stand-offs. He entered the minds of lobbyists and nimbys as the story came to a climax, and wondered if his protagonists had the ability to fend them off. The policy revealed itself as a quest. Until now he had misunderstood the central plot, and as he reworked the story's structure he felt his old excitement return.

He pulled faces to relax his muscles and stood in front of the mirror, ready for rehearsal. He was not as old as he felt: forty-three, six foot, and in good shape. He had a warm face you could put your trust in, although he no longer asked for it.

There was a knock at the door. 'You ready?' came Charlie's voice.

Michael nodded to himself. 'Yes,' he said, surprised. 'Yes I am.'

He stared at the 35 people crammed around the Cabinet Office table. Michael felt sorry that the ornate trappings of state – the chandeliers, velvet curtains and paintings – should have to endure this rabble.

'Good morning, everyone,' said Michael. There was a murmured response. 'I thought we could start on something I've been working on. It's about—'

'Well actually, Prime Minister,' said Sandra Cowling, the

Home Secretary, 'I think we're quite focused on how powerless the government's looking right now.' The rest of the table nodded into their coffee cups. 'The wolves are circling.'

'They're learning from the vultures, then,' said Michael.

'Michael, the media's baying for blood over our promised banking legislation,' said his Chancellor, Duncan Verso. 'With respect, it's a shambles and if we don't look as if we're dealing with this—'

'You're right,' Michael interrupted, 'appearances are everything, Duncan.'

He took responsibility for his government's failure and lack of direction; he was clearly not in control. But he felt his position more closely resembled a young prince who gets thrust into being king, his court ignoring his authority because he belongs to the realm of the child: a risk, Michael mused, of a leader who talks in fairy tales.

The Kidnap of Hanif Salah

> We have kidnapped the storyteller Hanif Salah. If you care for his release, watch online at www.serendipityfoundation.org tomorrow at 7pm.

The name was unfamiliar to the majority in the neighbourhood. The elder teahouse patrons remembered Hanif as a young man, but they hadn't seen him since the 1970s when the last generation of professional storytellers ebbed away from the public squares and cafés. He did not grow up locally; some recalled him arriving from a village on the banks of the Nile where he had learned his trade. But his history was soon confused with the onrush of nostalgia.

The demand appealed to a dark voyeurism. While many, especially from the younger generation, failed to register much concern for Hanif, the ransom stoked a desire to witness the consequences. All were united in their longing to see what would happen next.

Café owners set up streams from their laptops on to the televisions that hung on the wall. Grandparents pestered their grandchildren into giving brief tutorials on how to navigate the internet. The demand proved an ethical minefield. Some parents, fearing the worst, warned their children against watching, while other families sat down together as seven approached.

The online stream buffered at seven. The webcam revealed an elderly man, dressed in a traditional beige tunic – the galabeya. The figure was spotlit against the darkness of the room. Grey stubble peppered a hollow face. Hanif's expression was one of animation rather than fear.

'Please bear with me,' he said as he leaned forward towards the camera. 'My life will not be safe until I have finished what I have to say.'

All those watching on smartphones, laptops and TVs leaned in to meet him. For now, they were immune from the distractions that usually monopolised their attention.

'I have a story to tell you. It concerns a group of murderous bandits who terrorised the city of . . .'

For the next hour Hanif spun a story that flowed from modern Cairo to twelfth-century Baghdad. Characters pulled from *Arabian Nights* morphed with descriptions of groups that seemed unerringly familiar. They felt like clues, as if Hanif were trying to lead the audience to his cell. After 40 minutes a gun entered the frame, aimed at Hanif. A computer-camouflaged voice shouted, 'Come on, finish the story. You're out of time. Finish the story.'

But Hanif's story continued: one cliff-hanger followed the next; characters who had been introduced 20 minutes earlier reappeared.

The kidnappers once more demanded closure.

The audience were transfixed, as Hanif fought his fate with the continuation of a story that refused to end. Teahouses were silent as they willed Hanif to weave another narrative web to delay his captors. The young ignored the unread messages on their phones.

It was eight.

'OK, fine. You win tonight,' came the voice from the side of the camera. 'But let's see if you are good enough to do the same tomorrow night. See you at seven.'

The stream went down.

Miller and Jordie

Thursday, April 30th
London

'You've been AWOL over the last few days,' said Lucy as she joined Miller by the kettle in the grey, sparse staffroom. 'I thought you got back on Monday.'

'I know, sorry. We were given a few days off.'

'So what happened?' She was one of the few people he felt comfortable holding eye contact with. Early in their friendship there was a drunken embrace in a club. They formed a consensus that alcohol, not attraction, would be their chosen scapegoat. They both suffered private doubts that this was the case. Their colleagues were less private in their questioning. She once described Miller as nerd-chic in appearance, and in return he called her homely. Realising the mistake, he argued this was because he would happily put a mortgage down on her. In truth, he had not decided if she was beautiful or plain: her full cheeks and lips rested naturally in an open-mouthed, vacant frown, which transformed during conversation into a crackling vitality. He was much confused.

'Let's just say the relationship we built with the community was a little more abstract than we would've liked.'

Jordie approached across the staffroom. 'Lovebirds.'

'Nice shirt,' Lucy said.

Miller looked at him frostily.

'I read somewhere that stripes are a thinning pattern,' said Jordie.

'Shame you aren't wearing three shirts,' said Lucy.

'You cheeky mare. I was hoping you two might announce your wedding now and distract Fairweather with some good news before we go in,' said Jordie.

'A thoughtful offer, but I've come to accept my role as perennial bridesmaid,' said Lucy with a glint in her eye.

'Fairweather wants to see us now?' said Miller, uninterested in the whimsy.

Jordie nodded gravely. Lucy read the tension and decided to take her leave.

Jordie had initially avoided Miller when he arrived at the organisation three years earlier – as he did with anyone he suspected of harbouring idealism. But over a brief lunch conversation, Miller admitted that he had seen Jordie speak at a festival his mother had arranged in the Cotswolds 15 years earlier, and Jordie had since secretly taken credit for Miller's career choice. Miller was his protégé, and he vowed to continue his role as mentor.

'Keep calm. Coming clean now won't save us. In ten minutes we can put last week down to experience,' said Jordie in hushed tones.

Miller ignored him as they knocked.

'Come in,' Fairweather's voice called theatrically.

They entered to see him standing by a table in the middle of the room, where he was joined by Carol Sutton – the head of the Political Economy team – and an unfamiliar tall blond boffin. John Fairweather resembled a mad professor whose wife struggled to make him presentable. No one could remember seeing him without a bow tie. Carol's wardrobe consisted largely of black velvet and her movements were accompanied by an unaccountable clinking and jingling. Miller had no idea how they were taken seriously as the heads of a think tank: especially in Fairweather's office, which housed a mish-mash of paraphernalia from his world travels, including Amazonian blow-pipes, Malian masks and paintings drawn by Peruvian shamans.

'Gentlemen, welcome, I'd like you to meet Olaf from our Norwegian funders Nynorsk Solar. I sent him the skeleton report you sent earlier this week about your trip. He was as excited about it as I was,' said Fairweather.

Miller and Jordie distractedly shook Olaf's hand.

'In what way?' asked Jordie.

'In what way! The jokers!' said Fairweather as he put his arm around Jordie's shoulder and led him to the table. 'This village is perfect. Your work was brilliant: incisive, sensitive, you really brought the place to life even after the unfortunate event with the camera.' On the table was an enlargement of the map they had faked, using monopoly hotels for houses.

'Olaf spoke to his guys yesterday, and they're keen to push this pilot through ASAP,' said Carol. 'It's a huge relief: we've kept it quiet, but times are tough here at the moment. Your work might well have saved a few jobs.'

'It looks like you've received bad news,' Fairweather said in response to Miller's expression, as he pulled him towards the model village. 'He's a hard one to please,' Fairweather explained to Olaf. 'Incredibly high standards. Never known a moral backbone like it. It's as if poverty killed his family and he's seeking payback.'

'But . . .' said Jordie, his third chin wobbling, like his career. 'We made it clear in the report that an NGO was already doing a similar project in the same village.'

'What was the name of the NGO?' Olaf asked.

Jordie looked at Miller nervously; the other three followed

suit. 'The . . . er . . .' Miller's brain froze. 'The Foundation of Srinath.'

He was met by four vacant looks.

'Never heard of them,' said Olaf. 'Must be a local group. Sound a bit culty. Our organisation is a global leader in this area and we want to expand further into the developing world. This village is perfect, and you know what these local organisations are like. The village won't care who provides it.'

'But,' Jordie said, 'the, uh . . . the elder won't be pleased. Mr . . . Mr . . . Ranjiv.'

'What about Mr Ranjiv?' said Carol.

The question surpassed Jordie's creativity.

'Mr Ranjiv,' Miller took over, 'lives here.' He pointed to one of the monopoly hotels. 'His brother – who lives next door – works for the Foundation of Srinath, so I can't see him standing for us muscling in.'

'Ah.' Olaf stroked his stubble. 'That wasn't in the report.'

Miller blushed. Even given the situation, he did not like people finding holes in his analysis. 'No one else knows that Mr Ranjiv's brother works with the organisation. I only heard it privately. For some reason he doesn't want the Gavaskars to find out.'

'What could the Gavaskars possibly have against him working for a charity?' asked Fairweather. He seemed incredulous, as if this went against everything he previously thought the Gavaskars stood for.

'I heard it had something to do with their daughter.' Miller had no idea where these lies were coming from.

Carol shook her head, as if this were a microcosm of everything that was wrong with the world. 'You couldn't make it up, could you?' The five of them nodded at the complexity of real life.

'Well, that settles it,' said Olaf. 'I'll join you two on a visit to the village, and we'll have a talk with the Ranjivs and the Gavaskars and see if there's any way we can smooth things over. How about we fix it for when you two get back in ten days?'

'Sorry, get back from where?' said Jordie, confused. There was too much new information to know which bits he should object to.

Olaf smiled. 'I think that's my cue to leave. So . . . see you in ten days.' He shook everyone's hand and left the room.

As the door closed, Fairweather smiled and clapped excitedly to himself. He kissed Miller and Jordie on the cheek in turn. 'Brilliant. Amazing. You are the kings of this poverty-alleviating castle. The relationship with his organisation could save us. And it's all because of you two. He loves your work. And to think people were trying to convince me that you were turning into a loose cannon,' he said to Jordie.

'As part of this relationship,' Carol said, 'Olaf has just found a funder for a similar solar energy project, but in an urban environment, and he wants us to help implement it. But we have to move quickly.'

'When?' asked Miller.

'Tomorrow. For seven days,' Carol said.

'If that's too much of a turn-round, we can maybe look at bringing your India visit with Olaf forward,' said Fairweather.

'No,' Miller said loudly. 'No, tomorrow will be fine.'

'Where?' said Jordie.

'Ah, yes. I forgot about that detail. North Africa. It's an area that is invalua—'

'Fuck Africa,' said Jordie.

'Look, Jordie, I know you—'

'I've made myself clear on this before. I've agreed to work on African projects, but not to be sent there. I hate Africa, and Africa hates me.'

Jordie was the guy who hated Africa. It was his niche. It all started getting personal after he got posted to Sierra Leone two days before the outbreak of civil war. Four days later he was home with shrapnel wounds. He then had to evacuate a jungle village from armed gangs in Liberia, before bouts of malaria (Congo) and typhoid (Zambia) tried to bring him down from the inside.

'I know, I know,' said Fairweather. 'You're the MP who won't go to Westminster, or the cricketer who won't play at Lord's. I feel terrible for this being how I repay you. But jobs are at stake; think of your colleagues. Think of all the poor who'll suffer because of our cutbacks.' Fairweather motioned towards the pathetic model village on the table. 'Think of them.'

Jordie felt Miller's angry stare: a trip to Africa would buy time to work out how to avoid a visit to an Indian village of their own invention.

'North Africa, you say,' said Jordie.

'Cairo,' said Fairweather.

'It's barely Africa,' added Carol.

'It's barely African,' added Fairweather.

'Call it West Jordan, and I won't look at a map,' said Jordie.

'Well, just in case, consider the map of the Middle East redrawn in the name of progress,' said Fairweather. It wasn't as if reshaping the boundaries of the Middle East had led to any complications before.

They were on their second pint, in a crowded pub near Waterloo. They had negotiated a small table with two stools. Miller had so far refused to tell Lucy what had been troubling him all day.

'Here's the deal. As you won't tell me what happened, you can at least rate out of ten how close your troubles are to those of famous fictional protagonists.' Lucy's addiction to literary references was a trait Miller was on the fence about.

'First up. Meursault from *The Outsider*. Out of ten.'

'Who?'

'Gets dehydrated. Shoots a stranger.'

Miller lifted his glasses and rubbed his eyes. 'Um. I guess I got a little dehydrated. Say a three.'

Lucy sucked some of her shoulder-length blonde hair as she weighed the answer.

'Interesting . . . Let's try Josef K. from *The Trial*. You've always reminded me of a modern-day Kafka.'

He smiled while he tried to remember something about the book. 'Anxiety, a suspended sense of judgement. Say a five.'

'Ahhh.' Lucy stared at him intensely. 'It's falling into place now.' She nodded thoughtfully as if she had discovered a vital clue. 'Finally, I put to you Pinocchio.'

Miller narrowed his eyes at Lucy in mock angst. 'You've got me there. A ten,' he said, as if being forced to confess against his will.

'I knew it.' Lucy clapped. 'Heatstroke created an alienating system that's forcing you to lie. No wonder you've been so quiet.'

Miller shook his head dismissively while being taken aback by her deductions. 'I only meant that I have dreams of becoming a real live boy.'

Lucy scrunched up her nose at him. 'Liar. Anyway, it could be worse. You could be going on a seven-day trip to Africa with Jordie.'

'Thanks. Don't mind the plague as the apocalypse is coming.' Miller said it in good humour, but his face betrayed the panic that had built up since he met Fairweather, Carol and Olaf.

'Cheer up,' said Lucy. 'I know things are a bit shit at the moment, but you and Jordie are capable of going there and doing a great job.'

Miller held his pint glass and shrugged. 'I just don't understand what the point of what I do is any more. I'm a different person in the field. I get stage fright, as if all this is a performance. I can make the world a better place on the page, but not in reality.'

Lucy placed her hand on Miller's, her fingers flirting with interlocking with his. 'We all doubt what we're doing every so often. It's only natural. Things will get better. I promise.' She pulled her hand away slowly.

Miller watched it slide back, the silence between them saturated with possibilities. He realised he was holding his breath. The crackling energy of the unsaid pulsed through his fingers. And as always, in such moments of intensity, he instinctively tried to dispel it. 'Maybe I need to do something radical. Shake things up a bit.'

Lucy's smile, poorly supported by a brief look of sadness in her eyes, attempted to put the involuntary rejection behind her. 'Maybe best to start in your own country. Egypt may be a little weary of Brits going over there and shaking things up.'

'My sights were set below creating an empire. But just in case, be prepared to come and rescue me if things go wrong.'

Lucy took a sip from her pint. 'We going to rescue Jordie as well?'

Miller pursed his lips, giving her comment more consideration than she thought it deserved. 'On second thoughts, don't rescue us. It'd be nice to have an excuse to miss the next month or so.'

Liam

Friday, May 1st
London

'You should give your opinion on the actions of all current terrorist groups,' said Ronston, performing to his colleagues nearby as Liam took his seat in the office. 'Distract them from the violence they were planning. Lure them into heated debate instead of jihad. You could yet be a force for good.' Nearby faces smiled politely to appease Ronston.

Since the news had broken that a Yemeni group had asked him for a retraction, Liam's name had circulated internationally. His ego could not resist basking in the attention. It should have been a return to the moral high ground of his youth, yet #IStandWithLiamPowell remained immune from global trending. Instead, years of criticising others meant those he had wounded came out in turn to pull apart the myriad holes in his book's case studies.

Barrett entered the newsroom, coffee cup in one hand, phone at her ear in the other, with her handbag held in her inside elbow. 'Come with me,' she said to Liam without looking at him as she strode past his desk. Ronston smiled gleefully as Liam stood up and followed.

'Yes, I know. I'm talking to him now.' Barrett ended the call and put down her coffee cup and bag, then took a seat and looked at Liam.

'Sit down, for God's sake.'

'They still expecting an apology?'

Barrett adopted a stern expression. 'Liam, I get it – this situation is surreal, and you can't just apologise because someone doesn't like what you have to say. But they're now making veiled threats against the paper.'

'So on this occasion I'm going to be the sacrificial lamb?'

'On this occasion . . .' Barrett teased out the words.

'You got something you want to say?'

Barrett paused briefly. 'Let's face it, you're no stranger to sacrificing the odd lamb for the sake of your reputation.'

'So you're comforting yourself by saying I'm getting what I deserve?'

Barrett flicked an impatient smile. 'Be careful not to attack one of the few friends you've got. I'm trying to protect you right now.'

'How?'

'You know what these terrorists said? They wanted you to admit you could be wrong.' She stared fixedly. 'And to be honest, I wouldn't mind seeing that either.'

Years of silent recriminations filled the room, as Liam shuffled under Barrett's gaze.

'I've just come back from speaking to the board. They're anxious. As far as they're concerned, the only reason these threats arose is because of you, and they're wondering whether it's worth the hassle for a journalist whose recent tone is at odds with our readership.'

Liam's defensive expression lost its resolve, a hint of vulnerability entering his voice. 'You're . . . you're letting me go?'

Barrett held his stare for a few seconds silently, before shaking her head. 'The board wanted to.'

'And you?'

Barrett smiled gently. 'I told them to trust me.'

Liam nodded. 'Why?'

Barrett shrugged. 'Old times' sake.'

'Big gamble in the name of failed promise.'

Barrett remained silent and looked down at the table. 'Maybe what the group asked is what I should have asked you a few years ago.'

'What do you want me to do?' Liam asked tentatively.

'I want you to go and prove yourself wrong. I want you to go to Cairo.'

Liam remained silent.

'Have you actually followed this story at all?' Barrett said, knowing the answer. 'Jesus, Liam. The one thing I . . .' She trailed off, rubbing her forehead, eyes closed. 'Your inside scoop on this has all but gone. For the last week they managed to get 4,000 people to tune in each night and watch the hostage storyteller ramble on for an hour. He was released yesterday, and now he's performing on the street to large audiences.'

Liam had no response.

'You're going to Cairo tomorrow, and you're going to provide me with a story about this group. Find the kidnappers. Find the victims. Just give me something that I can use to justify your future at the paper to the board.'

She slid an envelope across her desk. 'Your plane tickets.'

He narrowed his eyes questioningly before picking up the envelope.

'Liam,' Barrett said before he opened it. 'This isn't the type of thing a reputable editor is supposed to do. You understand what I'm saying?'

He looked at her, nodded shallowly once, and offered a smile of thanks, then stood and left the office.

PART TWO

The Kidnappers

A Walking Tour

There was a village that if viewed from above would titillate even the most jaded urban planner. If pressed, they would likely conclude it took its design inspiration from the thermometer – unless, of course, they were familiar with the rababah.

A reputable walking tour would start at the village's most northerly point in the late afternoon sun. The mud buildings here formed stables, storerooms and granaries. Here, students explained at length their jobs in the running of the madrasa's farm. There was much to see but, boy, can these kids *talk*.

To the right, heading south on the only road, were the musical instrument workshops. Here, craftsmen moulded the bodies of tabla drums, stretched skins across tambourines, strung rababahs, and hollowed out flutes. Opposite lay the metal works and carpenters. Next were the textile huts, where cotton from the fields was processed, woven and dyed, then turned into clothing for performers and puppets.

The next 25 metres on either side housed the story rooms. Each had a stage. A blackboard hung to one side with names of protagonists, events and places, with numerous arrows highlighting potential scenarios. A large mirror covered the opposite wall, where students rehearsed their gestures and facial expressions.

All guests were invited to tell a story. While students found the idea of someone without a story unsettling, they had been warned to prepare for a silence. That was, after all, why they were studying.

Musicians would be heard practising in the rooms opposite. Guests might reflect on how traditional it all appeared; but the sun was starting to recline and they understood nothing yet.

Further down the street the buildings left their traditional roots behind. The earthen walls were punctuated by modern windows and air-conditioning units. In a large open-plan room, students in huddles learned the art of making and breaking computer code. Off this central space lay further rooms armed with video cameras, editing suites and radio booths.

Elsewhere, students were studying business, politics, international relations and constitutional law. Snatches of English and French grammar hung in the early evening air.

A large acacia tree stood in a circular clearing at the bottom of the road, casting its shadow over a fire pit. A middle-aged man invited his guests to settle here until dusk, when Al-Shā'ir would be able to join them. The man read the confusion on his visitors' faces. 'The Poet,' he said with a smile, as if the translation solved the misunderstanding.

Two students made a fire as the shadows lengthened, out of which a silhouette appeared and took a seat.

'I have a story to tell you,' the old man said, the flames picking out the deeply etched smile lines on his face, 'that is, and is not, so.' He motioned for a boy to serve his guests tea.

'It is said that, among us, a secret order lies in wait. They may have already sought out your company for pleasure, or be masquerading as your colleague, friend, or lover. Legend has it they shake hands just like us. Their wardrobes would betray no purple robes. Chanting and incense have no place in their world. We cannot rule out the odd pointy nose, but nor can we guarantee one.

'Their secret is such that members of The Order may unknowingly be friends. They live in constant doubt: when should they rise up, and what should they do once they have done so? Indeed, none of them has any certainty that any other of The Order is still alive.'

He looked up and smiled at his audience.

'Their prophecy, like many others, foretells the apocalypse, but not in the way so often promised, with horsemen and hell-fire. No, what The Order foretells is the end of the word, of the imagination. Don't pretend you can't hear its approaching silence. We all have blood on our hands. When it is time The Order will rise and . . . and . . .' Al-Shā'ir trailed off.

'The legend can be traced back to eleventh-century Persia. The Seljuk Empire, whose lands stretched from the steppes of Anatolia to the sands of the Taklamakan, was terrorised by a clandestine group called the Assassins. For years they worked their way into positions within the court, before shockingly and publicly slaying their masters.

'And if the peoples of the Seljuk Empire thought the Assassins inspired fear, along came the Crusaders. On the plus side' – Al-Shā'ir chuckled to himself – 'the Crusaders didn't hide behind curtains, and crawl from the shadows to smother you in your sleep. Instead they climbed over the city walls and killed everything. If your only fear was subtlety, they were a breath of fresh air.

'To summarise: if you were lucky enough to be in the

ownership of your head, it was likely to be filled with tales of the most monstrous kind.'

He looked across the flames to his audience of four.

'It is said The Order began as a collective of rich traders from all over the Muslim world, from as far as Fes and Tripoli along the Maghreb trade routes towards the great cities of the Levant. Surrounded by fellow tradesmen exchanging tales, they recognised a story's ability to inspire empathy between strangers. Where stories were absent, chaos ruled.

'At the end of the thirteenth century, the 43 founding members gathered in Cairo. Stories from across the world were performed, embellished, lengthened and satirised. They sang, they danced, they revelled in the wonder and power of story.

'One day, with a heavy heart, the member from Samarkand announced that he had to leave. The night before his planned departure, the member from the Persian city of Shiraz asked if she might tell one final story. It was a tale so full of adventure and truth that when dawn gave a polite cough from the horizon, it still hadn't finished. It was decided the return to Samarkand would be delayed, and the tale would seek a conclusion the following evening.

'The next evening saw the climax to her story, but also the beguiling temptation of another that would find no closure that night. None of The Order could bear to leave while the plight of a hero, or the revealing of a truth, lay in the balance. And so it continued.

'It is said that the member from Shiraz, who went by the name of Scheherazade, continued in this vein for 1,001 nights.

'The delay enabled a plan to emerge. Each would return home and set up a madrasa dedicated to the art of storytelling. Each would have two schools. The first would develop technical performance: delivery, expression, pace, drama, musical accompaniment and puppetry. The second would focus on repertoire, tailoring the narrative to the audience and the exchange of successful stories between madrasas. The rababah – a stringed instrument with a long neck and a small round body that was used as musical accompaniment to performance – would be their insignia.

'As the members returned home, the global influence of The Order began. From the cafés of Bukhara to the squares of Marrakech, huge crowds would gather to have their imaginations set on fire. No one knew where the performers had come from, but their powers of providing guidance and wonder led people to question how they had previously managed without them.

'The original 43 members quickly increased in number. From Morocco, The Order crossed the straits into Iberia. Ships from Alexandria crossed to Italy. In Europe the madrasas were the only centres of learning in town, and soon became known institutions. The first of these sprang up in Cambridge, Bologna and Salamanca.

'These European madrasas expanded their instruction to include grammar, logic and rhetoric as ways to captivate, reason and persuade their audience. This was The Order's Golden Age.'

Al-Shā'ir paused.

'Further skills were added that were intended to support the madrasas. Astronomy was added to take advantage of planetary superstition, arithmetic to do the madrasa's accounts, law because everyone makes mistakes. They soon became subjects in their own right. Men, called mathematicians, roamed madrasas with no idea how to craft words into worlds. Storytellers existed who had no stories, and were called philosophers. They all wanted more room and more departmental funding.

'Questions were then raised as to whether storytelling was a proper subject. In the sixteenth century a university was formed without any provision for storytelling. Its founders felt the extroverts in the courtyard were for lunchtime entertainment only.

'Around this time, the heads of storytelling at all The Order's madrasas met in Venice. From Fatehpur Sikri to Stratford-upon-Avon, members spoke of their disillusionment. They had been pushed to the margins, trumped by dogmas of religious intolerance, naïve to the politicisation of stories, which had been harnessed for the ends of power and greed. The world, as it always seems to be, was teetering on the edge.

'And if The Order was to save it they had to adapt, and nurture a few saviours of their own. Each madrasa would select their most promising students, and grant them the best education and social privileges. Keeping their loyalties hidden, they would climb up to the highest ranks in government, looking at ways to frame stories in ways that could unite rather than divide, to bring joy rather than hate – waiting for a time when a story was needed to pull the world back from the abyss. Each initiate would induct a younger replacement.

'The member from Stratford-upon-Avon was one such man. Excited with the prospect of saving the world, he produced 38 plays before later covering his tracks.'

Al-Shā'ir laughed and looked at his audience to gauge if they understood.

'Which figures from history belonged to The Order? How many of your heroes were also your saviours? How many told the wrong story and became your enemy? How many died alone and ignored?' Al-Shā'ir shrugged.

'We all have our lists. Yet the important question is how many remain? Over five centuries on, how could anyone keep such solitary faith? Where would you find anyone with the patience to be initiated? Maybe by listening to this story, you, too, have been initiated. You might be the last ones left.'

Al-Shā'ir took a sip of tea. The sound of the cicadas, the river and the fire reminded his audience of how far away from home they were.

'It was not long before storytelling was purged from the history of madrasas. The members of The Order who avoided destitution became tutors, analysing *Macbeth* one syllable at a time.'

His audience smiled.

'Others took to the streets to entertain an ever shrinking audience, but times had changed. Crowds left coins out of pity, the value of a story demeaned to that of begging. The modern world was no place for men whose imaginations had no ulterior motives.'

Al-Shā'ir nodded slowly.

'But there is one more story left to tell. It is said that an elite group of storytellers from the Cairo madrasa left one day at the start of the twentieth century. You would not find them in cafés or squares. They were gone. Rumours circulated that early one morning they had left the madrasa, trunks in tow, boarded a felucca, and set sail in a southerly direction.

'And with that, the story was said to end.'

A Bend in the River

Unlike other parents who celebrate each jumbled vowel, Al-Shā'ir's parents expected him to make a vocal mark upon the world only when he had something worth saying.

For the first four years of his life Al-Shā'ir was handed from his mother's teat, to musicians' laps, to orators' hips, to the stage where he received acclaim for his wordless comic timing. By his fortieth month he had mastered puppetry, and before his fourth birthday had performed what his father recognised as a silent performance of Hamlet's most famous soliloquy.

To outside eyes, this would not have been considered textbook parenting, but his parents had been raised in a similar way. They were born in the same village on the banks of the Nile after their own parents had fled Cairo in an event that became known as 'The Exodus'. Whereas the Israelites had parted water for theirs, Al-Shā'ir's grandparents sailed leisurely on top of it in a southerly direction: a fleet armed with an arsenal of musical instruments, props, costumes, puppets and the imaginations of 12 storytellers and their families.

Their retreat from the city was viewed as a temporary

measure. As the madrasa became established, they would re-forge their links with madrasas around the world.

The fields were fertile, and the madrasa soon grew in size. As the world experienced one crippling war after another, there seemed no compelling reason to re-enter the fray. Al-Shā'ir's parents grew up to marry each other, believing that everything of value in the world lay within the madrasa's limits.

As each of the next 40 years passed, the madrasa drifted further from the twentieth century. It was no longer a training camp for an army of stories, but a form of preservation. They were archives in a forgotten museum.

Four years into the life of their previously mute heir, a note of discord entered proceedings. As an evening performance recounted The Order's cosmopolitan origins, a wavering, high-pitched voice invaded a dramatic pause.

'Why do we speak of places we are too scared of visiting?'

The rest of the audience turned to the young boy. A mixture of proud smiles and disquieted frowns crossed their faces. It had taken a child to point out the madrasa's blossoming relationship with irrelevance. The madrasa more closely resembled a village than a school. No one graduated or left in search of bright lights.

The young boy was named 'The Poet' and he soon grew into the name. King Solomon of Sonnets, the Prince of Pentameter, the Verse Vizier: by the age of ten, he spoke solely in poetry. Disagreements over cleaning his room transcended into lyrical paeans to the stars.

By the age of fifteen he was said to have the largest repertoire of stories in the whole madrasa. From the fantastical, to the allegorical, to the comic, thrilling and erotic, he had a story suitable for every mood.

His fidelity to poetry was eroded by contact with traders

who hinted that the modern world favoured stories in prose. He adapted all his stories to both formats, causing uproar among the elders. By his twenties he argued that the madrasa had lost its way: a saviour whose time has come does not remain in hiding.

Around this time, he fell in love with Aliah, the closest person he had to a rival in the madrasa; but puppets, not words, were her chosen medium for magic.

As the madrasa prepared for the evening show, they would sneak into an empty story room, and by candlelight bare their feelings to one another, one performance at a time. Their trysts saw them chastely explore each other's hopes, fears, flaws and burdens. Their days were spent wondering how a plot twist revealed an aspect of the other's heart, or how the sudden introduction of a new character implied uncertainty within their relationship. Soon, their plots and protagonists intertwined, the different choices their heroes took became a conversation about the decisions they would take in their own life together. Their stories became less fantastical, and more domestic. How many children did the hero have? How much time did he spend at home? Their stories began to overlap in both content and timing. The frictions that mired certain forks in a story's path started to ease; puppets no longer shook their heads in disagreement with the words. On the one-thousandth consecutive night they told a love story together that had no leader or follower, no reserve or amendments. On night 1,001, they wed.

They decided that the only way for the madrasa to reconnect with the world was to try to understand it. First they took trips to the great cities of Cairo and Alexandria. Later visits to Jerusalem, Damascus and Beirut demonstrated that stories were political weapons battling for power and truth.

So Al-Shā'ir sought to drag the madrasa into the modern

world. They returned to their trading roots. Initiates were sent to the cities to study business and economics. Some returned to teach at the madrasa, while others embedded themselves within corporations. A similar route was taken with politics and international relations, with initiates rising up through government and international organisations. The public's obsession with TV and film saw a focus on media studies, production and acting.

No more would initiates be cut adrift from The Order. Those who left the madrasa submitted quarterly reports to what was now jokingly labelled 'HQ', detailing opportunities within their industries. Each month Al-Shā'ir headed a committee of orators, musicians, puppeteers and mimes to brainstorm their responses. It often took hours of revelry crafting them: be it relevant stories, strategies, or introducing fellow initiates from competitive companies or industries to each other. They spent hours mocking committees of storytellers in America who made 'ads', using their powers to create money instead of empathy. Within the madrasa, acceptance into the committee was seen as the highest honour, and was soon labelled the Grand Circus: the GC at HQ.

In 1975 Al-Shā'ir and Aliah had their first, and only, child. They named the girl Jalila. Unlike his own childhood, Al-Shā'ir encouraged her to talk as much, and as early, as possible. His parenting reflected the realisation that the world rewarded not the one who told the greatest story, but the one who told it the loudest. Yet in spite of paternal pressure, his daughter chose the path of listener over orator. She followed debates that raged for hours, before expertly providing a synopsis of the common ground and potential paths forward. She would extract the hidden truth from within a story's cliché. Her eyes could calm even the most nervous speaker.

Aliah comforted her husband. 'Every great storyteller needs

a great audience.' Al-Shā'ir nodded, unconvinced. She was right, except that it had been entrusted to them, The Order, to do the talking.

And so the differences between father and daughter continued as Jalila matured into a woman. With every disagreement, Al-Shā'ir used more words in his bid to convince his daughter, while Jalila became more patient. 'Father, I'm just looking for proof that someone is listening.'

He had none. He had been naïve to suppose that the world was a stage for him to use for free. No number of initiates in all the world's media and entertainment could change a simple truth: an audience only forms for a story they want to hear.

In academia, stories became theories; in politics they were propaganda; and in business they were PR. Cynicism stalked the stage.

By this time, a young man called Ramsey had fallen in love with Jalila, and although now a teacher of logic and reasoning, she could not help but love him back. Her eyes were sirens to his deepest secrets. They reached inside him and extinguished his insecurities.

Unfortunately, they could not extinguish the tuberculosis that took him four months after they married, and two months after Jalila fell pregnant. She now felt trapped by stories she had no affinity with. The one story that was hers, and hers alone, had ended before it had started. She was inconsolable, and spent hours sitting on the riverbank, dreaming of escape.

Al-Shā'ir and Aliah were similarly broken: parents haunted by their inability to ease their child's pain. Al-Shā'ir knew his daughter would see through his words, and reproach him for using wisdom he had not learned first-hand.

Soon after, the Grand Circus received an unusual request

from an initiate who worked in the book industry. It was an invite to something strange yet utterly familiar: the literature festival. The Order had been holding variations of them for a millennium. But the initiate reported how such festivals had become recent highlights in the diaries of the powerful. They had selected a couple of events with particularly influential attendees, such as the inaugural Festival of Good in Britain, and asked if Al-Shā'ir would like to perform. His initial response was no. It was Aliah who changed his mind. 'Since when did the great storyteller avoid an audience? Have we become too content with age, my love?'

He agreed so long as it was a family performance. That summer, suitcase of puppets in tow, Al-Shā'ir, Aliah, Jalila and the bump set off for Europe. At first, nothing eased Jalila's sadness. Strange cities only intensified the loneliness. Yet in performance she found comfort. Although her parents tried to hide it, Jalila noticed that they had never seemed so in love. They stole smiles during shows. She had forgotten their talent and chemistry when they performed together. She could hear belief return to her father's words. He felt vindicated by the laughter, gasps and applause.

Jalila thought of baby names. That summer was their happiest as a family.

It would also be their last. Aliah complained of nausea before they left their London hotel for the airport. By the time they entered French air space she was feverish, and as the Mediterranean stretched out below them, she was helped to the bathroom where she collapsed. As the plane descended, stewardesses cleared the back row and a solicitor with basic CPR tried to resuscitate her. The plane braked heavily, stopping prematurely on the runway.

Al-Shā'ir refused a post-mortem. Through her tears, Jalila arranged a vehicle. After three hours they boarded a felucca headed for the madrasa. They sat on the bow holding Aliah as the sun set and the stars awoke, as Al-Shā'ir recited poems of the eternal nature of love.

Aliah was buried on the edge of the madrasa, on a spot that overlooked the Nile. Al-Shā'ir sat by the grave all night. He remained all the next day, and was taken food, drink and a mat to sleep on. Jalila joined him, listening to her father describe to his sleeping wife the world around him. There was a patience in his voice that led Jalila to believe he would never leave this place again.

It was said that over the next 1,000 days he recounted every story that had ever been told. Jalila would join him every morning and evening with her newborn daughter, Aiya. At first Jalila would carefully place her in her grandfather's arms, but before long Aiya would crawl, walk and run down towards him. Years were passing, but the loss that clung to Al-Shā'ir and Jalila's hearts was not.

Then one day, Al-Shā'ir returned.

Jalila smiled at him as they took a seat by the fire under the acacia tree and called for refreshment. The silence that followed lay heavy with all the questions burning within Jalila.

'The river is a constantly changing story of where it has been, who it has met and what has been done to it,' Al-Shā'ir finally said. 'It's the witness of civilisations past, heavy with the load of hope and greed, politics and poetry. It's maybe the greatest storyteller that has ever come to be. And look how we treat it: it is now a mild poison, running with the carelessness of our world. When I was young, we respected the river as a member of The Order, telling stories from faraway lands. But now . . .'

Jalila stared at the fire, for once unable to find words of comfort: heavy sediment falling to the riverbed within.

'When your mother and I were young, we made a pact to

modernise the madrasa. Even then, the majority of boats that sailed past the bank were feluccas.' He smiled and looked at his daughter. 'And now I look out, and there are these cruise boats. On deck are all the people looking at the river through their screens, taking these terrible pictures of themselves, refusing to ask fellow passengers for help. They send these pictures of the river back home to their families in an instant.

'The river, the great storyteller, may not be what it once was, but what sails on top of it has created a global audience it could have never dreamed of.'

Jalila smiled, raising her eyebrows. 'Does my father wish to be the cruise boat?'

Al-Shā'ir shrugged. 'Maybe we were never quite as modern as we thought. I think I owe your mother one last attempt.'

At first the madrasa was infused with energy. Modern buildings were erected to house the new computer labs and recording studios, as external initiates were invited to return to give coding tutorials. Al-Shā'ir's calls to harness the internet inspired dreams that the whole world was a potential audience. For a while it seemed possible. When the Grand Circus was formed, they found their stories ignored by an audience captured by corporate money. But now they were promised a 'democratisation of storytelling'. They accepted the ugly language in return for the opportunities it promised.

But it wasn't long until Jalila could see the sadness of the grave return to Al-Shā'ir's eyes. The new world he had invested in cut him adrift from his earlier joys. Time in the story rooms had been replaced by the editing booth. Audiences were gauged not by smiles of delight, but by website hits. The Grand Circus became a bureaucratic chore, haunted by spreadsheets and an obsession with algorithms. Maybe it was for the best, yet he cursed the present for its lack of patience, craft and presence. He was an irrelevance cast aside by the tide of progress.

'Do you think the world is listening?' asked Jalila.

Al-Shā'ir looked at her with a tired look of love. 'The world does not exist. It is a distraction,' he said with wet eyes. 'Only stories remain.'

Jalila had no will to argue. She had learned how The Order was struggling – the promised huge audiences proved fickle and easily coerced by the corporate interests her father thought he had escaped. But Aiya was happy growing up within the madrasa. What do children care about ancient prophesies? She was precocious, and took her grandfather's sombre advice to excel in IT. At the age of six she hacked into government websites and placed nursery rhymes on their homepages. She was fluent in English, Italian, German and Spanish. Her horizons were widening, and her mother realised that one day soon she would want to take part in the world she was reading about.

Jalila walked with her father to the grave early one evening. A few minutes of silence passed.

'I have to believe in the world,' said Jalila.

Al-Shā'ir nodded. 'If anyone can save it, it is you.' He smiled at his daughter, who, holding his hand tightly, kissed him on the cheek, then slowly walked away.

The Fellowship of the String

It wasn't a separation; it would be a renaissance. Once more, the Mediterranean would be crossed in the name of a prophecy: this time in pursuit of something that had sailed centuries before. While Aiya's excitement was infectious, Al-Shā'ir had long ago been hardened against such optimism, and looking on from his wife's grave to the departing felucca that was carrying his family away, he thought he saw traces of the same resignation in his daughter's eyes.

They arrived in Alexandria after a day on river, road and rail, accompanied by Aiya's endless questioning about the world that passed by their window. A bored customs official nodded them and their chest of puppets aboard the ferry.

The three-day crossing was uneventful. To pass the time, Aiya begged her mother to tell her The Order's history one more time. Her eyes lit up with the evocation of the names *Salamanca*, *Bologna* and *Cambridge*. Her soul soared like the Venice skyline that eventually appeared through the porthole.

Soon they found themselves in the Piazza San Marco giggling with each other, almost in disbelief that the adventure had begun. Although Jalila's excuse for coming had been the re-forging of links to the European madrasas to escape the inertia of home, as they sat in the square, she couldn't help being caught up in her daughter's imagination.

For two weeks Aiya took to the daytime streets alone. At first her voice was timid, but her confidence soon grew. 'Deutsch? Español? Português? English?' she quizzed audiences from atop tables, lampposts and fountains, weaving multilingual tales clothed in her newly favourite black bomber jacket. 'Gentlemen, come close, *Denn ich muss eine Geschichte erzählen, die so ist, und auch nicht.*' Even those on the wrong side of the language barrier were transfixed by the music of her voice, where the meaning was understood even when the words were not.

Jalila, meanwhile, immersed herself in a world of horns, hand gestures and accusations. Her driving instructor was impressed by the lengths she would go to absolve herself from blame: 'You should tell stories for a living.' After nine days, the examiner nodded as she pulled in to the test centre. The next stop was a car dealership where she bought a 1970s white Fiat 500.

For the next three days, Aiya and Jalila performed together around the casino on the Grand Canal, where the Venetian order was said to have originated. Aiya's confidence infected Jalila as they performed in front of a black banner, embroidered with The Order's insignia: a secret calling to the initiated.

They spent their afternoons customising the car. The insignia was spray-painted on the bonnet and sides. They installed three angled mirrors, enabling them to perfect their own version of mime over the thousands of miles they were to drive.

On the fourth morning, they were on the road to Padua where they gave a matinee puppet show of *The Taming of the Shrew* in the piazza where it had originally been set.

The following day they were in Bologna where for two

days they performed in and around the medieval squares and university buildings.

In Florence, Aiya protected the decency of Michelangelo's *David:* he was, after all, one of them, and in Rome they performed in the Coliseum, before heading north via Perugia, Siena and Genoa.

At first, their hours on the road were spent refining their stories. A blackboard stretched across the dashboard from wheel to passenger door: a storyboard to hone their craft. With each passing mile, their silences grew longer: mime had become their chosen medium of communication. As their virtuosity increased, their facial expressions became subtler, to the point where the untrained eye would fail to notice any passing narrative between them.

They gave late-summer performances in Barcelona, Valencia and Murcia. After putting on a three-day retelling of *Don Quixote* in Salamanca for Aiya's fifteenth birthday, they parked their car for a few days to join the Camino de Santiago: a pilgrimage initiates had historically made in homage to the innovative madrasa at Santiago de Compostella. Modern-day pilgrims had their evenings brightened by a mother and daughter mind-reading act.

As autumn arrived the Fiat Madrasa boarded the Channel ferry at Calais. It was only as the days shortened and they reflected on their continental adventures that Al-Shā'ir's doubts started to prey on their minds: after three months they had yet to come across a single member of The Order. On the streets of Cambridge, Oxford and Stratford, they performed to small crowds who lingered at most for a couple of scenes, took photos of the spectacle, and moved on.

The long drives that followed were the first true silences that had passed between them in months. As they reached The Order's most northerly outposts at Copenhagen and

Uppsala, their breath frosted and their fingers seized in the Arctic air. *Father, I'm just looking for proof that someone is listening*. She understood his resignation now.

They arrived in Prague dreaming of the warmth of home. It was drizzly and dark as they set up in the Old Town Square. All the outside bar and restaurant tables were covered by tarpaulins. Pedestrians beelined across the square. For 20 minutes, Aiya and Jalila damply evoked a lost Baghdad, then dejectedly stopped mid-scene, packed the puppets away and pulled down the banner one last time.

Solitary applause cut through the rain's soft patter. They looked towards a bar doorway, where a waiter was sheltering, drawing on a cigarette. He gestured for them to come inside. Aiya shook her head uncertainly, but he scurried out with two umbrellas, placed them in their hands, and grabbed the chest before they could stop him. They followed meekly, too forlorn to care.

'Come on, let's get you warm. Tea? Hot chocolate? It's on me.' He guided them to a cramped corner table next to a heater and left to get their drinks. On the tables around them, agitated parents provided chips and technology to entertain their restless children. Couples sat largely in silence, sipping their lager. All the seats were angled towards a TV that hung above the bar, where a news channel looped grainy images of armed men, with the headline scrolling underneath.

So this was where their audience had been hiding. And who could blame them?

'Two hot chocolates.' The waiter placed the steaming cups in front of them along with two ragged towels. 'Where are you from?'

Aiya dried her face. 'Egypt.'

'Woah. Long way to come to perform in the Czech rain. But I liked your show very much.' Aiya nodded seriously, to which the waiter responded with a comforting smile. 'I see many performers come through here. Sometimes they get big crowds – but only in the summer, and never for long. Five minutes, maybe ten, and then the audience drifts away. Nobody would perform as long as you, and definitely not in the rain.'

Jalila smiled politely at the waiter, who was immediately apologetic. 'I'm sorry. I'm not criticising. No, no. I'm no expert. I just spend a lot of time watching people.' He motioned to his customers, who were playing on their phones, or transfixed by the muted tragedy on TV. 'People like to watch videos of cats doing silly things or they like disaster. That guy by the bar has been watching this kidnap on TV for an hour. This is the competition.'

Aiya and Jalila looked up to the screen, quickly piecing together their own story from the images of hostage, kidnapper and concerned company executives. Both instinctively understood the story's dark, addictive qualities.

'You know what I'm thinking?' said the waiter. 'If you really want people to pay attention, you should kidnap one of those silly cats.' He laughed out loud. 'People will love it. Nothing like cute mystery to bring everybody together. No?'

Still chuckling, he nodded an apology as he moved away to serve another customer.

They shrugged at each other. 'Fancy kidnapping a cat, Mum?'

Jalila smiled distantly, staring thoughtfully out the window. Aiya stirred her chocolate. The waiter's words had stirred something, but neither of them was thinking about cats.

The Hit List

At the first sign of dusk, Al-Shā'ir would make his way up to Aliah's grave, and take a seat. There, as the sun called a truce with the landscape, he told her the story of his day. It would always begin with anecdotes from the stage, or a piece of gossip involving one of Aliah's old friends. But this was all a prelude to what burned in his heart, words that only a woman who loved him for all his faults could understand; for every night, he would tell the story of a mother and daughter who left their home in a quest to save the world.

These stories were the most dangerous he had ever told. Worlds of genies and fantastical kingdoms were replaced with harsh dystopias filled with apartment blocks, traffic and poverty: he'd left a world he knew for one he did not. Their adventure was the only consolation remaining to him.

The antagonists were the most complex he had conceived; situations were no longer black and white, right or wrong. Evil was now replaced by background noise and apathy; the landscapes of their quests were no longer haunted forests and howling seas, but concepts and systems. It was never obvious to Al-Shā'ir if his stories were sad, thrilling, or comic. Yet it brought him great happiness to be close to them: the ghosts of his family, both dead and alive, united by a story once more.

But as the sun fell, the warmth of his stories diluted in the darkness, leaving him lonely and broken, in the knowledge that he had imagined the lives of his family too much, and taken part in them too little. And he wasn't now sure where to start.

Jalila had written: their European tour had come to an end, and they were headed for Cairo. Their purpose was vague, speaking of new creative ways of attracting a local audience. Their sole request was for a list – compiled by the Grand Circus every quarter, using information drawn from their global initiates – of powerful or influential figures who were to visit Cairo.

Had he not already tried and failed upon a public stage? Influence could not be won or lobbied for The Order's cause when no one was listening. No special pleading would change that, and he doubted they would be granted meetings with the elite in any case. But he decided that maybe they too needed to sample that bitter experience for themselves.

So every three months he would be handed a list to glance over before it was placed in an envelope and wax sealed with the rababah insignia. It was five o'clock one afternoon as the list was placed in his hand. He skimmed the surnames: *Johnson*, *Evans*, *Meyer*, *Sellwood*, *Darwish*, *Riaz*, *Pounder*, *Reichwein*, *Dwyer*, *Wilson*; and browsed the professions: *human rights campaigner*, *educator*, *programmes director*, *composer*, *anthropologist*, *comedian*, *philanthropist (former oil company CEO)*, *global health adviser*, *academic*, *explorer*, accompanied by columns indicating their date of arrival, accommodation in Cairo, and rough itineraries. He shrugged and nodded to the assistant.

He rested a while in thought, before he got up and

departed for his daily pilgrimage to a grave where the last remaining light suspended, if only briefly, his heartbreak with the world.

A Parable

15 years earlier
The inaugural Festival of Good, Oxfordshire, UK

It was day three of the Festival of Good. The English summer had arrived. Participants modelled summer dresses and shirts with undone buttons. While there were displays of community projects in India and photo exhibitions of famine in Africa, the atmosphere, with its strawberries and cocktails, was closer to that of a wedding reception, as a collection of the world's most prominent well-intentioned people milled around the marquee village.

Over the last two days they had been treated to presentations by activists, philanthropists and alternative currency economists. It was widely agreed that the high spot of the festival so far had been a charismatic speech by Richard Pounder, the new, young CEO of GoldBlue Oil who had set out his vision of a green oil industry. In the question and answer session that followed, he had been challenged by Liam Powell, a young journalist, who accused him of representing not genuine change, but a public relations exercise. This was compounded by a further challenge from the floor by a controversial NGO worker, Jordie Macpherson, who had wagered Pounder 50 quid that his principles wouldn't last as long as his employment at GoldBlue – that his principles had a price.

The same Jordie Macpherson had earlier shocked the crowd with his highly individual take on his reasons for leaving the World Bank and joining an organisation that worked in slum communities around the world: 'I've no idea what the fuck I was doing at the World Bank. It reminds me of when I was a virgin, I tried to get my hand down this girl's pants, but was so nervous I forgot about the belt. I ended up with my hand trapped, wiggling about trying to look busy. The girl was polite enough to give a half-hearted groan, but whatever . . . it was a pretty fucking terrible experience for all concerned. At the World Bank, the girl was a country, and the knickers, its economy.'

Sixteen-year-old Miller Carey was sitting in the front row with his mum.

It was a performance session, mid-morning, on day three. The lights were turned down. A man and two women entered the stage. The women went straight behind a four-foot-high screen on the stage. The man stood to the side. He was wearing a white shirt that came all the way down to his ankles. The women spent a few moments organising hidden objects behind the screen.

Good afternoon, ladies and gentlemen, boys and girls. The man's face conveyed many qualities: warmth and secrecy, humour and sadness.

I trust you are comfortable, as we have a story to tell that is, and is not, so.

Once upon a time there was a king. A puppet appeared in front of the screen, adorned with fanciful lace clothing and crown. *The king was a mild ruler, not like some of these beasts we hear of in fairy tales with a taste for tomfoolery and murder. He had a deep respect for the needs of his subjects, and acknowledged that his responsibility lay in preparing his people for the coming of democracy. When they were ready, he would step aside.*

In the meantime, the king's court ruled justly over its population. Proposed legislature had to be performed; puppeteers, dancers, soothsayers and drunkards were all granted a stage before the king and his advisers. The public filled the court's stalls to the rafters.

The marquee was transfixed. They had lost count of all the intricately crafted puppets that had entered the stage; their bodies were directed with grace and humour.

No policy was put forward until its supporters had transformed it into the lyrics of a 12-bar hoedown. Budgets were turned down for lacking a sense of rhythm, court expenses due to a lazy half rhyme.

The crowd laughed as the kingdom's absurdity unfurled.

Referendums took the form of two plays that had been inspired from each of the competing points of view, and performed in a random town. Whichever play entertained the crowd the most gained legislative approval.

No bills were ratified until the whole court had made love to their partners.

A queen puppet approached the king. Just as the queen pushed the gown off her shoulder, a curtain quickly fell, and the audience clapped with delight.

One day, a regal notice arrived, written by a baron from far-away lands wanting to visit and pay his respects. Before he arrived, an adviser stole the ear of the king, and confessed his fears that this baron might look down on the current practices of the court. 'Your Highness, I believe that abroad, governing is not considered a form of play.'

The king looked confused. 'Then . . . how on earth do they govern?'

'I believe they do so . . .' – the adviser paused nervously – '. . . seriously.'

The king's confusion was complete.

'In the name of kingdom security,' the adviser continued, 'we can't afford our particular mannerisms to be common knowledge.'

The king remained unmoved. 'Ah, yes . . . yes of course,' he suddenly exclaimed, realising his adviser's euphemism. 'Well, what on earth are we to do?'

For the next hour, the adviser tried to explain how kingdoms abroad were governed: their respected rituals, how participants felt the gravity of it all.

Eventually the king relented. Unable to comprehend what was being asked of him, he gave full authority to his advisers to manage this one-off event.

Once the king departed, the advisers called in the court fool.

'Where's my master?' asked the fool. It was he who ran court sessions, and whose responsibility it was to maintain a healthy level of reverie.

'We're in charge for now,' said one of the advisers, 'and we've decided it's best for the kingdom if you don't come to court this week.'

'You boorish cockscombs. You could never run court without me.'

'A foreign baron is attending, and the king thinks your presence would embarrass the kingdom,' one of the advisers sneered.

The fool laughed. 'I know my master better than that. This all comes from you, and your desires to run this kingdom like all the others. I know what you are.'

'And what's that?' an adviser bit back. 'A fool?' The other advisers laughed without humour.

'No. You're a . . .' The fool stared back with a smile, before whispering the following syllables as if they were a curse. 'Bu. Reau. Crat.'

The puppet fool exited the stage to be replaced by a line of bugle-playing puppets, greeting the baron's entourage at court, while the Festival of Good's audience watched, enchanted.

For all the orders and declarations made by the advisers for them to stay away, the public crowded outside waiting to attend the court session. The advisers sent in plain-clothed guards to dispel them.

Inside court were a group of men and women who failed to understand why they had been invited when so many others remained outside: their interests in law, banking and renting land were regarded as the least glamorous in the whole kingdom.

'You are here because you are the elite,' said an adviser, before issuing their instructions.

'The elite?' they repeated unfamiliarly. 'Must be French,' said one.

The elite desperately conferred with each other to try to grasp their new responsibilities. It was all very confusing. Those who initiated a Barber's Quartet welcome to the baron were quickly cut off by the advisers and escorted from court. 'The excitement of your visit seems to have driven some of our privy council positively mad,' excused a conniving adviser.

The session passed quietly. Only the advisers spoke, passing legislature, while the rest of the elite sat confused and afraid. But pass it did, and with a sigh of relief the ordeal was over, and things could return to normal.

Except they did not. The baron, tired from his travels, was encouraged by the advisers to stay for a month. Meanwhile the advisers convinced the king that the pretence must continue until the baron's departure. Palace guards were ordered to keep the protesting fool away from the king.

The public turned up to court once more, not expecting to participate, but as a protest against their exclusion. Guards forcefully scattered the crowd, with veiled threats to any future dissent. Within the court, the elites started to learn their new roles within a wholly different performance – that of raised hands and un-played consensus.

The fool could sense the changing tides. On his walks outside the palace gates he heard the confusion of the people. Mornings heralded new laws nailed to doorways, laws that bore little relationship to their lives, enforced rather than en-acted.

He could be idle no longer. Guards blocked his access to the king's ear, so under the cover of night, he visited taverns and squares, encouraging the continuation of the kingdom's traditions in the bawdy underground. The disillusioned came to hear his foolery, playing a clandestine opposition into existence.

The advisers soon learned of the swelling disillusion, although its ringleaders remained unknown. They intimidated people in their homes, demanding information. Plain-clothed guards spied in taverns. Yet the swell of discontent continued.

The advisers met, urgently seeking a solution. 'It is said that you cannot jail an idea,' said one. The others were impressed by his profundity, but anxious for his solution. 'But you can undermine it.'

'With what?' came the reply.

The adviser smiled. 'With fear disguised as reason.'

The following day, notices were found stuck to walls throughout the kingdom. Within its lines there were reports of neighbouring kingdoms preparing for war, of potential hard economic times ahead. Over family dinners, parents started to chastise younger generations for continuing such naïve play when the whole security of the kingdom was at risk. 'They are lovely ideas, but your sonnets fail to stack up.'

Families and villagers started to argue among themselves. Angry protesters aimed accusations and ridicule at the king: just another tyrant whose promise of democracy had descended into dictatorship.

The king had spent the preceding month entertaining the baron, who turned out to be an insufferable bore. His advisers assured him that the kingdom was happy, and that he should focus only upon the baron until his departure. The realities were kept hidden from him.

Their only challenge remained the fool, who stalked the palace waiting for a chink in security to grant him access to the ear of the king. The advisers ordered the fool to be followed at all times. The fool became careless; security soon followed him to a tavern where he was calling on his supporters for insurrection against the king's tyranny.

The king was heartbroken as his advisers spoke of the fool's treachery: of how his anger at not being invited to the royal party welcoming the baron had fuelled his jealousy; of how he had refused to come to see the king in a sustained fit of self-righteousness; of how, like a madman, he had defamed the king to an outraged public.

So play was confined to outside court. It was said the fool died a pauper. Ringworm of the soul, said the make-believe coroner. The advisers closest to the king protected him from all contact with his population. A continuous cycle of meetings and debates were held to distract the king from asking where his citizens had gone. His court reassured him it was being taken care of. 'Just sign here, Your Majesty.' And with a flick of his wrist he set his mind at ease.

It wasn't much fun, he lamented. The king missed a sing-song. Don't we all?

His population certainly did when they all started starving to death.

No, it wasn't much fun at all.

PART THREE

The Kidnap

May 6th
Cairo

Liam didn't believe any of them. He had met people who had been kidnapped before. Irrelevant of how brutal or calm the experience, they all returned with a heightened sense of description: the distantly heard daily cycle of the call to prayer or commuter buses; the focus and attention paid to food; measuring the length of day by shafts of light; the coarse texture of the floor. They remembered.

But while obviously being held by the same group, all the hostages he met described different cells. They were served different food. The number of kidnappers varied. They were reluctant to speak about their ordeal, but not seemingly because of the trauma it caused, but almost because they were trying to downplay that anything untoward had happened. The older woman refused even to call it a kidnap. Hanif the storyteller answered his questions with winding narratives of genies and princesses.

Commissioner El Sayed was a policeman, a man who supposedly specialised in details, and yet he had none to give. When asked about the state of the investigation, he looked confused as to what investigation Liam meant. Everyone he spoke to showed little desire to catch the kidnappers.

The hostages didn't feel like . . . victims. The way the head teacher had proudly shown the school renovations; the way her colleagues and parents interacted with her: not in the fragile way he had seen other hostages treated, but as part celebrity, part heroine.

But for all his suspicions, Liam was wary of accusing them of the conspiracies he suspected: as a last chance of saving his job, it would have been a bold strategy. After walking the morning streets, frustrated by the dead-ends he was facing in both the story and his career, he took a window seat in the corner of a teahouse, and closely observed the passers-by. He imagined each one as a co-conspirator – in what, he didn't know. The men sitting at tables around him were all suspects. But what were they guilty of? And did he have a right to solve a mystery that its victims didn't want solved?

His shirt stuck to his clammy body, the fan making little impact on the rising heat. He suddenly felt lost and vulnerable, impotent at solving a foreign puzzle he no longer had the energy or imagination for. In the time it took him to finish his tea, he decided to check out of his hotel and head to the airport. He was done.

He glanced out of the window as he waited for his change – no longer looking for answers, but for an alternative, a last chance to save what he wasn't sure he wanted saving. And there it was, trailing behind a huge vision in khaki, with a clipboard: serendipity found in the most unlikely of places.

Miller had tried a variety of liquor, tobacco and ginseng, but nothing could calm his panic. He stared across the lobby to the reception desk, where Jordie had gone to complain about the lack of toiletries.

'Success,' Jordie said as he joined Miller. 'I've sorted out the substandard tea- and coffee-making facilities as well.' The hotel was more luxurious than their projects usually afforded them: the generous philanthropic budget had upgraded them to marble floors, lobby water features and a disinterested piano player in the bar.

Miller returned Jordie's comment with a frosty stare.

'Ah come on, man. I'm sorry. I fucked up. I know. How many times can I apologise?'

Even if Miller wanted to, his body was incapable of forgiveness: it was preoccupied with the guilt of putting his and his colleagues' jobs at risk. Jordie's newfound sensitivities would have to wait.

They had only found out about Richard's involvement as they read the itinerary on the plane over to Cairo. Jordie could still clearly picture him up on stage 15 years ago, delivering a vision of big business that he thought either manipulative or naïve in the extreme. It had only just occurred to him that he might be owed £50 on an outstanding wager.

'Well, what should we order from the wine list, considering this is a reunion and all?'

Miller stared angrily at Jordie, shaking his head. 'You might have given up hope on your future,' said Miller, 'but for the next couple of weeks, can you at least pretend you haven't given up hope on mine.' So far, their best plan to avoid the India trip with Olaf was to contract dysentery.

'Well . . . we could just kidnap Pounder,' said Jordie, raising his eyebrows in an attempt to bring a smile to Miller. 'Rebalance the world's karma a little. Even for us it would represent new territory in the many ways to fail a development project.'

Miller signalled with his head across the lobby. 'Speak of the devil.'

Miller and Jordie both stood up. Richard headed in their direction; all he knew was that on his arrival at the hotel from the airport he was supposed to meet two Brits in the bar. It was only when he got closer to Jordie that he took on the face of a man who had forgotten where he had put his keys.

'Cotswolds. 15 years ago. Self-righteous festival,' Jordie said as he shook Richard's hand. 'I believe we made a bet over which one of us would become disillusioned first.'

'I trust the court is still out,' Richard said, with vague recognition sparking in his face.

'Cotswolds as well, I suppose,' said Miller, holding out his hand. Richard looked blank. 'I was 16,' Miller clarified.

Richard shook his head. 'You too. Jesus.'

'Well, it's nice that we're all back together. All passionate and motivated,' said Jordie.

'Isn't it?'

They made small talk around the flight, the oppressive outside temperature and whether it was their first time in Cairo. After 15 minutes, conversation was going to dry up unless one of the elephants in the room drew attention to itself, which elephants have a habit of doing after eight units of alcohol.

'So . . . uh . . . when did you rediscover your passion for solar energy?' said Jordie.

Richard stared back frostily, trying to hold his tongue for long enough to let his defensiveness subside. But the touch-paper was already lit. Richard had been looking for someone to argue with since the final board meeting.

'I've done more for the environment than you'll ever know.'

Jordie nodded. 'Ah yes, I hear that oil is like Nivea for seabirds.'

Richard was caught between laughter and anger. 'I remember you. The one who put himself on the pedestal because he left the World Bank so that he could play around with the poor a little more intimately.'

Jordie let out a patronising smile. 'Well, I'm so glad you've finally arrived down here to give us a helping hand. I suppose it's nice for you to be a little more . . . what should we say? Public?'

'Something like that.'

He instantly regretted coming to Cairo. He had no desire to see the project before investing, but had been convinced by Si from the philanthropic investment firm that it would let the team know he was committed. Larry, his supposed friend, had agreed with Si. *The bastards*, he thought.

The following morning, they left for the site visit: Jordie in the front, the other two in the back. Jordie played with the air conditioner but still couldn't halt the trickles of sweat sliding down the side of his face.

The day before, Jordie and Miller had started collecting household data on electricity use, utility bills and potential roof space. They had tried to limit the time lost in translation by using a simple questionnaire, but their translator Hashim, like a visiting relative, still talked for long periods at each port of call. Jordie and Miller spent most of their time declining endless cups of tea and sugary snacks.

They were all now on their way to meet Hashim at a local café for a tour of the neighbourhood. The tense evening had been carried on into the morning, coloured with a tinge of regret.

Their vehicle came to a halt. The fleet of dilapidated blue and white taxis that surrounded them showed no patience for diagnosis, and embarked on a cure of collective horn blowing: the traffic jam equivalent of kicking a broken television. Jordie grunted.

'Things like this just happen here. Strange things. Traffic jam with no jam. How do you say it . . . effect without cause?' said the driver.

Minutes passed. 'Maybe best you walk. Don't know how long this could take. Café only three minutes away.' None of them had any inclination to leave, but Miller eventually took the lead and opened the door.

'You need to walk down the second small road on the left,' said the driver, 'and then you're on the street with the café. You know from there. Remember, second on the left.'

They slowly made their way down the road. The stationary frustrations of the cars were in sharp contrast to the frenetic activity on the pavement. Hawkers and fruit carts encroached on it as pedestrians wove between obstacles. The smell of spice, fish, garbage and fumes underlined their foreignness to this environment, as did the inquisitive stares that accompanied them everywhere.

'Richard . . . Richard . . . Richard, is that you?'

They looked behind to see a figure slaloming between the traffic towards them. Jordie and Miller both turned to Richard, who gave no sign of recognition as the man approached them, hand outstretched.

'Liam Powell,' he said, holding out his hand. 'The, er . . .' – an embarrassed edge to his voice – 'journalist.' Richard offered his hand before he fully comprehended who was in front of him. 'What a coincidence to see you here like this.'

Jordie's laugh broke the silence. 'What are the fucking chances? That's perfect. Bit of early publicity for your altruism.'

Richard looked less impressed. 'What are you doing here?'

'Oh, just doing some background on a story.'

'You chasing another kidnap victim around the world?' said Richard, deciding against the pleasantries.

Liam smiled, embarrassed, as he leaned in towards them to let a pedestrian pass. 'No . . . I'm, er . . . I'm looking into the radical ways urban communities solve crises.'

'What a coincidence,' said Jordie. 'Richard's investing in

something like that. Aren't you, Richard?' He nudged him with his shoulder. 'I tell you what, why don't you come around with us and have a look at what we're doing. We can give you some inside information, and, you know, maybe you could give us a mention.'

'I, really, I was just about to go back to the hotel.'

'I thought you were an investigative reporter.'

Liam stared at Richard. Despite their animosity, the look signalled a common bond of enmity towards Jordie, who had already turned and continued walking.

They reached the second street on the left: a service road that provided access to the abandoned warehouses that graced both sides. They strode down it with increasing anxiety as they left the din of the traffic behind. There were no signs of life. Halfway down they approached two garbage piles that rose over six feet, heaped against the warehouse walls.

A wolf whistle pierced the quiet.

They looked to their right to see a figure dressed all in black crouched between the piles. The figure held an AK47 and aimed it at Richard's forehead.

'Don't even think about it, gentleman,' said the figure. 'We have the whole area covered.' The voice was female.

She motioned to the opposite side of the lane where another gunman emerged from the shadow of a doorway and waved them inside. The men exchanged glances, their imaginations filled with images of bloody consequence rather than of heroic escape. In a city of millions, they found themselves alone without hope of rescue or even a witness.

'If it helps I can ask you to come inside and have a look at our carpets. Just look, no buy, cheap price. I can make you all some tea.' The voice lacked malice, as if making an attempt at humour.

Liam closed his eyes to try to calm himself. *This must be*

them, he told himself, but the gleam of the rifle barrel dispelled the previously benign image he had constructed. Next to him he could hear Richard mumbling swear words.

'Get a move on,' said the gunwoman to Jordie who kept glancing towards the intersection.

'Heeeeeeelp. Fucking help us,' Jordie shouted as a figure passed the intersection. Before he had time to see the passer-by disappear into the sea of noise, a shove forced him towards the door, knocking him off balance. He looked up to see the rifle in his face.

'Make no mistake, fatty, I will shoot you in the face right here. But I would prefer to cook you lunch. Now get up and go inside.'

The others watched him get up in stunned terror. The countless hostages they had seen on TV, the drawn-out negotiations and the gunshots that had been heard echoing down corporate conference-call speakers – and here they were, seconds from being the photos that would titillate a global public obsessed with tragedy.

They found themselves shuffling towards the door.

'If you please, gentlemen, a little more pace. It is very hot out here,' said the armed female as they crossed the threshold.

Inside was a room six metres by six with two doors: one to their left, and one in front of them, guarded by the silent second gunman who had gone in ahead of them. The entrance behind them slammed shut.

'Welcome, welcome,' the gunwoman said. 'Now, before we continue I must ask a favour. I'm sorry to trouble you, but could you put all your phones and wallets in the basket in the middle of the room. Please, don't worry, I won't steal or sell them on. You know where I live.'

The men stared at each other, helpless, handicapped by fear. 'Phones and wallets, gentlemen. I won't ask again.'

One by one they placed their phones and wallets into the basket.

'Thank you. There's no reception in there anyway, but I don't want you to be distracted with thoughts of escape.'

The small room was painted beige and had darkened over the years. The only other marking on the walls was a simply painted black symbol. On first impression it looked like a thermometer.

'It's sort of our family crest,' she said, as if this was the detail from the last minute that played heaviest on their minds.

The silent gunman opened the door to their left, which revealed a staircase leading down into the basement. At the bottom lay another door.

'Make yourselves at home,' said the gunwoman, gun by her waist. '*Mi casa es su casa*.'

The door shut behind them after they entered.

The windowless room was 12 metres long by 6 metres wide and split into two halves. The half to the left had two bunk beds with a chest of drawers between them. The other side had two sofas that were turned to face each other, a modern-looking TV against the wall on the right and an L-shaped bookshelf that ran the whole length of the wall closest to them and around behind the TV. Opposite the entrance was another door that led to a bathroom with a shower and western toilet. A small table with four seats stood in the centre of the room. The walls had crisp beige paint; carpets covered the cement floors; an air conditioner welcomed its visitors from the oppressive heat outside.

They explored the cell, unsure how the unexpected comfort of the room squared with the terrible fates they each imagined. Had they been locked in a dark cage they could have understood their plight better.

In the corner next to the TV stood a small desk with a menu, writing paper and a laptop without internet connection. The menu fused east with west; all dishes were priced 'FREE'. It stated: 'If you have any special dietary requirements, please let us know. Please place your order under the door two hours before lunch and dinner, which are served at 1pm and 7pm respectively. Breakfast is served at 8am and should be ordered before 8pm the night before.'

The bookshelf contained a range of fiction, a spiritual collection covering the major religions and philosophies, and self-help books with titles such as *What I Believe in When I'm Stuck in a Room*, *A Flexible Amount of Steps to a Happier Life*, and *How I Became a Successful Noun*.

'What the fuck are we going to do? Fuck. Fuck. I knew I never should've been talked into coming. Fucking people. Fuck,' said Richard as he paced the room.

The silence gave way to recriminations and hopelessness.

'Would you shut up and let me think,' said Jordie from the sofa.

'Oh, you need to think now, do you? About what? We've been kidnapped. No one knows where we are. And I've had first-hand experience of what these type of people do to hostages. And as for you,' he said to Liam who sat opposite Jordie, 'why the fuck are you here? A minute after we meet this world expert in kidnapping we get fucking kidnapped.'

There was a loud knock on the door. 'Gentlemen, please. I know that after such an ordeal people like to blame each other, but I'd prefer it if my mum didn't have to hear the swearing. It's a bit awkward.'

They heard the footsteps disappear, replaced by the sound of uncontrollable sobbing. Miller sat against the wall, doubled over, his body shaking violently.

They were beset by a jumble of regrets and worries. Images

of friends and family hearing the news of their capture were punctuated by the bloody spectre of their own mortality.

It was the most complete loneliness they had ever felt.

'More to the point,' Richard said, as if the last hour of silence had never happened, 'how did they know where we were going to be? Or are there patient terrorists waiting on every abandoned side street?' He glared at Jordie and Miller, who looked up, surprised that in spite of their private torment, they were in fact in a room with others. 'It must have come from you. You've been here for two days. Let slip a millionaire was visiting, did you?'

'Yeah,' said Jordie, 'I speed-dialled straight through to al-Qaeda.'

'How mature. I meant let it slip to someone in the neighbourhood.' Richard paced behind Liam.

'Because everyone around here has two degrees of separation between themselves and Bin Laden. Fucking hell. Trust me, your presence wasn't something to brag about. You're as desirable as rubella in a fucking nursery. And to my knowledge you're the only one with a background in hostage crises, and the precedent you set is pretty fucking worrying.'

'Well, they didn't just magic out of nowhere. Someone must have told them we'd be walking down that street.'

'Why *did* you walk down that particular street?' said Liam, speaking up for the first time. 'It felt dodgy from the moment we got there.'

'We got told to by our—' Richard broke off.

Jordie breathed deeply. 'Our fucking driver.'

Richard escaped the tension he had instigated by visiting the toilet. As he peed, he noticed four new toothbrushes, a range of shower gels and shampoos, fresh bath mats and lavender air fresheners.

He re-entered the room with greater focus. 'We can sort this out,' he said, as the other three stared at him blankly. 'We need to tell them that we're here to help . . . you know . . . Muslims.'

He walked to the door and banged it repeatedly. 'We're here to help Muslims, not harm them.' By the third repeat, a sad desperation had entered Richard's voice.

Miller walked over and put a hand on Richard's shoulder, whose forehead now rested against the door. 'Come on, it's OK. That's enough.'

But to their surprise a knock came back.

The young voice from the other side of the door said, 'Are you here just to help Muslims, or are you here also to help sisters, carpenters and storytellers?'

Richard stared at Miller, confusion contorting his reddened face.

'I . . . I suppose so,' Richard said out loud.

'That's good. People have many identities and it's dangerous to focus on just one. And whatever makes you think we're Muslim anyway? You should say, "We're here to help *people*, not harm them."'

Richard looked nervously at the others. 'I . . . I understand. We're here to help people, not harm them.'

'Excellent! Now please, relax and have a read of the welcome literature.'

'Here's how I see it,' said Jordie. The four of them sat on the sofas. 'They haven't made demands, but the air conditioning, Bible on the bookshelf, and chicken kiev on the menu don't scream al-Qaeda. If they were going to kill us, why provide spare clothes?'

'They might just be using us for something first,' said Richard.

'Like what? Fashion models in their summer catalogue?' said Jordie.

'Let's just try to relax,' said Miller, attempting to ease the tension. The mental focus these deductions required had overcome the darker sides of their imaginations and diverted their initial terror.

The morning passed slowly. At 1pm the door opened. A couple of trays were slid into the room before the door slammed shut. Chicken shashlik was an absurd culinary accompaniment to the situation: it refused to sit with the despair of being a western hostage in a Muslim country and hinted at a slim optimism that subsequent events might not involve bloodshed.

Liam lay on his bunk, choosing to keep what he knew to himself. The strangeness of his surroundings made him think they must be the kidnappers he had been looking for. But why kidnap them? It felt out of character: the others had all been local people and concerned local issues, seemingly without the need for the guns that had been pointed at his head.

None of them fell asleep until the early hours. As a result, none of them heard the door open as an assortment of coffee, toast, jam, fried eggs and fruit was slid through the door on three trays. Breakfast was served with serviettes, salt, pepper, with metal knives and forks. A sole red rose stood in a vase. On the tray was a note:

Good morning, gentlemen! I hope you slept well. First, some housekeeping. Please leave dishes by the door along with any clothes you need washed. We don't do ironing. Sorry.

We are setting you some homework. Today you must read a book from the myths and beliefs section of the bookshelf. It doesn't matter which. Later today I will send you some activities to complete based on your readings. No excuses, please.

Scream if you need anything!

Aiya

'This is fucking ridiculous,' said Jordie. 'We've been kidnapped by a renegade book club. The girl's going to pull off her balaclava and reveal Oprah Winfrey. I say next time she delivers food we jump her.'

'We've got knives now,' said Richard, pointing to the dishes by the door.

'And she's a midget,' said Jordie. 'Miller?'

'I don't know. Maybe we should watch her deliver it again.'

'If she sees us watching too closely she'll be prepared for next time. I say we use our element of surprise,' said Jordie.

They sat in silence for a minute.

'Let's take a vote,' said Richard. 'All in favour of doing it this lunchtime?'

Jordie, Richard and Miller slowly raised their arms. Liam remained unmoved.

'What's up? Scared?' said Jordie to Liam with a hint of ridicule. 'You've been a little too calm for my liking. Do you even *want* to get out?'

Liam flashed Jordie a malicious look; but it was a pertinent question. If the kidnappers were who he hoped they were, he was interested in sticking around. This was balanced by the terrifying consequences if they weren't. 'Forgive me if I doubt tackling armed terrorists is your destiny.'

The comment silenced Jordie: it was a poor motivational speech for a break-out.

'Well,' said Richard, 'three to one. It's on.'

It approached 1pm. The escape plan had been agreed and rehearsed. Miller would hide to the right behind the door and wait for a nod from Jordie. Richard was positioned to the left to help Miller in any struggle. Due to Jordie's physique, he would be in front of the door to create a distraction.

Liam had sat reading on the sofa all morning, claiming that his presence there would create a further diversion. The others took it as a cowardly refusal to take part, but they had no desire to draw his negativity into their operation.

Miller's body had been shaking all morning. The hand that held the knife no longer made sense to him. What was he supposed to do with it? The actions required of him seemed impossible. Once more, events had been set in motion that he was unable to halt.

They heard footsteps approach the door, took their positions, and nodded at each other expectantly. But out of keeping with their run-throughs, the steel door was thrown open violently, hitting Miller on the side of the head. In front of Jordie were the two gunmen, both holding AK47s, wearing all black and balaclavas, their heights mismatched.

'Does the one behind the door mind coming out and standing against the back wall with the other two?'

So this was it. The two rifles pointed at them as they took their places against the wall. They wouldn't even hear the shots.

But as they closed their eyes they heard a clunk and the sound of footsteps. They opened them to see the tall, silent gunman placing moussaka, grilled chicken, rice and bread on the table.

'Gentlemen. You're in our room. We can hear everything you say. Now enjoy your lunch. Mum's moussaka is legendary. And after that I think you have homework to do.'

Jordie and Richard closed their eyes and rested against the wall in hopeless relief, as Miller collapsed to the floor. Liam continued to read in his place on the sofa. He wore a smirk and held his silence: no one likes an 'I told you so' in captivity.

After a silent lunch they went to the bookshelf and selected their reading.

They were out of practice: Richard didn't read books, Liam only for work, Jordie had given up a decade ago, and Miller only while commuting.

Without events or the tracking of sunlight, time lost its significance.

Evening arrived and the door opened. Two trays were slid in with a variety of mezes: hummus, baba ganoush, matzo balls, vine leaves and pitta bread. To the side of the trays stood a bottle of red wine and four glasses.

> Gentlemen. I thought you might be hungry. Apologies for my violence earlier: Mum says I misjudge my own strength. Please accept this bottle as an apology.
>
> I've cancelled this evening's activities as you have had a long and stressful day. Please post your breakfast order soon. Sweet dreams.
>
> Aiya

They ate, and drank a glass of wine each. Jordie and Richard made tentative enquiries about the books they had been reading. They continued reading until they went to bed at eleven and quickly fell asleep.

*

Richard was coming out of the bathroom when the door opened to reveal Aiya, without balaclava or gun, sliding in their breakfast trays. She made eye contact and smiled. Richard, without thought, smiled back: it was a natural reaction to a girl he guessed was no more than fifteen. She had plaited hair, an undeveloped slight frame, and puppy-fat cheeks. Her expression carried an innocent whimsy ill-fitting for a terrorist.

She closed the door. On one of the trays was a note.

> Good morning gentlemen.
>
> Today's homework is to read a book from the hope and community section of the bookshelf. Before dinner, please explain to one another what your book is about, and how it might have relevance in your lives and work. I will bring some shisha in at 6.45 so you can discuss things like real Egyptian men.
>
> Knuckle down,
>
> Aiya

After breakfast they chose their books: all focused on individuals or groups that had achieved great things against the odds. These ranged from local-scale stories of dedication, such as doctors risking their lives in war zones, to a biography of Nelson Mandela.

They discussed Richard's encounter with Aiya before Jordie and Liam retired to their bunks, Richard and Miller to the sofas. They took time to settle, but soon adjusted to their newly enforced schedule. Lunch crept up unnoticed. The afternoon waned between turning pages, yet the strangeness of spending a whole day immobile gradually drew attention back to the stark realities of their detention. The prospect of performing for their kidnappers rekindled their anxieties.

At 6.45 the door opened. Aiya delivered four shishas, along with a metal container with smouldering coals, then left.

They looked at each other, before bringing them to the sofas. Miller had some expertise in making shishas from his time at university; a friend had made a trip to Turkey and gained a short-lived notoriety for being worldly before his friends started seeing them appear in middle-class knick-knack shops and stores selling hash pipes.

Miller offered one to Liam who shook his head.

'You're a washed-out journalist. You must smoke,' said Miller.

'I took up self-loathing instead.'

'Well, sunshine, this is double-apple flavour,' said Jordie, patting Liam on the cheeks to incite him. 'Consider it two of your five a day.'

At first the conversation about their books carried the awkwardness of saying hello to the person waiting to use the shared toilet after you have just had a bad stomach.

Jordie took the initiative. His tone held a trace of disdain for the story he described, continuing a habit of dismissing the moral actions of others. In the desire to fulfil Aiya's challenge, Richard asked further questions. He had come to view the world through a similarly cynical lens, but his keenness to contradict Jordie saw him champion the cause of hope. 'At least they're trying to do something!'

They struggled through the remaining three book descriptions, unsure of the purpose of their task, or the qualities they were expected to display. No questions were asked. Liam seemed at ease in the tension, leaning forward as if to absorb the conflict for a later date.

Once they had all given a synopsis, Miller reminded them that Aiya had asked them to explain how the books had relevance to their lives and work.

'Well, Mandela was, of course, a huge inspiration in my life,' said Richard. He gave a nervous laugh; the self-deprecation was an attempted apology.

'Yeah,' said Jordie aggressively, 'I've heard that apart from him you're every African's beacon for democracy.'

'Don't give him too much credit,' said Liam. 'The idea of Richard being this evil puppet master is off the mark. He was powerless rather than evil.'

Richard eyed Liam suspiciously. 'You are kidding, right? After framing me as the wicked face of capitalism, you now say I was irrelevant?'

Liam shrugged and turned away from Richard.

'You think you can just shrug it off? Do you have any idea what that did to me?' Richard continued. 'You don't give a shit about what you do to other people, do you?'

Liam sat back and folded his arms.

'For Christ's sake. Listen to me,' Richard said loudly. 'What right do you have? How can you live with yourself writing stuff you know is a goddamn lie?'

Liam rolled his eyes. 'This world isn't about fair. I didn't give a toss what you did during Crest Voyager. In all likelihood you probably tried to negotiate and your board shut you down. I didn't choose this. I didn't choose you. Everywhere in the world people find themselves in positions they don't want to be in because they don't hold the chips to get out of them – too much debt, too much responsibility, playing out the demands this shitty world places on us. I was held ransom by my reputation as much as you were. I, along with every reasonably well-thinking person knew you had no ability to change Crest Voyager. I'm not always proud of what I write, but this is who I am now. This is what *we* are now. This is what we do. You can't negotiate with a world that doesn't give a shit.'

The silence that followed was only broken by the sound of bubbling water: Jordie and Miller's shisha inhalation had increased in direct proportion to the tension. Richard paced around the room. Liam watched him.

'And don't go believing the story I'm sure you've told yourself all these years,' Liam continued, 'that you're some misunderstood warrior for good. That you're chipping away at the periphery, doing things that others in your position wouldn't. There's no glory in futility – only misplaced vanity.'

'Well, my book chartered the history of an initiative I've often copied,' said Miller, tentatively trying to move the discussion on. He had read a book on the founder of micro-finance that lent small amounts of money to people so poor that banks refused to lend to them. 'It just feels like they were the pioneers, and we're the second-rate followers who suck the magic out of it.'

'Fucking hell,' said Richard, angrily turning towards him. 'We're all here locked in a room because I was convinced to fund a project that was supposed to be pioneering and cutting edge.' He shook his head, continuing to mutter under his breath.

Miller looked puzzled as he momentarily forgot all the reasons for his life's accumulated disappointments.

The note Aiya delivered the following morning told them to read something from the literature section. Instead of sliding the trays in on the floor, Aiya had walked calmly into the room and placed the food on the table. As she left, Miller called out, his eyes remaining glued to the page, 'Thank you, Aiya.'

'Pleasure,' she replied as she closed the door.

At 6.45, shishas arrived and they broke from their books to

discuss their thoughts on the day's reading. None of them realised they had not been asked to.

The next day, they were advised to read from the poetry section. It required patience to find reward in these lines. But what else were they going to do?

Liam privately did the maths. This was day five. The ransoms for El Sayed, Fathima Ahmed and Salma Mirza appeared a week after the kidnap. He would soon discover if the kidnappers were who he hoped they were.

The following morning they received another note from Aiya.

> Gentlemen. Today is self-help day. On the shelf is a range of titles that might take your fancy. Pick the one that appeals to you. All the pages are blank inside. It is your task to write that book. Write as much or as little as you desire. I won't ask you to read its contents. All I want to know is how the book you thought you were going to write at the start of the day compares to the one you ended up writing
>
> Author away,
>
> Aiya

They approached the bookshelf, their eyes trying on each title to see if it would fit the disappointments they were harbouring inside. Miller selected *Change Yourself to be the Change You Want to See in the World*. Richard chose *I Am Not My Job: Finding Identity Beyond the Workplace*. Jordie took some time before pulling out *Better the Devil You Are: How Nasty is the New Nice in Changing the World?*. Liam saw a title that challenged his negativity, much as Barrett had done in their last conversation: *A Firm Affirmative: The Art of Saying Yes*.

After lunch, six bottles of wine were left on the table, a liquid companion to their deepening introspections.

Each wrestled with their books in a different way: Jordie's pages were filled with crossings-out and rewrites; Richard wrote a stream-of-consciousness tome; Miller was controlled, deliberating over each sentence; Liam spent the day making a list of every yes/no question or decision he could remember making in his life.

At 6.45 Aiya delivered shishas to the sofa. 'Thank you, Aiya,' they said, as if she were the well-treated domestic help. She dutifully retired to the sound of laughter as they sloppily refilled their glasses.

They smoked for a few minutes, the nicotine enhancing their stealthily acquired drunkenness, before Liam broke the silence. 'I've written many autobiographies, hidden within the criticism of others,' he said with a strange smile. 'In all of them I'm the man who says "no". I choose the wrong fork in the path, the one of reproach, of negativity—' He broke off. 'But I'm not sure I've actually said "no" to many things . . . I've drifted here . . . an accumulation of all the times I never fought for *yes*.' He sat back and crossed his arms as a way of signalling his conclusion.

Miller spoke next. 'You know . . . I grew up thinking I could change the world simply by reading books and committing time.' He paused before giving his audience a rueful smile. 'I'm coming to think what I thought was altruism was arrogance.' A swaying shrug indicated he had finished.

They turned to Jordie, who had been quiet all day. He sat back against the sofa and ruffled his hair. 'What the fuck do you want me to say?' He looked at each of them in turn. 'Ten years ago I was working in slums helping families secure housing and safe drinking water. Look at me now. Do you really think I find my current state acceptable?'

Legs were crossed and faces rubbed as the awkwardness of unchartered emotional waters took its toll.

'We're all hypocrites here,' Richard said. 'I was a hypocrite when I started writing; 43 pages of self-analysis and a bottle and a half of wine hasn't changed that. But you know what?' He looked around the group. 'Writing this down made me wonder why I'd given up so early. I'm not talking redemption here; what's done is done. I'm merely saying, if the chance appeared, would I recognise it as an opportunity to be who I wanted to be?'

That evening they put the world to rights. They did not suddenly become best friends, nor did their flaws dissolve in confession. They did not say anything overtly profound. But talking together seemed to ease their personal disappointments. They would blame the moments of empathy on the alcohol.

They woke the next day with a feeling of having had a convivial evening without being able to sketch in the details.

At 8am the following morning, they awaited breakfast. At 8.30 it still had not arrived. At 9.00 they became restless, more through a breaking of routine than hunger. By 10.00 it was hunger. By 10.30 they became self-righteous in a way hostages rarely feel entitled to. At 11.00 Miller noticed that the door stood slightly ajar. They stared at each other in confusion. Liam took the lead, edging towards the door and slowly opening it.

Aiya sat on the chair in the room they had first entered from the street. 'You're the four most unobservant people I've ever met. I've been here three hours. My mum's waiting. It's time for some reintroductions.'

'How long has the door been open for?' asked Liam.

'It's never been locked,' said Aiya.

*

Aiya led them up the stairs to the small room where they had first entered from the street, and then through a door to their left, up a set of dirty wooden stairs. The air was stale and humid. They entered a dark, sparse room with a small table, a sofa of faded brown, three wooden seats, some black and white photos of men sitting in an arc, wearing galabeyas, playing drums and exotic stringed instruments; and an armchair that was filled by a figure who they presumed was Aiya's mother. A creaking fan attempted the impossible task of ventilation.

'Curiosity won't kill these cats, Mum,' said Aiya. Her mother's brown hair was in a ponytail; her lips were raised in a permanent closeted smile; her eyes had stolen all the room's available light. Her oval face was beautiful, but unconventionally so: the lines and muscles gave the subtle impression of activity.

The four men soaked up the setting.

'I, of course, am Aiya, and this is my mum, Jalila. And Mum, these are my friends.'

Miller looked at her with curiosity.

Jordie shook his head, unsure which avenue of confusion to address first. 'We're friends? You kidnapped me and made me read Wordsworth. I'd have forgiven the kidnapping. What is this and who the fuck are you?'

Jalila smiled warmly; the men could see her right cheek moving slightly, yet purposefully; her pupils moved subtly around the whites of her eyes.

Aiya giggled. 'She says she likes you, even though she imagines many others don't. Now, I imagine you've a lot of questions. So first . . .' She curtseyed to the floor. 'I'd like to warmly welcome you to the Serendipity Foundation. Please.' She gestured for the men to sit. Jordie and Miller tentatively took seats on the sofa. The others grabbed a stool each. 'As you can see, we spent most of our money renovating the guest suite.'

'A fucking guest suite?' said Jordie with a grunt. 'What do you want from us?'

Jalila coughed and looked sternly at Aiya, who blushed. 'Language!' She leaned towards the men. 'She's a bit conservative, but she's all right, really.' Jalila coughed louder. 'Muuuum, please. I know I'm fifteen, but you let me carry a gun . . . Yes, they're fake, but it's still not textbook parenting.'

'How the hell are you doing that?' said Jordie. 'You reading her mind?'

Aiya looked at her mum and smiled. 'Kind of.'

'Look,' Richard interrupted, unenthused by the change of topic. 'Can you just tell us what your demands were?'

'Were?' Aiya said. 'Who would we have made them to?'

Richard looked uncertain. 'To . . . like . . . the world.'

Jalila and Aiya laughed at each other. 'That sounds messy. There'd be people looking everywhere for you.'

Richard looked nervous. 'So this is about money. How much?'

Aiya looked at Jalila who nodded. 'We're looking for £40,000.'

The men looked puzzled, as if such a small figure hid a more sinister purpose.

'You do know how much he's worth?' said Jordie.

'Why are you asking for money this time?' said Liam.

The other three men looked at him in surprise.

'What do you mean, *this time*?' said Jordie.

Liam ignored him. 'Your ransoms so far have been staging football matches and crowdsourcing. So why are you now kidnapping foreigners for money?'

Jalila let out a laugh with Aiya.

'What the f—' Jordie stared at Liam. 'You knew something about them and didn't say anything. You—'

'I wasn't sure then.' He turned to Aiya. 'But I am now. Why us?'

Aiya clapped her hands together in delight. 'I'm impressed, Mr Liam. But you only know our more . . . public events.'

'Sorry. What the hell are you talking about?' said Richard.

Aiya smiled and nodded. 'We arrived in this neighbourhood because we wanted to create an audience. But we soon realised how dislocated the community had become. Old support networks of friends and family were disappearing. People were scared about the future and became more isolated. So we had to develop our audience. We set up the Foundation to secretly create events that drew people together: issues that needed to be collectively solved, enjoyed, or grieved; events that people thought were everyday but were no longer so; situations that would encourage people to listen.'

It seemed to Jordie more like a performance than a conversation. 'Like kidnaps?'

The scepticism knocked Aiya off her guard; she looked at Jalila to calm her nerves. 'Kidnaps are only a minor part of our events programme. We started off by leaving toys in the street so children would play together. We encouraged people to act crazy' – she stuck out her tongue and waved her arms in the air as she stomped around the room – 'to fuel conversation in the market. We'd get people to fake serious illness to get old support networks out for the family. We had musicians, dancers, storytellers and' – she smiled – 'puppeteers to perform publicly once more. We cleaned the streets.'

'Outside was a mess,' said Richard. His tone reflected the growing confidence of the four hostages to their situation.

'Yes, but that's for our anonymity. When we eventually go

clean, the pile outside will disappear. I mean the wider neighbourhood. People want to laugh, listen, eat, sing, play and cry with their neighbours, but they're too embarrassed to know where to start. We provide them with opportunities not to look too intrusive or forward.'

'By kidnapping people.' Jordie bought the attention back to the immediate situation.

Aiya looked at Liam. 'When you met the hostages, did they seem like victims?'

They all looked at Liam, who after a moment's hesitation shook his head.

Aiya continued. 'You see, our kidnaps give the hostage an opportunity to fix things they can't do alone. They ask for things so easy to achieve, that it's impossible to turn down. They are things people would demand from themselves.'

'Do they all have to pay £40,000 before they leave?' said Jordie cuttingly.

'We believe in the power of people, Mr Jordie, but we are not idealists. The computers we later donated to the school didn't pay for themselves. Then there's rent, living expenses, general funds we use as safety nets for people.'

'So what do we get in return?' said Richard.

Jalila smiled at Aiya. 'Our previous paying residents have mostly been sad, cynical foreign men. So in return for their money, we'd give them some time to think. A chance to decide if they wanted to give the world another shot.'

'How romantic. How successful has it been so far?' said Jordie.

'You tell me.'

They remained silent.

'How many have you kidnapped for money?' said Miller.

'You're our third batch.'

'And what are we paying for?' said Miller.

'Connecting every house in the neighbourhood to clean water that hasn't already got it.'

'How did you arrange this?' Miller hit back quickly.

'We have . . . er . . .' She looked at Jalila for guidance. 'What would you call it? A network. But old school.' She said the last sentence slowly, as if showing off.

'So you knew I was coming to Cairo?' said Richard.

Jalila smiled again, as she gave a non-committal nod.

'Traffic jam with no jam? Effect without cause?' said Aiya.

The four guests nodded, knowing it was a clue, but not sure what it led to.

'We've texted your employers. The project's going so well you've decided to stay on a few days,' said Aiya.

'So no one knows we've been kidnapped?' said Richard.

'Technically you haven't. The door was unlocked. You've just taken a week's holiday in a little-known homestay.'

There was a calm. 'So what now?' asked Richard.

Aiya seemed on more comfortable territory. 'Everyone so far has paid up, left on good terms and put it down to experience. We'd like to think some have changed their lives a little. At the end of the day, who admits to being held hostage by a fifteen-year-old girl in an unlocked room?'

As it was Richard's money being held to ransom, the others left it to him to respond; but his facial expression implied he was thinking beyond the £40,000.

'So . . . there's no chance of a ransom video?' asked Richard.

The men looked at him in shock.

'It's not part of our standard package.'

'What if I wouldn't pay without one?'

Aiya stared at Jalila. 'Yes . . . But what if? . . . Really? . . . I suppose so.' The others dared not interrupt the surreal silences that interspersed Aiya's questions.

Aiya turned back towards the men. 'Why do you want one?'

Richard looked embarrassed. 'I know the last five days have been all touchy-feely, but . . .' Richard leaned forward, rubbing his face. 'Look, I know this sounds silly. But I have nothing to go home for. My career is . . . well . . .' He shrugged as he took a deep breath. 'When it all ended I realised I had made only acquaintances, not friends. I spend my evenings on my own at home. The people I worked with will never trust me again, and those I didn't work with never will.'

He fell silent, attempting a laugh to break his own awkwardness. 'Fuck. You know what? I don't fucking know. Quite frankly I feel as trapped at home as I do in here. This project was my attempt to try to change direction, and after all that's happened, you want me just to go back home to a life I hate? Fuck that. I'm interested. You've got my attention. And if you want my money, I want something in return.'

'Can we wait for the epiphany at home?' said Jordie.

Jordie looked at Liam and Miller who seemed deep in thought.

'Miller?' said Jordie.

'You know what?' Miller said. 'Richard has a point. Why are we so keen to go home? A kidnapping is about the only excuse that will save our jobs and potentially some of our colleagues'.'

Jordie's face screwed up, as if stuck doing long multiplication. 'Liam?' Jordie said. 'You have anything you need to get back to?'

Liam pursed his lips, and shrugged.

Jalila looked puzzled but relaxed. Aiya looked around the group. 'Maybe we all need some lunch. We'll meet again at three. How about enchiladas?'

*

'You think the public will suddenly forget your legacy because you've been kidnapped? If anything they'll view it as a sign that there's some justice in the world,' said Jordie back in their suite.

'Look, kidnaps are hardly my favourite thing, trust me. But we're not faking the fact we were kidnapped. We were. Video and payment: they're the two main kidnap ingredients. We're just changing the order.'

They decided to spend ten minutes with their own thoughts. They were in no rush to get home, but were uncertain what the proposition being put forward was.

'The way I see it,' said Miller, getting up from the bed, 'we've already dealt with their demands, so we can make up our own.'

'You what?' said Jordie. 'Have you just lost your fucking mind?'

'So what do you recommend we do?' said Miller, his frustration with Jordie rising. 'We can't send a ransom video without a ransom, can we?'

'Well . . .' Jordie stalled. 'I don't know. Why don't we just stay here for another week, keep our heads down, and wait for the India trip to pass?'

'And then what?' said Miller. 'We go back, claim that things went really well out here, and then we've got two imaginary communities on our hands.'

Liam smiled, and took a seat on the sofa opposite Jordie. The way Miller looked at Jordie reminded him of the way Barrett had come to look at him.

'What? Faking my own kidnapping is going to undermine the capitalist system?' said Jordie. 'Do me a favour. Who are we going to make demands to? What are they going to be? You know governments don't negotiate with terrorists.'

'It depends on what the demands are,' said Miller.

'How profound,' said Jordie.

'Stop being a prick,' responded Miller.

'Prick?'

'Yeah,' said Miller. 'We talked about having the courage to take an opportunity if it came along . . .'

Jordie was momentarily silent. 'So what type of demands are you talking about?'

'I don't know exactly,' said Miller, his excitement receding.

'Can I suggest something?' said Richard. The others turned to him. 'From experience, we should make demands that would be seen as unreasonable to turn down.'

'You're really honing this,' said Jordie.

'A perfect ransom,' said Liam with authority, 'is like a perfect con. It needs to ask for something that both parties want. Look, we've been kidnapped by the experts in this. Maybe they fancy scaling up their stuff.' Liam took stock of the first solution he had put forward in years.

They played with the idea for a few moments.

'What if our ransoms aren't met? Are we going to kill one of us to show we're serious?' asked Richard.

'For your sake,' said Jordie, 'I hope not.' The four of them smiled.

'What have any of us got to lose?' said Liam.

There was a knock on the door, and in came lunch.

Enchiladas proved a surprisingly decisive source of nutrition. They ate in silence as internal debates raged. It had been a long time since they had felt this type of excitement. The more they thought about the proposition, the more they saw no option but to follow it. The time for excuses had come to an end.

They retired to the sofas and spent 30 minutes in deep discussion before Aiya entered and asked if they were ready to come back upstairs. They climbed the stairs and for the next 20 minutes, to mounting laughter, they discussed their lunchtime deliberations.

The history of the world is shaped by the loneliness of good ideas. (So keep them company.)

'It's agreed,' said Aiya. 'Today's the first merger in the history of the Serendipity Foundation. Welcome to the family.' Aiya poured mango juice into six glasses, jumped on the table to reach the others' eye line, and made a toast. 'Gentlemen, may we not ask of others what we would not ask of ourselves.'

They drank.

'Now,' said Miller, 'we're going to need to get our hands on a video camera.'

PART FOUR

The Ransoms

A Grainy Image

Thursday, May 14th

'Turn the TV on,' Charlie said, storming into Michael's office. His heart sank. Good news was in short supply.

Michael remembered wistfully a time when he could watch the latest natural disaster without it reverberating with his sense of responsibility. He could get overwhelmed by death, confuse which country the last earthquake shook, guess which sub-Saharan nation the most recent famine ravaged. He kept up to date because he was an educated citizen who *cared*. He now understood that *caring* and *being up to date* were two different things.

Charlie found the channel. Michael's reaction to the first images was one of relief: he was not in it.

The main headline read: EXCLUSIVE: CAIRO KIDNAPPING; the scroll bar: EX-OIL CEO RICHARD POUNDER KIDNAPPED ALONG WITH TWO HUMANITARIAN WORKERS AND JOURNALIST; KIDNAPPERS BELIEVED TO BE LINKED TO AL-QAEDA; NO DEMANDS YET MADE BUT HOSTAGES APPEAL TO BRITISH GOVERNMENT AND PUBLIC TO SAVE THEM.

In a sparse, dimly lit room, the four hostages sat dishevelled, hands tied behind their backs. Their faces showed signs of bruising. Standing to one side, a figure dressed in black held a Kalashnikov. Behind and above the men hung a black banner displaying white Arabic script framed by a frieze of guns, swords and what appeared to be pens.

The hostages, their eyes downcast, read out their names one after another, before the youngest, Miller Carey, spoke:

'We call on the international community, in particular the British government and the British public . . . to listen to the demands of these . . . people. Please . . . we just want to go home and back to our jobs . . . helping people around the world . . . We beg you, listen to them . . . our lives depend on you looking within yourselves and . . . and . . . not giving up on us . . . please . . . take responsibility for us . . . please . . .' At that point the message cut out.

Memories of Crest Voyager flooded back to Michael.

The news anchor was speaking to the first educated Middle Eastern man the station could find, leaving no stone unturned in their analysis of the clothes the hostages and kidnappers were wearing and the fact the hostages 'looked tired'. Links to Islamic terrorist groups were insinuated. The kidnap was either an attack on the evils of western oil companies, or a statement against the liberal values inspired by development. Alternatives were not viable at this point without the facts.

An aide entered and handed Charlie a sheet of paper.

'Well, we have the translation of the banner,' said Charlie. 'It apparently translates as: "The pen is mightier than the sword, and everyone will get a Biro."'

'Wh . . . I mean . . . is that a Koranic reference?' said Michael.

'Um . . . I think the Koran predates the Biro.'

Michael rolled his eyes at Charlie. 'So what does it mean? Is this a call to arms against the west?'

'Using Biros?'

Michael smiled, his original anxiety relenting. 'At least I'm bringing ideas to the table.'

'I'll try harder to speculate on matters of national security in the future,' said Charlie with a grin.

Barrett sat in her office, holding a tumbler of Scotch, watching the news. Everyone was telling her it wasn't her fault. But she knew, by giving Liam an ultimatum to track down a group of kidnappers or be fired, that it was. Just as the Scotch began to take effect, an anonymous message pinged into her inbox.

> Dear Editor,
>
> Do not tell anyone you have been contacted. Later on today you will be sent an article. You must publish it on the front page or you risk the life of your employee.

By mid-afternoon the kidnap dominated all media outlets. The *Financial Times* held Richard up as a 'visionary'. The head of his old board, Ted Monroe, pleaded for Richard's safe return: 'He held the interests of Muslims all over the world close to his heart.' Cynical commentators privately noted the absence of the word 'best' before the word 'interests' in the statement.

The broadsheets placed a stronger focus on the meaning of the Biro. Although the involvement of fundamentalists could not be discounted, the pen hinted at a more progressive group advocating literacy over violence.

The Foundation had shot the video the day before. Aiya had bought four new phones and SIM cards to replace their old ones, along with a digital camera armed with video settings. Jalila had applied expensive theatrical make-up to their faces. They judged their needlework unworthy of a global audience, instead using a glue-stick to apply the letters and pictures to the black banner.

There were multiple takes. Miller stumbled over his unscripted lines. Jalila's knee ached after the fifth take, but adamantly continued: the watching world might not be intimidated by a terrorist who had trouble standing.

After they finished they sat down on the sofas while Liam worked on the computer composing their first press release, which they would send to Barrett later the following day. He nodded as he finished. 'You want a read?' The others took turns in front of the laptop. The article received silent nods of approval.

Aiya sat behind the computer and entered an encryption code that would make their emails untraceable.

'How do you know how to do all this?' said Liam.

Aiya smiled. 'My grandfather was keen I should know my way around a computer from an early age.'

In the early hours of Thursday morning, they released the video, and later that day sent the following email to Liam's editor, Jane Barrett.

> To the Editor,
>
> Put this on the front page of tomorrow's edition, or your employee and his three friends will be on the front page the day after.
>
> Many thanks.

> I write these words from a dirty floor in a bare, windowless room. There is a bucket in the corner. For the majority of our waking hours we lie in darkness, suffering our own personal hells, imagining the natural next steps from the beatings we received in the first few hours.
>
> We are now the characters in those videos we used to watch with detachment. We are the dark grainy figures

hoping the world will care more about our fates than we did when others were in our place. We are terrified of our fates becoming a guilty entertainment to those who could, if they wished, save us.

We don't know our kidnappers' motives or demands. They say the government will let us die, hiding behind its refusal to negotiate with terrorists, but that the average citizen will refuse to have our blood on their hands.

In the next couple of days they will release their demands. I pray it does not involve the release of terrorists, or betraying a cause I know is more important than our lives. I hope against hope it is a demand you conclude is worth meeting in return for four innocent lives.

Charlie sat with Michael in his office as they consumed Friday's newspapers. Only the *Daily Voice* had published the article that morning, but it had since been duplicated on every international news site, and all publications were centring their Saturday editions on the story. Charlie had left his phone on silent, but a knock at the door saw an aide brief Charlie on developments.

'And?' said Michael impatiently, as Charlie returned to his seat.

'Two things. First, intelligence has discovered that the area in Cairo where they were taken has had a spate of strange kidnaps recently.'

'Strange?'

'Yeah – with demands to mend school roofs and visit the elderly, apparently.'

'Hmm.' Michael paused. 'So is this the same group?'

'The video and article are highly uncharacteristic. Egyptian intelligence has spoken to former hostages: they don't think it's the same group. So we'll take it as a coincidence for now.'

'And the second thing?'

'Well . . . tomorrow's *Mail* runs with a picture of the four men in captivity and the headline: WILL THE PM STAND UP AND SAVE THESE MEN?'

'And do they think I will?'

'They decided to take a poll. The good news is only 18 per cent said no.'

'18?' said Michael. 'That's the good news?'

'Everything's relative. 45 per cent said maybe.'

Michael looked to the ceiling as he did the maths. 'Still, that's 37 per cent who think I'll rise to the challenge. That's higher than my approval rating.'

'A hollow victory, but a victory nonetheless. I'm pleased to see a glint of the old "silver-lining Rayburn" through the dark clouds,' said Charlie.

Under the joking, Michael was hurting. He understood the parallels being drawn with Quest Voyager.

He forced a smile. 'Maybe we should just agree to everything the kidnappers demand. It could be liberating. Maybe they'll have some well-thought-through demands on running the NHS. We could form a coalition.'

'Of the damned,' said Charlie.

Everyone became an expert, except for the actual experts who pointed to the absence of leads. 'Don't you recognise the room?' asked an MI6 operative, shocked by the expert's unwillingness to speculate.

'Maybe they've painted it,' the expert responded sarcastically.

The media gleefully accepted the news: a story tailor-made

to satiate the addiction of a population drawn vicariously to horror and bloodshed.

This was tempered by Miller Carey's sudden ascent to national heart-throb status. Blogs appeared with pictures of him out with friends. A shot on a beach in Greece with an ex-girlfriend a few years earlier would charitably be awarded 'Torso of the Week' in a gossip magazine. His dedication to helping those in need meant his appeal united both adolescents and their mothers. #savemiller trended with an unfortunate consequence that his supporters appeared a little apathetic to the lives of the other three hostages.

'We need the first ransom soon. Someone else's scandal will take centre stage before long.' They had grown accustomed to Liam's ability to see the potential for failure everywhere, but on this subject they accepted he was an expert.

All afternoon, the Serendipity Foundation had discussed ransom ideas. But for all their experience, most of their suggestions felt too preachy, too righteous.

'We just need to have faith in our convictions,' said Richard.

Jalila had not drawn attention to herself all afternoon, but now gestured to Aiya, who translated. 'We're in danger of turning into yet another group convinced their vision of a better world will be everyone else's.'

'But . . . but we are,' said Richard. 'Otherwise what's the point of us being here?'

'That's not what we're about,' said Aiya. 'We deal with means rather than ends. Let me put it like this: would you want a country where everyone has strong convictions, and nobody's willing to compromise?'

Richard shook his head.

'So what do we want to encourage people to be?' said Aiya.

The four men remained silent. A minute passed.

Miller looked up from the floor. 'Pragmatists.'

Jalila smiled and nodded encouragingly.

'Almost,' said Aiya. 'What the world needs are pragmatists with hearts of gold. We create ways for people from different positions to start working together.'

Richard remained unconvinced. 'What would that look like?'

'You've never held a community meeting in a place where everyone hates each other,' said Jordie warmly. 'The first thing you do is tickle each other's balls – I apologise, ladies, for the analogy, but only once the nuts have been titillated will people consider rubbing them against people they hate. The goal of ransom one is to inspire taut sacs.'

The others shuffled awkwardly.

'Moving on,' said Richard, 'what you're basically saying is that we need a country-sized ice-breaker. Well, how about this . . .'

Operation Taut Sac

Monday, May 18th

The front page of every Monday daily carried the following article:

Do as you would be done by?

We have four of your citizens.

Will you stand idly by watching from the sidelines, or will you save them?

Our first demand is as follows: Wednesday is Prime Minister's Questions. During this session, all the business of the house will be conducted in haiku poetry. All questions, answers and procedures must be expressed using three lines – each consisting of five, seven and five syllables respectively. Kireji and Kigo will not be necessary.

Failure to do so will have severe consequences. There will be no exceptions. We will respond on Wednesday evening with further instructions.

What do you stand for?

A COBRA meeting was called. Michael preferred these to Cabinet meetings, surrounded as he was by a range of police, army, intelligence and assorted boffins. Uniforms and badges hinted at a greater sense of discipline, if not competence. The combination of low-level lighting and large bright screens was about as sexy as government got.

The room stood up as Michael entered, with murmurings of 'Prime Minister', and followed Michael's lead in sitting down.

'So what can you tell us? Have we been able to trace roughly where the hostages are being held?' said Michael to no one in particular.

'Prime Minister,' said a member of MI6 whose name Michael always forgot. 'So far we've had little luck tracing the emails. They've been encrypted and as long as the kidnappers don't make any mistakes, we won't track them. The hostages' phones have been offline for ten days. The last confirmed sighting was with their driver who dropped them off here.' He pointed to the enlarged map of Cairo on the screen.

'From here they were supposed to meet their translator in a café . . . here . . . We're working closely with our Egyptian counterparts to search the area. We're using aerial heat sensors, but as the neighbourhood is densely populated, it's not straightforward.'

'So the chances are that we won't find them before Wednesday?' said Michael.

'That is our suspicion, Prime Minister.'

'Do we know anything at all about the group?'

'Nothing yet. Their behaviour doesn't fit with established Islamist cells. Japanese poetry is inconsistent with seventh-century Arabia. And then there's this other group, who've previously asked for under-16s football matches: the demand seems more in keeping with their style.'

'But Egyptian intelligence can't confirm this?'

MI6 shook his head.

'And even if it was, does it mean we should be less concerned?'

MI6 added a shrug to his shaking head.

'So . . . we know nothing,' said Michael, hoping to be contradicted. The room remained silent. 'We're not seriously considering letting four men die here, are we?'

'We wouldn't be *letting* them die,' said Rawlins, the General Chief of Staff. His uniform and medals were a reminder to others that he knew the balance between individual life and national security. He had a ginger moustache that for some reason made Michael want to call him Brigadier. His jacket buttons were resolute in the face of a growing paunch – his round face a further testament that he was a soldier who lunches.

'Prime Minister, the greater national interest will not be served by showing potential terrorists around the world that we're now open for negotiation.'

'With haiku.'

'With all due respect, Prime Minister, we don't know where this could lead. This could be an attempt to humiliate us in the eyes of the world before more dangerous demands are made.'

'Or our vanity could be sentencing four men to death.'

'All great leaders need to understand the difference between blood on their hands and blood on their conscience,' said Rawlins with vague battlefield wisdom.

'Am I seriously the only one who has a problem with Rawlins's thinking?' Michael sighed as he stared at the glaring overhead shot of Cairo that remained on the big screen.

'As I see it,' offered Sandra Cowling, the Home Secretary, 'the kidnappers have called directly to the public to put pressure on us. They might vote for a TV talent show, but I'm not sure they'll care too much about saving human life. We'll make a contingency plan, but for now we don't negotiate and wait for the kidnappers to contact us again or get caught before Wednesday.'

The room nodded cautiously.

'So sketch this out for me. What is a haiku exactly?' said Michael.

'I'd like to introduce Professor Chiyo Matsuke, an expert on Japanese poetry,' said Rawlins.

Michael nodded her a welcome.

'Prime Minister,' she said, with a quiver in her voice. 'As you might remember from school, haiku is a three-line poem, with the first line having five syllables, the second seven, and the third five. In most British classrooms that's as far as it gets. But it's a form with deep traditional roots that would have to include kireji: a juxtaposition of two different images or thoughts; and kigo, which gives a seasonal context. Indeed, haikus don't always maintain the five–seven–five syllable structure. Also, in Japan a haiku is not structured by syllables, but by om, which are often parts of syllables.'

'Comforting,' said Michael. 'This all sounds a little complicated.'

Chiyo smiled. 'I understand, Prime Minister. But the demand says you don't have to worry about kireji or kigo.'

'Meaning?'

'Kireji and kigo transform haiku into art rather than just counting syllables on your fingers. Without them, they're the haikus you did when you were eight.'

'So . . . ?'

'This is a guess . . . but most eight-year-olds do it at school because it's fun. I think the demand is less an intellectual riddle than an excuse for parliament to have some fun together.'

'Or for the world to have some at our expense,' said Michael.

Chiyo smiled. 'Laugh and the world laughs with you.'

'Seven syllables,' Michael said, repeating Chiyo's maxim to himself, returning her nervous smile from across the room.

'Shirta! Shirta!' called voices accompanied by a banging on the door upstairs.

The four men looked up nervously. 'It's the police,' Aiya said. They stood up and looked anxiously around the room, evaluating routes of escape.

'Is there another exit?' said Richard.

'You expect a fire escape in a hostage cell?' said Aiya.

'Can we climb out of an upstairs window?' said Richard.

'Some of you may struggle with that option,' said Aiya.

'Why are you looking at me?' said Jordie.

'Go and hide in the bathroom. I'll see what they want. Do I look like a kidnapper?' she said nervously.

Aiya picked up a scarf and fixed it over her hair as she walked towards the door; the four men went to the bathroom. Jordie sat on the closed toilet seat, the others squeezed in tightly alongside. The atmosphere combined the gravitas of a police raid with the awkwardness of a crowded elevator.

Upstairs, they heard Aiya open the door. For the next minute they listened to muffled voices, alternating between police bass notes and Aiya's higher frequencies. They heard the door close and footsteps returning downstairs.

'You can come out now,' said Aiya.

They shuffled towards the sofas, waiting for their adrenalin to subside.

'So what did they want?' said Miller.

'They wanted to find four European men.'

'What did you say?'

'I said my mother was out, but they could call back later. They then moaned about having to be out in the sun all day and said it wasn't important.'

The Foundation sat in silence for a minute.

'That's it? That was our SWAT team?' said Liam. 'We've evaded the intelligence of two countries with the line "Mum's not in". Thank Christ we don't want rescuing.'

'I understand . . . really . . . mmm-hmm . . . yep . . . OK . . . thank you anyway.'

Charlie stared at Michael, as he hung up the phone. 'That was Rawlins. He says the Egyptians found nothing. It looks like I'm going to have to make a decision.' Michael curled his bottom lip. 'What are you hearing?'

'It's not great. I've spoken to a few of the rally organisers and they're expecting up to 100,000 out tomorrow, not including people who may travel in to London.'

Barrett's paper led a united front including all the print media in demanding government action to secure the hostages' release. An inside source claimed Michael was set to ignore the demands.

Analysts were wary of supporting the idea that a man's life was not worth a haiku. Even Michael's few remaining supporters created distance between themselves and the potentially fatal decisions of a government on its way out. The rally had widespread support across the political spectrum.

Michael's every instinct was to follow the will of the people. He could be at peace with his conscience, and for once be the leader he had dreamed of being. But throughout Tuesday his senior advisers lobbied heavily for resolve against what they saw as weakness.

'What are you going to do?' said Charlie.

Michael sank into his chair and flicked a pen around his thumb a few times before throwing the pen across the room.

'Do you think evil prevails when good men do nothing, Charlie?'

Charlie rubbed his face and let out a sigh. 'At the very least, when they believe everything's futile and no longer roll the dice.'

They both remained silent as Michael's face adopted a solemn expression.

'Well, let's go roll some dice, then.'

Parliament Square was a sea of heads, snaking down Victoria Street, Great George Street and Whitehall. The crowd were packed in along Westminster Bridge and the South Bank, directing their discontent across the Thames. Vans sponsored by tabloid newspapers were parked, armed with speakers and broadcasting live TV images from inside the House of Commons. Independent experts estimated the number of protesters had reached upwards of 150,000. Central London had shut down.

But they were not protesters *yet*, and that somewhat confused the atmosphere. Even now, with ten minutes to go before the start of Prime Minister's Questions, there was no announcement on the government's stance. Michael felt the decision was not his to make alone, and had met with opposition leaders, chief whips and the Speaker that morning.

The crowd had tried its best to lead by example, substituting grammar for a strict syllable count with chants such as 'What we want? Haiku/ When do we want to hear it?/ Now now now now now'.

Michael walked down the second-floor corridor in the House of Commons. He could hear the distant whirr of helicopters, the crowd, the police megaphones. There was danger in the air, and Charlie's expression revealed that he felt it too.

The Prime Minister entered an anxious chamber. The eyes of every MP and the crammed public gallery followed him to his seat on the front bench. He nodded to the Leader of the Opposition, who returned an empathetic grimace. He nodded to the Speaker, who closed his eyes and took a deep breath.

'Welcome dearest friends/ Questions for Prime Minister?/ I think we have some

If I could call on/ our honourable colleague/ Edward Hughes to start.'

Most of the crowd had their fingers up, counting the syllables of the Speaker's introduction on their hands. As five fingers followed the seven fingers that followed the initial raised five, a roar came through the windows and doors of Parliament. For the next minute, Parliament listened to the acclaim from a population that had grown weary with it. Some faces turned to smiles, basking in a rare moment of pride. MPs directly behind Michael patted his back; Michael deflected the praise, and waited for silence to descend.

Hughes stood. 'Thank you one and all/ Number One Mister Speaker/ I'm pleased to take part.'

Michael stood and approached the despatch box with his notes.

'Thanks, Mister Speaker/ I'm sure the house will join me/ in paying respects.

First to service men/ who fell so tragically/ in line of duty.

We owe it to them/ to recall their sacrifice/ every single day.'

A backbencher called loudly, 'Hear hear,' at which the whole house looked in terror in his direction. Realising his mistake he quickly added, 'Hear, hear, hear, hear, hear, hear, hear, hear, hear, hear, hear, hear, hear, hear, hear.' There was a deathly silence within the chamber, but outside they could slowly hear a cacophony of thousands of voices shouting 'hear', presumably seventeen times each. Smiles slowly turned to laughter within the chamber, and each MP joined in the one-syllabled heptadecathlon. Michael tried to regain his composure.

'Tenth Battalion/ Lance Corporal James Heathton/ twenty from Plymouth,' and Michael listed the other notable deaths over the last week as well as stand-out achievements. He was nearing the end of his prepared section. His initial excitement subsided: he would have to make up haikus on the spot from here on in.

'So Mister Speaker/ this morning I had meetings/ with my Cabinet

And in addition/ to my duties in this house/ I'll have more later.' And with that he nodded at the Speaker, who nodded at Hughes to begin the questions.

'The hostages saved/ One more day of coward whims/ When are losses cut?' said the MP, and sat down again.

Michael stood up to the despatch box. He took a breath near the microphone as if about to speak, but laughed and stepped back. Laughter rose within the chamber, but for the first time in years all the members laughed with each other. Michael sat back down and spent thirty seconds with a pen and pad before standing.

'Once more, but slow friend/ This battered brain unlocks not/ questions laced with Zen.'

The house laughed again, and Michael pointed to the Leader of the Opposition and mouthed, 'Your turn next,' with a grin on his face. Hughes rose and repeated his question slowly for Michael to write down. Michael then scribbled a response on the pad and double-checked its syllables.

'Hands should still be held/ when in unknown worlds we

walk/ Hearts of smiling tears,' Michael replied. MPs nodded earnestly in agreement. Michael was impressed by how profound evading a question could be when delivered in haiku.

Hughes stood once more to respond. 'Easy to avoid/ seventeen syllable flights/ pretence denial.' Michael had never had much time for Hughes, but he had to admit he was a tough haiku adversary.

Michael took his time to answer. 'Easy to disdain/ without power to provide/ action to your rile.' His Cabinet and backbenchers waved their fists in the air.

The Speaker struggled to be heard. 'May I,' he shouted three times before a Mexican wave of shush worked its way around the benches.

'May I ask to speak/ Leader of Opposition/ Mister Phil Greenham.'

'Thanks Mister Speaker/ Following the people's will/ no plagues in our house.'

Although both sides of the chamber admired the Shakespearean reference, Michael was confident he would be able to out-haiku Greenham.

'I ask my dear friend/ what of the tax we spoke of/ at this time last week?'

Greenham's attempt at haiku brought a torrent of seventeen-syllable abuse.

'Order, order, please/ I will not have such manners/ in this house of law,' shouted the Speaker. But it was hard to silence a crowd when four lives depended on them not falling silent prematurely.

Looking around at his own MPs and pointing at Greenham with a grin, Michael said, 'My child is better/ at words structured from the soul/ than men of breeding.'

No one understood the second line's pretence, but there

was a haiku class war at stake, and the house erupted with laughter and derision.

'I'm happy that when/ history writes your failures/ you'll still have haiku,' said Greenham, trying to be heard above the ribald parliamentarians.

Michael had not had this much fun in a long time, and clapped Greenham's attempt with gracious acclaim. 'I'm praying that when/ electorates come to vote/ all you'll have's haiku,' replied Michael. All parties quickly concluded that debating the details of government policy were futile. 'Sonnet would allow/ rhyme to undermine your lies/ where haiku will not,' said Michael.

What took place was a celebration of the ridiculous. Political point scoring was replaced by a desire to hear the laughter from the crowds outside. Agendas were unable to fit through the narrow syllable requirements.

As the session reached a close, Michael said, 'I'd like to thank you/ Be proud of who we can be/ when forced to behave.' He nodded at Greenham, who smiled, nodded back, and started a solo clap, which quickly multiplied into a round of applause that dominoed out of the House of Commons, through the Central Lobby into Parliament Square, conducted its way through the streets of central London, then reverberated through TVs, radios, computers and smartphones into the ears of hundreds of millions of people around the world. There was a strange type of warmth and camaraderie that only a Prime Minister's Questions conducted in haiku can provide.

For a few minutes, the festivities led people to forget about the four hostages, who were sitting in a luxury basement in Cairo, sipping lattes and planning their response.

Life is Beautiful

Wednesday, May 20th

Lucy, along with all her colleagues, was given compassionate leave on Wednesday, and she spent the day at her mum's. As she arrived, her mum hugged her tighter and longer than she had done since Lucy's father had died. Her mum had met Miller and picked up on the confused chemistry between the two.

The tears Lucy had fought all week finally welled over. She had barely eaten or slept.

'Oh, before I forget, a letter arrived in the post for you yesterday,' her mum said.

Lucy rubbed her eyes as she walked to the sideboard in the kitchen where she found a brown envelope addressed to her. On the top right of the envelope were two stamps adorned with pharaohs and the word 'Egypt'. She opened the envelope to find no note inside. She turned it upside down; a lonely SIM card fell into her hand. She retreated to her old bedroom and switched the SIM card in her phone. Two new messages were received. The first welcomed her to the UK and gave the price for calling home to Egypt. The second read: '*This is your Pinocchio, washing fruit in iodine. Text when you get this. Don't call the police. I am safe. X*'

She read the text three times. A rush of chaotic emotion took over. She struggled to believe the nonchalant text could be from Miller; she toyed with the idea of it being a sick prank. But they often joked about the clichéd dangers of working abroad: avoiding salads, pickpockets, Imodium. She quickly remembered their last conversation in the pub: Pinocchio – a codename that no one else could possibly know.

She wiped her tears and texted back. '*Is this you, Miller? Are you hurt? Where are you? X*'

She found an old phone for the Egyptian SIM. She decided against telling her mum. As the build-up to Prime Minister's Questions approached, she swung between optimism and despair. Three minutes into the session, with her mum crying tears of hopeful relief, she received a message. '*I'm safe, but very important you do not contact anybody. Will call at 3. Make sure you are alone. X*'

At ten to three she made her excuses and went for a walk to the nearest park.

'Miller? Thank Christ. How are you? Are you hurt?'

'Calm down. Relax. I'm fine.'

'What the hell's going on? You've no idea how terrified I've been. Have you got hold of anybo—'

'Lucy. Calm down. This phone call's costing a fortune.'

'I . . . I don't understand.'

'Do you promise you'll keep this a secret? Before I tell you anything you have to promise.'

'I . . . I . . . Yeah. Of course. What's happening?'

'Listen. Things are not exactly what they seem . . .' Over the next ten minutes Miller told Lucy everything: the imagined Indian village, the kidnap, who the Foundation were, and why they had decided to join them.

Lucy was silent throughout.

'Come on . . . say something.'

'You're nuts,' Lucy said, as she struggled to comprehend what Miller had told her. 'Absolutely crazy. You know how much trouble you could get into? This is insane. The whole world just watched you ransom Parliament. Hundreds of thousands came out to support you.'

'But everyone had a great day out, right?'

'That's not the point. You've just taken advantage of people's goodwill. You've lied to everybody.'

'I disagree. That's exactly the point. No one came out to save us, but to support the principle that human life should be valued. Imagine what else we could do.'

'Like what? Is haiku going to overthrow the capitalist regime next?'

'It has huge untapped potential,' he said, frustrated.

'Miller, how long do you think people are going to stand for this?'

'For as long as people enjoy it. That's the point: we're the ransomers who demand what people would demand of themselves. I know theoretically you'd support this, and for once I'm doing it instead of just talking about it.'

'Miller the pragmatist.'

'Miller the pragmatist with a heart of gold.'

Lucy laughed and broke the building tension. 'Where's my timid Miller gone?'

Lucy could hear Miller breathe out deeply. 'He got tired of being scared.'

Lucy skirted the edge of the park, past a couple of dog walkers, and looked out towards the grass where three games of football were taking place. Such normality added to the current absurdity; and yet cutting through all her anxieties and questions was a giddy excitement that it was her he had chosen to call.

'So why are you calling?' Lucy's tone was ambiguous;

Miller took a moment to evaluate the many potential subtexts.

'You're going to think it's stupid, or that we're being delusional.'

'A modern *Don Quixote*.'

The literary reference went over his head. 'But what I was hoping you might do is . . .' He paused. The request was harder to articulate than his last ten minutes of confession. The boundaries between reality and fantasy were in flux. 'Well, I was hoping you might pretend to be my girlfriend.'

Lucy laughed awkwardly. 'Miller . . . people know we're not together. No one will buy it and without you here I could get myself into some serious trouble.'

'People know we're not *publicly* together.' He had barely slept the night before in panic at how he would explain his request to Lucy. 'Look, I know we know that we're not together, but, well . . . look. People in the office constantly, kind of, you know, joke about us . . . you know, about us in the club that one time, and . . . well, I was thinking we could kind of maybe pretend . . .'

'I get it,' she said, putting an end to his tortuous reply, although the silence that followed proved even worse. 'I don't understand why this helps you?'

'Because . . . well . . . a worried lover gets opportunities to meet people. Important people. It keeps that option on the table.'

'I'm an option on the table?'

'I thought you said you'd help me get out of trouble.'

'This is not exactly what I had in mind.'

Miller felt suddenly guilty. 'I don't know what I was thinking. I'm sorry. I guess I just liked the thought of you being a part of it with me.' Miller could hear Lucy breathing deeply on the other end.

'Look, Miller. Can you give me a little time to have a think about it?'

'Of course,' said Miller. 'Like Anna Karenina.' He felt a literary analogy would act as an apology and she was the first female literary character that came to mind. He instantly regretted tingeing his proposition with a narrative that climaxed in suicide.

Lucy laughed at Miller's attempt and hung up.

Anna Karenina's decision was between a life of safe comfort, or that of likely ruin by investing in the man she loved. During Wednesday evening, both Miller and Lucy nervously reflected on how accurate the analogy really was, selectively overlooking the train tracks.

Michael and Charlie were sitting in Michael's office drinking beer out of the bottle. They had not heard from the kidnappers yet, but the safety of the hostages seemed less important now that Michael had done everything he could to save them.

The evening papers were filled with praise. A LEADER AT LAST chimed the *Evening Standard*. Internet blogs and media were equally complimentary.

Some 100 million had watched events live. Replays had since gone viral online across the world. Opinion polls had seen Michael's approval ratings jump an unprecedented 15 points.

'They're a fickle bunch.'

'Who are?' said Charlie.

'The public,' said Michael, taking a swig of beer. 'But I suppose they pay the bills.' He sat back in his chair, and let an emotion that he had not encountered for a long time surge through his veins. Pride.

*

The Foundation had sent a brief congratulatory response to Parliament, via an email to Barrett, and were in the process of getting drunk.

None of them had dared hope the day could have gone so well. They started brainstorming for ransom two. But most of their ideas turned out to be no better than poor relations of their first theme: merely substituting haiku with rap freestyle, alliteration, or interpretive dance. Their euphoria soon turned to despondency. Kidnapper's block had taken hold. They, in turn, had turned to alcohol.

'No offence, gentlemen, but your imaginations are terrible. It's best to start with what you know,' Aiya said, topping up Liam's glass. 'Let's start with you. I feel you've broken a few demands you would've made of yourself.'

They all looked at Liam. 'Oh right. So I'm supposed to be the greatest disappointment to myself out of the four of us?' he said, his small eyes narrowing.

'Pretty sure you've carefully crafted self-loathing to be your niche,' said Jordie. 'We like to do ours a little more privately.'

Liam took a sip of the home-brew, grimacing as he swallowed, and scanned his audience. 'Look at all of you, sitting in judgement,' he said with a light slur, his eyes also giving firm clues to his intoxication. 'Did I dream of this when I was young? No. But at least I'm not in denial. Richard can pretend all he wants that he's been unfairly done by, but if I was him, I'd hate myself. Whether he likes them or not, he made his decisions. He's a self-made disappointment.'

'Whereas you're a victim, I'm guessing,' said Jordie.

'You made me what I am,' Liam snapped back bitterly. 'You, the public, the consumers of the shit that's served up to you; sexualising everything around you, picking on others to make your lives seem less depressing. I was forced to give you what you wanted. Is it any surprise the young Liam gave up fighting, with you throwing all these incentives at him? I haven't given anyone the benefit of the doubt in years. But why should I? None of us deserves it.'

A silence descended. They were all struck by the ugliness of a man who had forgotten how to forgive.

'I like it,' said Aiya, nodding at Jalila.

Liam looked confused, as if his outburst should have put paid to any note of positivity.

'Like what?' asked Richard.

She smiled at her mum before turning to the others.

'National Benefit of the Doubt Day.'

Lucy found a bench near Hyde Park Corner, and sipped her coffee as she read a newspaper with Miller's face adorning the front page. Next to it was a response from the kidnappers to yesterday's events in Parliament:

> Alive! Smiles of hope
> On faces that see no sun.
> Buoys on melting lakes.

She wondered if they were Miller's words. He would smile at the academic analysis visited upon them. As an English professor at Oxford put it: 'The poem is clumsy, yet profound. We are forced to imagine the hostages as b(u)oys, being freed from their icy slavery on the visible surface, yet such buoys remain roped to the bottom of the wintery lake.'

Would the nation believe she and Miller were an item? Could she deal with the intrusion? The spotlight would inevitably fall on her attractiveness and the depth of her grief.

Lucy and Miller. Miller and Lucy. She had stared at her pictures of the two of them together. Would the public confuse the chemistry as romantic, or had she confused it as platonic? She recalled specific moments where joking colleagues had alluded to their relationship. Their blushing denials replayed endlessly in her head. She could no longer imagine turning down Miller's request.

She had texted Miller the evening before, simply writing '*I'm in*', to which Miller had replied 30 minutes later giving the meeting place, the need for her to find a couple of photos of them together, and a request to keep all recent revelations to herself except for the one concerning her love for him. It was only on her way to the meeting point that the full enormity of what she was doing became clear. Her legs felt weak as she imagined all the things that could go wrong.

Without Lucy realising, a woman had taken a seat next to her on the bench. She was dressed in a skirt and a crisp blue office jacket. She stroked her red hair behind her ears. 'When a person who's waiting for you doesn't notice you slide in next to them, you can feel pride at realising the anonymous look,' said Barrett, smiling warmly at Lucy. She offered her hand. 'I was tempted to wear leather gloves, a trench coat, and Grisham it up, but I'm unsure if this is conspiracy or farce.' She looked enquiringly into Lucy's eyes, searching for signs she might know more than she was giving away.

'I decided to go for the "drinking a coffee" look,' Lucy said. There was a promise of summer in the mild breeze; her scarf and woolly hat showed a more conscious effort at disguise.

Barrett had received instructions on her private email the night before. Only a handful of people, including Liam, had the address. She was to publish an article on Lucy and Miller, and was given details of the meeting point.

Lucy handed the pictures to Barrett on a pen drive. She provided a few autobiographical details, and some background to their relationship.

Barrett gently touched Lucy's arm, ready to take her leave.

'Do you think it's right we're not telling the police?' Barrett said. 'I'm presuming you've been contacted with the same vague threat for compliance?'

Lucy smiled warmly and nodded. 'Why are you doing it?' she said as Barrett got to her feet.

Barrett pursed her lips. 'I guess to try to find a way to forgive Liam for what he'd become before he left.' She paused for a moment, distracted by the traffic that edged around the park. 'And, I guess . . . to find a way to forgive myself for forcing him to go in the first place.'

Lucy gave a sympathetic smile. 'Do you think you'll succeed?'

'Redemption is a tricky one to predict,' she said as she turned to walk away.

*

To the esteemed editor, please forward this to the editors of all registered print, online and television news, with the urgency you think it deserves.

Dear Ladies and Gentlemen of the News Media of Great Britain,

On behalf of the four men sitting on the floor next door, we would like to thank you all for so warmly embracing our recent campaign to give poetry a more central role in government. You have regained the trust of the nation.

We have decided to capitalise on this by making you the centre of ransom number two. We trust that you will once more rise to the occasion.

Sitting on our floor is a man who has worked in your industry for a long time. He is not a model for happiness. Years of probing and hoping for the worst in everybody and everything has left him numb to the beauty of life. So in his honour, we have chosen you to inaugurate National Benefit of the Doubt Day this coming Monday.

To commemorate the event, we ask all media outlets to guarantee that at least 75 per cent of their content is positive. Do not try to be clever, lives are at stake. It will be amazing, once you are allowed to focus on positives, how quickly negative stories can be transformed.

But does this go far enough? The public will still be inclined to mistrust you after years of falling standards and the absence of rigorous reporting. Journalists are as loved as politicians. It's a mystery you remain in business at all. So this is our gift to you.

On Monday, you will score every news feature you release out of ten.

This score will reflect how much genuine value the piece represents to the public's understanding of the issue. You might wish to consider how much you actually know about the subject, or if the article has axes to grind.

We will judge the scores you award yourselves against those that our esteemed hostage-journalist gives the same pieces. He will be shown them without seeing your scores. Let's hope there are not large discrepancies between the two.

On Sunday we will send an editorial that is to be placed on the front of your newspaper under the headline 'Life Is Beautiful', and as an opening segment on your news channels.

Many thanks,

The Foundation

'Michael, you've got to see this,' said Charlie as he stormed into his office, and handed Michael a print-out of the email that had just been disseminated to all the editors of news media in the United Kingdom. He sat tapping his feet impatiently as

Michael read. He could tell Michael had finished by the grin that passed across his face.

'Did you write this?'

'I only wish I had.'

Michael sat back in his seat and rubbed his head. 'Have we had any feedback from the editors yet?'

'We've arranged a meeting this afternoon. I get the impression they're looking for you to help them out of their hole.'

'Ha. I'm sure they are. But they were happy ushering in my demise yesterday. What do you think?'

'I think we should maybe tone down our smiles. It is, after all, the whole of the country's news media being held to ransom.'

'To be better.'

'Quite, but maybe concerned helplessness is the tone we're after.'

Michael weighed it up. 'I can definitely do helplessness.'

Barrett walked to Downing Street. She felt strangely excited. Meeting Lucy, a co-conspirator, made the situation feel less abstract, even if she was in the dark over what they were conspiring against. But she instinctively felt she had been drafted in for a cause more worthy than mere terrorism.

This was the first time she would be meeting any of the other major media players since the kidnap, and she was practising looking guilt-ridden. She had a firm alibi: she was merely fulfilling tasks delivered by kidnappers who threatened her staff.

She was escorted to the meeting room where she joined the other editors of the national news media, before the Prime Minister, his press secretary, a few aides, and a scattering of ministers made a grand entry. The press secretary gave a short introduction, before opening the session to the floor.

'Obviously the press can't be held to ransom,' said Wilcox, the editor of a daily tabloid. Many of his fellow editors nodded in agreement. 'This threatens the life-blood of democracy. If we agree to this, where will it end?'

Barrett couldn't help but smile.

'I don't really think smiling is particularly helpful right now, do you?' said Horner, a broadsheet editor. 'It's our moral responsibility to pull together as an industry and show that we're not for sale.'

There were murmurs of approval as people looked towards Barrett.

'Such rallying words,' said Barrett. 'You almost made me a convert. But on Monday I'll be upholding the kidnappers' demands. I'm meeting with my staff later this afternoon to make sure we deliver our best ever paper. I have responsibilities to my team, and, for that matter, my conscience.'

The room shuffled uncomfortably. Many had come relying on a unanimous refusal of the demand, that a vacuous rally behind 'the freedom of the press' would be sufficient. Now they needed a champion, an enforcer. They looked at Michael, who was sitting back in his seat, flicking his pen around his thumb.

'Oh sorry, you're wanting my opinion?' he said as he leaned forward. 'Well . . . of course I'm very concerned,' he said, looking at Charlie, 'but at the same time, I am very, very helpless.' He looked around the room. 'Concerned, yet helpless,' he said as a timely synopsis for those who missed it. 'You see, after already bending to the will of the kidnappers, I have no moral authority to stand against them now. If only you had been against the first demand you might have some' – he clenched both fists trying to find the word – 'arghh . . . you know. But here we are,' he finished, unclenching his fists to open palms.

There was a moment's silence. 'Prime Minister,' said Fitz-patrick, the editor of a 24-hour news channel, 'if you could put yourself in our shoes for a minute and—' Michael cut her off with his hand.

'I have already put myself in your shoes. First, and imagine this with me,' he said, gesticulating to the room. 'I got what I thought was your right shoe and put it on my right foot, but it felt all cramped and I realised I had put it on the wrong foot. So imagine what I did?' He looked around the room. 'I took it off and I put the shoe on my left foot, and I asked myself a question – one that I would like to ask you all now – and that question is: "How does the shoe feel on the other foot?"'

And with that he pointed to his watch and looked at a bemused Charlie. 'Now, I have some very important government business. After all, I've only three days to deliver some really positive news for you all,' he said, and walked out of the room.

In Friday's *Daily Voice*, hidden on page seven, was the headline MILLER'S GIRLFRIEND: 'PLEASE DON'T PRESUME THEY'RE SAFE YET'. Below was a picture of them at a Christmas party: Miller's arms around Lucy, kissing the top of her head in a drunken embrace. Classy it was not, but Barrett was strangely transfixed by the tenderness in both their faces. The article spoke of Lucy as if she were already cemented as a character in the hostage drama. Lucy was quoted as saying: 'Miller would be so grateful to the media. It gives me so much hope that they're doing everything they can to bring him back safe.'

It came as a surprise to the rest of the media, who had failed to detect the girlfriend. The poignancy of the story increased as the secretive nature of their love was revealed; colleagues spoke of how the two of them had tried to hide their relationship in the workplace. The think tank's head John Fairweather spoke of how he had suspected it for months, and could tell by how devastated she had been during the last week that they were more than just friends. 'It's amazing that through it all, she remained dedicated to helping the poor communities she was working with and came to work. She's a truly remarkable woman.' He had now forced her into compassionate leave.

'Heartbroken vixen enter stage left,' said Michael as he read the Friday papers. 'How has it taken a week for her to appear?'

'The value of privacy?' ventured Charlie.

'Hmm. I suppose in due course she needs to be invited over, eh? You know, so I can express my concern in person.'

'You seem to be doing a lot of that recently,' said Charlie.

'I've got a lot of concern to go round.'

Friday was to be a particularly busy day for Michael. He had no desire to stop Monday's challenge, but felt he should at least be perceived as part of the solution: it was his responsibility to deliver some good news, and this took him out of his comfort zone.

He sat down with his ministers and made a list of all the new hospitals, schools and initiatives they could open or announce between then and Monday. Funding was wrestled from an impending bank bailout and used to save hospices and sports centres.

For one ethereal day, the entire civil service became focused on clearing blockages to projects in the name of Good News Monday. The threat of being held responsible for murder was a much more efficient incentive than public service. Paperwork miraculously appeared. Committees were bypassed. There was little time to add jargon to briefing papers.

'We should threaten to kill someone every week,' said Michael. 'Maybe we could do it inter-departmentally. Pick a different aide to place the guillotine over each Monday, and hand the department their targets.'

'After witnessing the lack of chemistry in these departments, I'm not convinced that'll provide the right incentives,' said Charlie.

'Win-win. Government becomes more efficient, or smaller,' said Michael. 'You know, a great man once asked what a country could achieve if it could replicate the spirit of wartime during times of peace. You know – the togetherness, the drive, building solar panels instead of warheads.'

'That's the magic imminent death brings to the table,' said Charlie. 'The best you could do is to have a fake threat, and try to control it.'

Michael nodded and sank deeply into thought, as if Charlie's comment had profound repercussions.

The offices of Britain's news media were in an existential frenzy. If the whole industry had stood together it would have been a *principle*, but Barrett's stance had injected a moral scale into proceedings: what price were they willing to pay for a human life? Each organisation reluctantly agreed with its owners that it was best, if only this once, to try to be on the right side of the moral compass.

Each faced a different problem. The worst of the rags were content to admit their all-round pointlessness, as their readership prized breast above integrity. But for the more respected organisations, the demands forced them to address the divide between the perception of them being the torchbearers for truth and what they had become: cosy groups that had confused integrity with neutrality, the internet stripping them of their ability and dedication to investigate. They were understaffed and under-skilled. Content had been commercialised and sexed-up. Monday demanded a frantic search for the best of themselves.

A couple of publications concluded that the public's ability to combine strong loyalty to a paper and extreme disinterest in integrity would see them survive the low scores they would be forced to award themselves – possibly wearing the judgements as an ironic badge of honour. Their readers didn't consume the news to be informed, but to be entertained and told that they were better than everyone else.

Others were not willing to take the risk. They cajoled the best journalists from their Sunday sister papers to contribute to Monday's edition. Freelancers auctioned their skills. Offices became hives of nervous tension. World-weary hacks became enthused with purpose, sending their self-evaluated prose to the typesetter, who, like everyone else, eagerly awaited the words that would fill the blank space on the front page.

National Benefit of the Doubt Day deserved an editorial with flair. The Foundation originally envisaged a piece that detailed the amazing strides humanity had taken over the last century: in increased life expectancy, cuts in preventable disease, and improvements in education and gender equality. It gave perspective to today's troubles by outlining how problems from the past had been solved. But they soon disagreed.

'The reason some humans live in such luxury is because people like him,' Liam said, pointing at Richard, 'have pushed a system that has used up millennia's worth of resources in one generation.' Liam had woken up on Thursday with a thumping hangover and sense of remorse, yet two days later remained stewing in his bitter casserole.

'Yeah. It's all my fault. I made you consume it against your will.'

'No, but you sure as hell killed the alternatives.'

'And you're a man so full of solutions.'

Pessimism surrounding overpopulation, inequality and the financial system soon followed. Miller pointed out that the world's resources could not provide for the billions of the future. Jordie added that if that did not wipe out humanity then a third world war would. National Benefit of the Doubt Day was struggling to empower four professional naysayers.

'Stop being so childish. Like any of you know the slightest thing about the end of the world. Honestly . . .' Aiya sighed with disappointment at the newly abashed adults. 'You're here because you had a solution.'

They all sat in silence, not sure how to progress. Jalila had not spoken for the entire session, and it was only now that she gave a little cough to announce she had something to say. Aiya explored her mum's features.

'Yes.' She smiled. 'I like that one.'

Aiya turned back to the men. 'A while ago I was told a story by a wise man . . . It is a story that is, and is not, so.'

On Sunday, an email appeared in the inbox of every news media editor in the country.

As promised, the editorial for Monday. Regards.
The Foundation.

Once upon a time, there was a village. It was poor, as were the majority of settlements in the age of once upon a time. Families battled with the land in a desperate fight for survival, their miserable existence nourished by parsnip, radish and a gnawing sense of injustice.

As we know, poverty is not defined solely by a lack of food, shelter and currency, but also by the lack of hope in your soul, the inability to chase and fulfil your dreams. The depressed village in question no longer even had dreams. During the day they dwelt on their muddy fates, by night their energies focused on fighting the chill that came knocking at their bones.

That was until one autumn day. Radishes were drying in the weak October sun; the icy winds were freezing their square-mile pigsty into wintery roads of discontent. Down such a road came a stranger from faraway lands. You could tell by his unsuitable footwear.

'Who are you? And what do you want?' snapped the locals.

His deformed face disgusted the villagers: his lips had the ability to turn upwards, and there were strange lines around his eyes. 'I come bearing dreams,' said the stranger, 'and the ability to make them come true.'

'What are dreams?' said the villagers.

'Dreams,' said the stranger, 'are what give us hope.'

'What is hope?' said the villagers.

The stranger knew he had his work cut out.

But the stranger persevered. He began leading courses in dreams and their fulfilment with the children. The younger villagers – having been marinated in bitterness for fewer years – were more susceptible to his dark arts and soon a rumour spread that strange transformations were taking place among the young.

The stranger soon opened up his sessions. No one could resist his illicit visions. Before long couples talked about *the future*. The truism that carrots could not grow in soil with such high melancholy levels was questioned. The words 'why' and 'not' started being put together with devastating repercussions.

Such news quickly reached other villages. The stranger soon became a guru. His reputation spread across the land as the man who took on hopelessness, where others had said it could not be tackled. Followers came to learn his methods and disseminate them elsewhere.

But over time, the villagers tired of the stranger. They started to take his legacy for granted, forgetting how life was before his arrival, and how radical his ideas had been. They began to believe that if the stranger had not arrived, someone else would have inevitably introduced such ideas: such as the mayor and local aristocracy who had grown tired of this stranger hogging all the praise and challenging the status quo. Their jealousies grew, and they sought to undermine the stranger, instigating rumours, embellishing mistakes, seizing on misunderstandings, as hearsays became regarded as facts. All the stranger's actions became framed within a story of ego and corruption.

The stranger felt this irreversible changing of the tides. Gleeful rumours circulated that he was under investigation. It came as no surprise when the court writ finally arrived, notifying him of the case against him.

'But what am I accused of?' asked the stranger at court.

'Accused?' said the judge. 'We have irrefutable proof of your lies. For years you have been treated like a saint for the creation of dreams and their fulfilment. But this is lies. Lies, lies, lies.' There were gasps from the public gallery. 'Only 48 per cent of dreams have come true. That is 52 per cent of dreams that remain broken, wretched, haunting their owners, while we hang on your coat tails.' There were screams of 'liar' and 'fraud' from the gallery.

The stranger let out a warm laugh. He clapped his hands

together, excited that someone had pointed out this fact. 'Isn't that amazing? Absolutely amazing.' The court looked puzzled. 'How could we have ever imagined this only years ago? 48 per cent of people! 48! Not only having dreams, but having them come true. Isn't that the best news you've ever heard?'

And you know what? The court thought about it, and it probably was.

Ladies and gentlemen, boys and girls, today marks the inaugural National Benefit of the Doubt Day. Its premise is simple. What would happen if we chose to see the best in people and events? What if our natural reaction to an event was to suspend judgement? Today we do not see wicked deeds lurking in grey areas.

National Benefit of the Doubt Day starts at home, with your family, fellow commuters, pedestrians and colleagues. Remember, every day can be National Benefit of the Doubt Day if you choose to make it so.

LIFE IS BEAUTIFUL stood at the top of every paper in the newsstand, adorning the centre of news channels' scroll bars. The nation rose to find a world that had shifted slightly on its axis. They would quickly learn that the headline was just *pretend*, but few would forget their initial reaction: the excitement, the consequences.

While the premise was, of course, sentimental and naïve, there appeared a greater courtesy between drivers. Colleagues chanced a smile as they wished one another good morning.

There were no reports of anyone being fired or students expelled. Perhaps some friendships were re-evaluated and relationships saved. It would be foolish to over-claim on the day's behalf. But you could see its presence in the doorways being opened for strangers. It was the social elephant introducing itself to the room.

The first thing Michael noticed was the sport section. His team had won the night before, and, national incident or not, he was more interested in the manager's post-match interview. But the bad refereeing decisions were described as 'understandable considering the atmosphere'. Poor substitutions were today regarded as 'brave'.

Barrett took the opportunity to make the best paper she could. She got the best journalists writing about what they knew and brought in experts to write editorials. Rather than the ransom being an attack on journalism, the *Daily Voice* heralded it as its potential saviour. No articles scored below an eight.

Not all journalists enjoyed the day. Some were forced to write rubbish and score it accordingly. One news anchor introduced a segment by saying, 'This report is unlikely to help you understand the issue in any tangible way.' But for many it offered a little respite, an outline of where the bar could be redrawn.

Polls suggested an approval rating for National Benefit of the Doubt Day of 66 per cent. 23 per cent decided to reserve immediate judgement.

Mainstreaming

Tuesday, May 26th

Michael was watching daytime television in his office. It was ten thirty. The phrase 'on the taxpayer's watch' gnawed at his conscience, but after the weekend's productivity he felt entitled to watch live audience debates populated by people he would never wish to have dinner with.

The debate topic blazoned across the bottom of the screen was 'Kidnappers: friend or foe?'. The majority were in the friend camp. Michael reminded himself that the majority were not geopolitical strategists. 'They're the best thing to happen to this country in years,' said a middle-aged man with frightening conviction.

The hostages were becoming a sideshow to the main event. Michael found himself transformed: the current crisis was the most productive period he had known in government. He was having fun. Even Greenham had called looking for news and asked if he fancied a beer.

The Foundation sent a message to all the editors of the British media at midnight, which read simply: 'It's good news!' The relief mixed with uncertainty as to what they should do next. Barrett decided upon a paper much like the day before. Other papers followed suit: a headline read: EVERY

DAY IS NATIONAL BENEFIT OF THE DOUBT DAY. Online debates asked what this meant for the industry. Did the population really want to be bombarded with negativity?

'Unfortunately so,' said Charlie. 'People will soon return to finding comfort in the seediness and misfortune of others.'

'Maybe,' said Michael. 'It just seems people are a little more . . . upbeat.'

'As are you.'

'As am I. It's this or looking at banking reform. Now there's a story that isn't worth telling. The best I came up with was Hansel and Gretel with our dear Chancellor Verso as the witch.'

'He loves a gingerbread.'

'He'd probably have eaten the house before the kids arrived.'

'At least he'd be too full to eat *them*.'

'Eat them? Verso's more likely to home school them. Hansel and Gretel will return a year later with impeccable Latin.'

Charlie smiled and turned the TV over to another news channel.

'You know what time it is?' said Michael. Charlie turned towards him. 'It's time to show a little more concerned helplessness.'

That afternoon Lucy received a call from the Prime Minister's secretary inviting her to Downing Street. Lucy gave short submissive answers. When she agreed to Miller's proposition she understood its potential gravity, but never believed it would get this far. A couple of press photographers remained loitering outside her door. She now felt dizzy, staring down a precipice that had appeared without warning. She texted Miller. '*What should I do?*'

Miller texted back: '*He didn't invite my mum. Stay calm. Will have a chat and get back to you.*'

The Foundation had yet to decide how they would use a link to the PM, but Jordie argued, 'It's better to wish you hadn't put your car key into the bowl than to wish you had.'

Lucy responded surprisingly well to the directive of being their car key.

'*Just be yourself. Don't ask specific questions. Just try to see where he stands.*'

Immediately after, she received a second text: '*And thank you. X*'

There was a sense of purpose in the Cairo head office. The success of the second demand gave them confidence; it looked to the outside world like they had a plan.

'At this point,' Aiya said to Liam as they sat on the sofas, 'I'd like to offer my congratulations. The ransom was a success because of you.'

Liam remained unmoved. He struggled to accept compliments from adolescents, no matter how prodigious. The idea for the demand was not his. The ransom publicly mourned his potential: his was a cautionary tale. He felt confused and defensive, and the others picked up on this fresh melancholy. Jordie stood up from the sofa, waddled three steps towards Liam and offered his hand. Liam stared at it momentarily before shaking it. Jordie nodded sagely and sat back down.

'So who's next?' Aiya said excitedly.

'The way I see it, it's a battle of the most miserable,' said Jordie, 'and while I'm no Desmond Tutu, I'd say Dicky's the next most downcast bastard in the room.'

No one objected.

'Home brew?' said Aiya to Richard.

*

Lucy passed security into Downing Street on her way to Number 10. She wore a long grey skirt and jacket: she had spent the evening imagining what a grieving girlfriend should wear and settled on her work clothes. She was met at the door by an aide and escorted through the building to the Prime Minister's office. The aide knocked and opened the door. Michael and Charlie stood up to welcome her.

'Miss Smalling,' Michael said. Lucy smiled shyly back. 'Sorry, would you prefer me to call you Miss Smalling or Lucy?'

'Lucy's fine.'

'Of course. Lucy, can I get you a coffee?'

'Um, yes . . . thank you.'

Michael nodded at the aide who left.

'Please, take a seat.' Michael and Charlie joined her next to three seats that had been arranged by the bookcase. 'I really wanted to convey my deepest sympathy over what has happened. We're doing all we can to find out where they are. Our best intelligence is working with our Egyptian counterparts in Cairo. It's our number one priority to bring them home safely. I can assure you of that.' It sounded like such a natural reaction he briefly believed it was true.

Lucy felt smothered by the situation and tried to calm her shaking hands. She recognised the characters' names from *1984* written on the whiteboard. The photos on the wall, Pooh Bear on the bookshelf, the full-length mirror: the office seemed to further the farcical turn her life had taken.

'Thank you,' Lucy said. The muscles on her face struggled to coordinate the necessary emotions. 'So, is there any news?' At least her fragility and fear were authentic.

'Let me be honest. We have leads, but are unfortunately waiting for the kidnappers' next move.'

Lucy nodded, absent-mindedly sucking on her own hair.

'So . . .' Michael ventured. 'I can't begin to imagine how hard it must be waiting around for news.'

Nor could Lucy. She gave a brave smile, nodded and searched for some words. Under pressure, her remarks had a habit of turning literary.

'I feel like Penelope waiting for Odysseus to return,' she said, staring longingly through the window. She closed her eyes as a means of escape. Drawing the parallel between herself and a universal symbol for marital fidelity missed the restrained humility Lucy hoped to parade.

'Let's just hope it doesn't take this Odysseus 20 years to return to Ithaca,' Michael said with a warm smile. 'I'm usually the only one who makes literary analogies around here.'

'Is that one of them?' Lucy said, gesturing with her head at the whiteboard.

Michael laughed nervously. 'It's one of my more recent attempts.' The board was split into four sections, with a jumble of arrows, names and circles muddling the middle two. In the first column the words 'Airstrip One, Oceania', 'Big Brother' and 'Ministry of Energy' were underlined, and in the final column read: 'Town runs on 100 per cent renewable energy.'

'How'd it work?' asked Lucy with interest.

Michael uncrossed his legs and leaned back in his seat. 'Not great.'

'I'm happy my Prime Minister tries to govern with Orwellian analogies.' They both smiled, the earlier frost now a puddle on the floor.

The aide knocked and entered the office with three cups of coffee. It gave Lucy a few moments to re-enter character.

'So have you ever had kidnappers make demands like this before?' she said.

Michael shuffled slightly. 'No. No, it's all rather strange. We don't know exactly what their motives are.'

Lucy's hands covered her face, as if to hide her stubborn tears. Michael leaned forward, his hand outstretched ready to descend on her shoulder. It quickly drew back as Lucy sat up again.

'I'm at least consoled that the ransoms have asked for things Miller would support. That maybe there is a happy ending. Is that silly?'

Michael shook his head. 'No, not at all.'

'As terrible as it sounds,' Lucy continued, 'I can't help but wonder what the next demand will be. It's as if so long as the ransoms remain benevolent, their treatment of him will be too.'

Michael felt a growing respect for this young woman: mature, selfless, wise, a listener. 'I know. These events inspire mixed emotions. I suppose we've all wondered what could be asked for next.' He immediately apologised, aghast at his own insensitivity.

'It's OK. Really,' said Lucy. 'It's only natural. I've done it also, as a way to distract myself from the other images . . .' She attempted a sad smile. 'I'd be interested at some point to hear what you've come up with.'

'Oh,' said Michael, who was keen to move on and pretend he had never brought it up. 'Yes. Yes, I suppose I could do that.'

Lucy gave a reserved smile. 'I'd like that.'

'So, Richard. Oil executive. Environmentalist. You must have broken a few demands you'd have made of yourself,' said Aiya.

Her voice made Richard feel he was playing doctors with his niece. He refilled another home brew.

'When I was younger, the only thing I demanded of myself was that I'd jump from GoldBlue if it looked like it was going wrong. I didn't. Fine. But it was never my job to demand things from myself. People had to demand things of me. And by me, I mean the market.'

'Wasn't me, guv'nor,' said Jordie in a terrible cockney accent.

Richard shrugged. 'If I didn't maximise profits, I'd have been fired, and someone else would carry on as usual.'

Jordie shook his head. 'A position worth fighting for has risks attached.'

'Coming from Mother fucking Teresa. Have you tried changing the system recently? I get all this crap about *me* being the system. *They're* the system. Shareholders make money from people buying their products. People. Not me. I'm the scapegoat for a population with double standards. GoldBlue got crucified after Crest Voyager – but did our profits drop? Did anyone stop buying our petrol? Of course they fucking didn't. Show companies that profits rely on change, and they will.'

'So it's the people's fault?' said Jordie.

'Of course it is. Everywhere there are people who don't live by their values and blame people like me for their weakness.'

'But is it a moral choice if you know your own sacrifice won't affect anything?' said Miller, who had often thought about becoming a vegetarian. No one had an answer.

'To summarise, there're many people who would've wanted to screw you over,' Jordie said to Richard, 'but they were too uncoordinated to place a demand serious enough to threaten your shareholders.'

'I could go along with that.'

'So let's get them coordinated.'

Over the next hour they made a list of the companies they felt were owed some demands. There were many candidates.

As they began to debate whose list was best, Jalila, who had sat quietly throughout the discussion, raised her head and smiled at the others. They studied her face as she looked at Aiya, fascinated by the minor movements that formed their conversation.

'Mum thinks the world would be a better place if you were the leaders of it,' Aiya said. 'But you're not. We're not here to change capitalism; we're not going to end inequality. We're here to help people realise that they have the power if they only knew it.'

The men looked deflated.

'I think, gentlemen,' said Aiya, 'a good starting point is to ask if your demand would fit on a banner.'

'I wasn't expecting you to give a veiled tribute to the kidnappers in front of a hostage's girlfriend,' said Charlie to Michael once Lucy had left.

Michael looked pensive. 'Indeed, I'm a man full of surprises recently. She didn't seem too upset by it, though, did she?'

'I don't think so. It was nice to see you bond with a fellow literary mind. Anyway, do you want me to brief the press on the meeting?'

Michael was staring at his bookshelf and scanning the titles on the spines.

'Michael? Did you hear me? What do you want me to do?'

Michael looked towards Charlie. 'I want you to clear me a couple of hours today so that I can have some thinking time.'

'For what?'

'I'm going to sketch out what my demand would look like.'

'*Good news: they have no idea where you are. Bad news: I'm not sure I appeared too concerned about it,*' Lucy texted Miller once she got home.

'*Sounds like we've been in a relationship for years,*' replied Miller.

It took time to decide on their targets. GoldBlue was an obvious choice, but the tactics lacked the required visual symbolism. Boycotting online companies would similarly fail. Their targets needed to sell exclusively from physical outlets, and options were fewer than they imagined.

'So, we'll send the letters to the companies tomorrow and give them until Monday before phase two kicks in. Agreed?' said Liam.

'Are we sure it's going to get to phase two? What happens if phase one succeeds?' said Miller. 'We'll seem like unimaginative bullies.'

'Trust me,' said Richard. 'I was one of them. It'll definitely get to phase two.'

'And then what if phase two doesn't go as we hope?' said Miller.

There were a few nervous looks.

'Until then,' Aiya put in to refocus minds, 'Miller and I build the website. Mum, you've got the board game, and you three experiment with the colouring and cornflour.'

The following email was sent to the head offices of two businesses, as well as the national press on Wednesday morning.

Dearest Companies,

We realise that people will frame our relationship as one in which we came after you. And we came after you because you were bad.

So from the outset let us be clear: we are approaching you because you have been let down by the public. Because of their apathy, your unethical actions were inevitable.

We are aware that your shareholders block attempts to inject morality into your business practices as it reduces profits, so we have come to offer our assistance. Simply fulfil the demands detailed below. You have until Monday to meet the demands, and if you do not, unsavoury action will be taken.

Kind regards,
The Serendipity Foundation

Demands

- The Fullbean Coffee Company must stop its attempts to block the trademarking of indigenous coffee beans by the Eritrean government.
- The Happy Burger Company must register itself and all subsidiaries connected to its UK operation as UK based, placing it under the remit of UK tax law.

The afternoon papers ran with the demand on the front page, and the analysis continued on TV and online. The large plasma screens at London stations beamed the news to commuters. The population seemed largely satisfied that big business was next in line. But in his office, Michael was less content.

'I mean, it just doesn't make sense.'

'Why?' said Charlie. 'They've challenged government and the press; this seems a natural next step.'

'But why two companies? They're hardly unique in their disregard for the common good.'

Charlie shrugged. 'Maybe the kidnappers have specific grievances about them.'

'Well, Fullbean Coffee does consistently over-roast its beans to leave a bitter residue on the palate. I don't know,' he said more seriously, 'their last two ransoms were . . . cleverer. There was a complexity to them that hinted at a greater purpose. This one . . . it's just a little basic, a little uninspiring.'

Charlie let out a little laugh. 'It's as if your favourite band just released a disappointing album.'

Michael gave a forced smile.

'Michael, this shows they're running out of ideas. We can soon focus on governing a country with a little bit of public approval for a change.'

Michael failed to notice Charlie's silver lining. 'It's just . . .' Michael started before falling back into silence. Charlie urged him to continue. 'It's just a bit of a wasted opportunity.'

'In what way?'

'I think my ransom is better.'

The two companies initially held their silence. They each felt a sense of injustice at having been singled out for actions they had simply copied from their competitors. It was the closest they had come to self-righteousness in years.

With less than three working days until the deadline, they had little opportunity to address the demands. It was as if the kidnappers hoped they would fail to respond positively. The CEOs knew their boards would not consider bowing to such ultimatums. All the operations being questioned had been deemed legal by highly paid law firms.

Polls indicated the public largely supported the demands, highlighting the belief that corporate law and regulation failed to ensure moral behaviour; however, many civic organisations were angry at the blame for unethical business practices being laid on the public. There was a feeling that the ransomers, who had so far appeared to be on the side of the citizen, had slightly betrayed them.

On Friday the companies prepared statements detailing the legality of their current operations, the impossible time restrictions placed on them for implementation, and an analysis of how such demands threatened the principles of the free market and, therefore, the cornerstone of civilisation. Vague invitations were made to the kidnappers for dialogue, but this was phrased as if speaking for the government rather than their own organisations.

Private capital did not negotiate with terrorists.

'Where did you learn to do all this?' asked Miller.

Aiya shrugged. 'I started using computers from the age of four.'

'Where? At school?'

'Kind of.'

'I didn't realise that schools out here were progressive enough to teach girls how to build a website.'

She smiled as she typed. 'Nor are they progressive enough to teach you how to hide four foreign men in your basement.'

Miller smiled back. 'You and your mum never seem to talk too much about your past.'

'Mum especially.' Aiya giggled and broke from typing. 'Mum saw that everyone was talking over each other, so decided to focus upon listening for a while.' Aiya turned back to the computer screen; Miller withdrew his follow-up questions.

It was Friday lunchtime. The website was to go live the following evening. The design was sparse. At the top right-hand corner stood the Foundation's logo as dictated by Jalila: a simple black outline of the thermometer-looking shape from the lobby wall. Wrapped around the bottom of the logo was their newly agreed motto: 'Unreasonably demand the reasonable'. Jordie tested the page; it appeared idiot-proof.

Cabin fever had set in. They had become sensitive to the enforced intimacy with each other's bodies. With phase two due to start on Monday, they decided they needed a break. Three weeks of facial hair growth provided a natural disguise, and it was agreed that with a combination of the sunglasses, white robes and turbans that Jalila had purchased, their identities would be safe so long as the females led. No one was looking for them in a museum.

On Saturday afternoon they granted themselves day release. They left in two threes: Aiya accompanied Jordie and Miller, while Jalila entertained Richard and Liam. They left separately and flagged taxis on the main street; Jalila handed the address to the driver. Security barely noted their existence as they entered the Egyptian Museum.

They inspected sarcophagi and golden masks. They read stories about Hapi, the god of the annual flooding of the Nile that kept Egypt alive; of Isis, the goddess of magic and motherhood; of Ra the god of the sun. On the one hand these gods were there to console and give meaning in a world of death and hopelessness. On the other, they were there to legitimise demands placed on populations. They were not the source of good deeds, but the excuse for doing them.

The Foundation had also become more powerful in the imagination than as flesh and bones. They had become myths, modern excuses for good deeds, contemporary gods in Arab disguise, with tired legs and a lust for ice cream.

On Monday, the rumours of non-compliance were confirmed. The country braced itself for the news that would spell the end of an enjoyable journey.

Michael found it impossible to focus. He stared unseeing at his computer screen, waiting for the drumming of feet racing towards his door. At 12.15pm the sound of Charlie's purposeful size nines came down the corridor and into his office. Michael stared at him urgently.

'And?'

'The demands they made last week seem to have been an entrée. Here is the main course.' Charlie handed Michael a sheet of A4 paper, which Michael snatched eagerly.

Dear All,

Our last demand was unreasonable and unimaginative. It was the type of demand you would expect from a common kidnapper.

Our key piece of advice to anybody placing a demand is this: you've got to hold the right people to ransom. Don't ask for change from people who do not have the power to change it. You, the people, are the ones with the power, whether or not you choose to acknowledge it.

But getting a country to boycott a company is complicated. How can you guarantee your neighbour will likewise go without a juicy burger?

We have a solution to your coordination problem. Anyone who consumes a product of Happy Burger or Fullbean Coffee will be held directly responsible for the deaths of the hostages. The last thing the hostages will see is the enlarged face of the person responsible for their deaths.

How do we get your pictures? We get them from you. At www.serendipityfoundation.org there are links to every outlet of the two companies involved. You, the public, will dissuade others from supporting these outlets by taking pictures of anyone who enters them. The website offers clear steps on how to upload these photos successfully.

This will last for as long as it takes the two companies involved to implement the demands previously detailed. All members of staff in these outlets are advised to wear uniforms and name badges at all times. The demand will commence at 9.00 tomorrow morning.

Regards,

The Serendipity Foundation

It was four in the afternoon and Michael was in a COBRA meeting. The Minister for Business had recently spoken to the two CEOs: their resolve remained unshakeable.

'They reiterated that consumer choice is the bedrock of our democracy, and that they've a moral duty to stand firm against undemocratic demands.'

'Of paying tax and letting the poor make a living wage: the first steps on the road to tyranny,' said Michael.

'We have four options,' said Rawlins, moving the conversation on. 'We either force the outlets or website to close, encouraging people to carry on as normal, or we enforce a picket line outside. Either way we need to mobilise every last law enforcement officer as it could turn ugly.'

'And if you were to focus the mind just a little more, which option would you take?' said Michael.

'Prime Minister, my job is national security—'

'Don't we bloody know it?'

Rawlins collected himself and continued. 'And as a man who cares only about safety, I recommend we shut down the website and encourage people to continue as normal. If it ends in four deaths, then we'll put on a charming service at St Paul's, but we're talking about flashpoints potentially arising all over the country. More than four people could die through the ensuing chaos.'

'Or maybe people will just grab a coffee somewhere else,' said Michael with annoyance.

'Prime Minister,' said Cowling, 'this could spiral dangerously out of control. We should encourage business as usual.'

There were nods around the room.

Michael shook his head. 'Really? So long as enough people are responsible for murder, that's OK, is it? Listen to me very carefully: under no circumstances does anyone make a statement. Mobilise law enforcement all you want, but they're not to be deployed anywhere. No websites will be shut down. Someone has asked the public to rise to a challenge, and we'll bloody well give them the opportunity to mess it up by themselves.'

Tuesday, June 2nd

If you found yourself outside the Fullbean Coffee outlet in Trafalgar Square at 8.45 you might have believed you were on the front line of an attack on the economic system. Protesters rolled police tape across the entrance, declaring it a crime scene. Activists held placards. Human shields braced themselves for clashes with callous caffeine addicts. Camera phones scoured the audience for suspects.

Nine o'clock arrived. There was electricity in the air: nerves and fear, fun and excitement. For some it was hard to link the event to a genuine threat: it was a curiosity, rather than a violent challenge. Yet the barricades at Trafalgar Square held firm.

Similar scenes took place in front of Happy Burger and Fullbean Coffee chains across Britain. Campaign groups had mobilised all available members to man camera phones. Local newspapers and everyday witnesses discouraged those who contemplated entering. At ten, there had been no reported incidents of murderous consumption.

No one knew exactly when the spell was broken. Many would-be protesters were at work: there were not enough bodies to man all the outlets, and the first to fall were in suburban areas where attention was least focused. Some rumoured that right-wing groups entered the Fullbean Coffee store in Aberdeen with the intention of drinking lattes. Others said the demand was broken by an old woman in Armagh whose TV had broken and was unaware of the demand. Some blamed it on a government conspiracy, some on the intrinsic evil hidden inside every one of us. It did not seem to matter; there was no shock it had happened.

Social media went into morbid hyper-drive. It seemed as if the whole country was waiting for news. Would all four hostages be killed? Would the execution be live?

Charlie entered Michael's office to find him sitting on the floor leaning against his desk. He threw a tennis ball against the wall in a way reminiscent of Steve McQueen, as if planning his own Great Escape. The TV showed images of the public slowly returning to the stigmatised businesses. They weaved through dejected protesters slumped on pavements. Michael could not decide if this was a symbol of good versus evil or idealism versus realism.

Michael had sat in the COBRA meeting room as events unfolded. His advisers and ministers pleaded with him to block the website and avoid potentially violent recriminations. He agreed, embarrassed by his original faith in the public.

'You've got to be fucking kidding me,' said Jordie.

Richard smiled as he stood over the Twister board. 'Jordie's T-shirt's bigger than the mat.'

This was Liam's idea of hell. Miller fancied his chances.

Aiya clapped as she took her position next to the spinner. 'Good luck, gentlemen.'

The first instructions were announced to each of the four players. Left foot red. Right foot green. Left foot blue. Left hand red.

The 20-dot mat lay on the floor in the middle of the room. Miller was the only one crouched on the floor, mat-to-hand.

Left hand red. Right hand yellow. Right hand yellow. Right foot blue.

'Get your arse out of my face,' said Richard to Jordie, whose main chance of victory was in taking up most of the mat rather than his yogic prowess. He had now spread himself across the mat's width, facing downwards, the cruelties of gravity on full display.

Aiya and Jalila stood to the side, grinning.

Liam went out first. An uncommitted lunge to right foot green failed to arch over Jordie's hide. Richard soon followed him: the approach to left hand red required a tunnelling under Jordie's stomach. A faint touch of elbow on belly disturbed the balance, and Aiya spotted the faint grounding of Pounder posterior.

'Left hand red!' said Aiya with glee. Jordie reached over Miller's head for a corner position. Miller failed to duck away, and found his head trapped under Jordie's shoulder and breast. Miller's move to right foot green saw his downfall under the human wall. Jordie collapsed victoriously on top of Miller shouting, 'You shall not pass! You shall not pass!'

Aiya's uncontrollable laughter reminded them of quite how young she was. Then, as soon as she recovered: 'Jordie! You win! You get to choose. Who are we killing?'

Charlie burst in to Michael's office. 'A video's been released.' He turned on the TV. A grainy image showed the four hostages sitting on short wooden stools. Their heads down, the large shadows around their eyes ran into three-week-old beards. They wore dirty oversized shirts and jeans, with tears around the knees and collars. They held takeaway coffee cups. The black canvas background aided the impression of dark, violent austerity. The time – 16.23 – showed in the bottom right-hand corner.

A figure dressed in black approached Liam Powell, who was sitting furthest to the right. The figure pointed a gun at him, and ordered him to stand before pushing him off screen to the right. The image cut out. Five seconds later the same scene appeared with Liam Powell absent. The clock read 16.33. The camera zoomed in on Liam's empty stool, where a takeaway coffee cup stood alone, Liam's name written in black pen at its base. The cup was overflowing, crimson drops running down its side. The image panned out to show Miller Carey, next on the right, a coffee cup in his right hand, his face covered by his left hand. In the cup stood a small olive branch.

Wednesday, June 3rd

The image of the overflowing coffee cup burned itself on to the conscience of millions. It spoke not just of the terror of its filling, but of how simple its avoidance had been in the first place. It overflowed with guilt, with repentance. It haunted the minutes before sleep: the brutal substitution of warm liquids. Of course, it crossed people's minds: *where's the body?* But it seemed too callous to air doubts and once more deny responsibility. Analysts agreed that the liquid in the cup had the consistency of blood.

Wednesday morning's live pictures beamed in to the Cairo head office. Police tape once more covered outlet entrances, but this time a collection of flowers interspersed with pictures of Liam were placed directly in front of the doors. Memorials were harder to breach than entrances. Those who had protested for four lives on Tuesday returned to protest for three. The symbolic olive branch: the peace offering, spoke of a second chance to save the remaining hostages. Some took up the symbolic challenge: potted olive trees blocked the entrance to some outlets.

The live stream cut to a Happy Burger in central Birmingham. The video camera pointed through the outside window. Three young men had forced their way through the protest outside and perused the meal deals.

Jordie patted Miller on the knee. 'I'm sorry, mon protégé. This looks like it's done for you as well.'

The others smiled coldly.

The three men approached the till. The staff looked on anxiously as the cashier became embroiled in an argument with the customers. Fingers were pointed. The staff moved forward away from the fryers and grills. They huddled in a semicircle behind the cashier. Then, in a later immortalised image, the fourteen staff took off their aprons, caps and name badges, threw them at the customers, and walked out of the door. The three men inside turned around as a sea of flashes relayed their identity against the backdrop of an abandoned restaurant.

The early afternoon saw news spread of countless copycat walkouts. Calls for high-level talks were made. The personal implications for quitting meant many workers stayed inside and hoped to remain idle, praying they would not be put in a position to choose.

The closure of some franchises allowed the slowly swelling numbers of protesters to refocus efforts on those that remained open. After five o'clock, thousands of extra bodies arrived on the streets, driven by the reproach of an overflowing coffee cup.

Thursday, June 4th

No news was good news. Michael had sat through a COBRA meeting that was devoid of any intelligence or foresight. Rawlins had pushed Michael to make a statement to the kidnappers, including words such as *values*, *choice* and a tip of the hat to *our way of life*. But Michael shook his head. 'This is not the government's challenge: it's the public's. It's their story, and they're responsible for its ending.' Ministerial eyes rolled at the word 'story'.

'Prime Minister,' said Rawlins, exasperated. 'The kidnappers are merely picking on two companies. Their equally conniving competitors are benefiting. This isn't fighting injustice, nor is it writing a damn story.'

Michael expected no less. 'It could be any two companies. That's not the point. This is not an end, but a showcase of a means.'

'This is appeasement!' Rawlins said, as he slammed his fist on the table.

The protest gathered force. Tens of thousands of idle students, parents and unemployed took to the streets. They were not all humanists, nor did they all dream of a change in the economic system: some were bored, some thought it would be fun, some followed their friends, some hoped for a riot.

Jobless burger chefs set up temporary barbecues. Newly unemployed baristas brewed coffee on street corners. A Frisbee may have been thrown. Amateur Hacky Sackers may have formed circles.

Everything was controlled until the afternoon. As schools finished for the day, parents brought their children to experience the atmosphere. Outside the Fullbean Coffee in the centre of Bagshot, crowds surged all the way down to the main road. At 15.32 a car hit an eight-year-old girl as she weaved around the crowd on to the road. She was concussed, broke her femur, a collarbone and two ribs.

The companies claimed enough was enough, and that children were almost dying through these reckless demands. The police and local councils started taking a similar view.

'Michael, we're under serious pressure to look at our policing directives. We can't allow large groups to remain on busy streets. You need to make a decision,' said Cowling. 'Michael?'

Michael felt Rawlins's gaze burn into the side of his head. He also felt three years of frustration burn in his veins. He took a couple of deep breaths and tried to separate passion from decision-making.

'Michael.' Cowling cut off Rawlins before the situation became irretrievable. 'What do you want to do?'

Michael returned his gaze to the table, avoiding Rawlins's glare. 'Shut them down,' he said.

'Shut down the shops or the picket lines?'

'I mean shut down the roads.'

Friday, June 5th

Commuters woke up to road diversion signs. Policemen directed traffic away from the centre of towns and shopping streets in cities. The temperate reactions of most drivers were said to be a lingering effect of National Benefit of the Doubt Day. But evidence in support of this statement was, at best, circumstantial.

Many were ambivalent to the news. But some entrepreneurs saw opportunities. The first to act were the newly set-up food stalls that placed picnic tables in the middle of the road to tempt their customers with al fresco dining.

By mid-morning, some activists were planning their own stalls and by afternoon had located tables and literature. Pedestrians didn't know how to react to organisations simply wanting to explain their work without asking for credit card details.

Streets filled during lunchtime, but remained sparsely populated. The odd game of football and cricket inspired light jealousy in the hearts of those caged in offices.

By the afternoon, councils received queries asking whether permits for bouncy castles were needed for these newly pedestrianised areas. The councils had no idea: an absence of bouncy castles from main roads had previously been considered a matter for common sense rather than regulation.

By Friday evening, many towns had declared that there would be fairs in the town centre that weekend.

Financial losses between the two companies had broken the £50 million mark.

Saturday, June 6th

In future years, the day would be known simply as Saturday Sixth. As with all past events that embody an aura of mystique, rumour would replace fact. People struggled to remember their own experiences without flooding their accounts with the experiences of others, to the point that it is now impossible to say exactly what took place where.

What can be confirmed is that on Saturday morning, rather than the streets merely being closed, the streets had been reclaimed.

Trucks and vans all over the country were unloading an assortment of fair rides, five-a-side goals, skate ramps, tables and chairs, stilts, gymnastic equipment, bouncy castles, padded sumo wrestling suits, fancy-dress wardrobes, synthetic cricket wickets, barbecues, ponies and one, singular elephant.

Volunteers of all ages came together to make feasts. Pictures were posted online of ramshackle street bakeries, giant pasties and paellas big enough to swim in. Tables and chairs lined streets and squares, as strangers made introductions to each other as they took their seats.

Accounts told of how, once initial defences had been withdrawn, strangers came to appreciate how they had misjudged their neighbours. There was nothing to fear after all. Amid the laughter came a realisation of how many skills lay between them, and common interests among them. There was mingling.

On social media, trending images saw hooded adolescents giving middle-aged men skate lessons on the ramp.

Games of cricket and football took over the roads.

Videos showed samba drums pulsing through the early evening air, the audience dimly basking in the flames of controlled fire pits and torches juggled by men on stilts.

Details now became hazy at best: estimates varied wildly as to the number of those on the streets. Memories recounted different performers and atmospheres. Some said the streets were *jumping till sunrise*; others that the parties barely reached midnight, and *that* was being generous. Everyone experienced a personal variation of the evening.

Most of all, newspapers relayed how, with a glass of wine in hand, strangers talked about their communities, the potential that lay within them, and the dream of what they could achieve. The next morning, few remembered the details of these conversations, but recalled with clarity the feeling of optimism, and the desire to bottle the emotion as a future panacea against the apathy they would inevitably face in the future.

What remained outside the realm of myth was how the companies' anxious board members flew in on Saturday afternoon in response to a boycott that had transcended a pinch on their shareholders' dividends.

'We're in danger of this undermining the last decade's branding strategy,' said the CEO of Happy Burger. 'The amount of tax we paid last month is now exactly the same amount as we turned over this week, which, in case you missed it, is zilch. A core mission of this company is to turn over more money than we pay in tax.'

These were facts that didn't need spreadsheets.

On Sunday morning, after total losses in turnover and share value of nearly £100 million, the two companies released statements outlining their compliance with the demands. The public had forced their hands.

Or maybe the public had given the CEOs wiggle room to do what they had always wanted.

Monday, June 8th

Rawlins felt as if he were about to vomit the sickly sweet excess of the weekend over his fellow Monday morning commuters. Their satisfied demeanours shocked him. He liked lunching outside as much as the next man, but doubted it was the panacea against inequality and injustice.

'Rawlins,' came a voice as he made his way up Whitehall.

He turned around to see Cowling struggle on her heels to catch up. He stood still and tried to hide his annoyance at being spotted.

'Were you out on Saturday?' said Cowling as she patted down her dyed-brown bob.

Rawlins scowled. 'I led the foxtrot lessons before telling all the ugly people how beautiful they are.' He had always struggled with humour. Cowling was the closest he had to a champion in Cabinet, and he regretted his poor diplomacy. His scowl softened. 'I walked to my village green and saw three boys in hoods getting high and a girl being sick on pants that were closer to her knees than her skirt. Life-affirming stuff.'

'Hmm. Yes.' Cowling wished she had never asked. 'Well, at least that week is over.' She looked at her watch.

'Quiet week ahead now that the world is saved,' he said. Cowling looked at him, confused, before Rawlins continued. 'I just got an email saying the Taliban have packed it all in to set up an organic farmers' market.'

Cowling smiled awkwardly.

'Well, this has been a pleasure, but I'm heading in there,' Rawlins said, pointing towards the Ministry of Defence, 'where I'll be dealing mostly with stopping people blowing us up.'

Cowling smiled. 'And I'll be heading down there,' she said, pointing in the opposite direction towards the Home Office, 'where I'll be drafting a press release congratulating the public for making salad.'

The Museum of Regret

Monday, June 8th

Michael and Charlie had spent the last 30 minutes with the speechwriters trying to forge a government position on the weekend's events.

'This is a seminal moment. Everyone will remember where they were on Saturday Sixth. It could change everything,' said Michael.

'What exactly do you mean by everything?' said one of the speechwriting team.

'Bush's speechwriters understood the concept of "everything" back in 2001. This is a spiritual 9/11,' said Michael.

'With respect, Bush was dealing with the greatest act of terror ever committed on American soil, whereas this weekend we witnessed a lot of people baking bread.'

'Suicide bloomers,' said Charlie.

'Nice.' Michael noted the effort, mulling a few puns of his own.

Michael wasn't alone in not being able to put his finger on why the weekend had felt so special: the whole had added up to so much more than the sum of its parts. Unlike the previous ransoms, the savouring of Saturday's climax was a more personal affair.

While the previous week had been a poor one for sales of Happy Burger and Fullbean Coffee, a little known CD, *A Haiku Analysis of the Tetragrammaton*, climbed the Amazon sales chart steadily to a place in the top 5,000, riding the recent wave of popularity encountered by the diminutive Japanese art form.

Jordie compared the Foundation's experience of Saturday with the sensation of waking up hung over to see a beautiful stranger putting their clothes back on. 'You're feeling chuffed with yourself, but just wish you could remember the fucking details.'

After a surreal weekend, the image of an overflowing coffee cup seemed more bizarre than terrifying. With the redemption of Saturday Sixth easing Wednesday's guilt, commentators floated the idea that remorse for the death of Liam should be suspended until a body showed up.

'You're the second coming of Christ,' Jordie said to Liam. 'Dying for the sins of others, controversy over the hows and wheres, similar upbeat personalities. Your resurrection will be epic.'

It seemed that Britain was having a moment of contemplation. Jalila was nervous that a new demand so soon would blow such vulnerability away; but Miller reasoned that a clever demand could capitalise on it, turning it into a force for good that could extend beyond the purchasing of a charity single. They decided to remain open to suggestions as they embarked on the ritualistic pouring of alcohol that fuelled their creativity.

'Jordie,' said Aiya, 'as the third most depressed, you're up.'

The others smiled as Jordie stood, sarcastically gave a fist pump in celebration, then wobbled and sat back down.

'So how are you feeling?'

Jordie took a few seconds before laughing at the scene's ridiculousness.

Aiya continued. 'Anger? Resignation? Regret?'

Jordie slumped his large frame against the back of the sofa. 'Talk about a leading fucking question. If you're wanting me to ball my eyes out, we're a few units away from that.'

'At least the tears are waiting to come out in time,' said Aiya with a smile.

'Smile all you want. One day you'll be old enough to have regrets.'

'So what are yours?'

'You're not going to get me that easily,' Jordie said, taking another swig.

'You're a man who faked a poor village instead of visiting it. It strikes me that you may not be the man you hoped to be,' said Aiya in a serious tone.

'I beg your fucking pardon. You know nothing about what I've had to endure in my life.'

Aiya shrugged. 'I'm sorry I made you so defensive.'

'I'm not being fucking defensive. Do you know what it's like? Spending 15 years in places with no proper friends. Fifteen years of being the fat white bastard? So I got tired of it. So I moved home. You want me to sit here and confide my life's disappointments? Yeah, I now write papers that will never be read. I do feasibilities on projects that will never be implemented. The same inequalities in the world persist but I now chew the fat with analysts in grey London offices. Slums I helped upgrade have been bulldozed.' Jordie paused, taking a couple of calming breaths, looking more vulnerable than the others had ever seen him.

'And it's all bollocks. I've spent the majority of my life helping people in the most tangible way possible. I've saved or improved thousands of lives. I'm not going to apologise or feel regret for that.'

Aiya allowed a brief pause. 'So what do you feel regret for?'

No one broke the silence. Jordie stared at the ceiling as he quickly wiped the inside of his eye.

'Look at these two,' he said, gesturing to Liam and Richard. 'I already know them better than I did my mum and dad, than I know my best friends . . .' He pursed his lips. 'And then you realise that for the last few years you've gone through a job like mine without the slightest interest of the lives of those you're changing; poverty's now an intellectual exercise, people are just part of the puzzle. I stare at suffering and all I'm left with is . . . is . . . indifference. What does that say about me?'

All eyes remained fixed on Jordie.

'I mean,' Jordie said, rubbing his eyes, 'when did I stop caring about the feelings of others?'

The results from an online search of 'Lucy Smalling' had changed radically in two weeks. Photos appeared she had previously thought lost. In some ways it was nice to have them found for her. Far from people dissecting her relationship with Miller, magazines analysed her style, applauding her professional chic.

She got recognised in Tesco.

On Tuesday evening, the following statement was released.

Dear Britain,

We would like to think we are all one giant team now. And communication is key to a team becoming great. So we would like to take this opportunity to get to know each other better: how are you all feeling, and where do you think we could improve?

We thought we would start the ball rolling by confiding in you all where we think we could have done better. We found it a useful exercise, and what developed was more a list of our lives' regrets. We felt some of you may wish to add your own thoughts to the list. We ask you to visit www.museumofregret.org and tell us of your greatest regrets.

Quickly register, and add your confession. Your details will remain private; we have no special offers to push. Entries close at midnight on Saturday.

Yours in service,

The Serendipity Foundation

'Well, it's not exactly the Bhutanese Human Index of Happiness, is it?' said Michael to Charlie. They were drinking tea this week. 'Instead we'll have millions of people detailing to the world exactly where their lives became irretrievably rubbish.'

'Britain is back: the safest depressed place in the world,' said Charlie.

'If we overlook being held accountable for murder for buying an onion ring.'

There was a knock at the door. 'Come in.' It was Rawlins, who nodded, and took a seat without invitation. Michael hated seeing army uniforms and medals in his refuge: two visions for ruling a country colliding.

'How are you, Rawlins? Join in the weekend festivities?' said Charlie.

Rawlins chose not to acknowledge him and addressed Michael.

'I came to find out the details of your statement.'

'My statement?'

'A British citizen was executed last week and it seems

everyone, including the Prime Minister, is choosing to ignore it.'

'Well . . .' said Michael, as he shuffled nervously in his seat. 'We have no proof yet. Intelligence has yet to rule out completely that it could have been a cup of red liquid. No body. No verbal confirmation they killed him.'

'So ask them to show you the body,' said Rawlins.

'What exactly are you hoping to achieve by such a request?'

'A modicum of control.' Rawlins's moustache twitched with frustration. He stared with a military disdain saved for those who are too weak to handle the means that achieve the ends. Michael doubted they shared ends.

'Fine,' Rawlins said as he stood. 'This charade cannot continue.'

Universities held seminars with titles such as 'Benevolent Terrorism: a new paradigm in democratic rights'. People sent their own demands to the letters pages of newspapers. Academia analysed how the demands could be improved *for next time*.

Councils received countless enquiries about how individuals could get more involved locally. New associations were registered. NGOs discussed which companies could be targeted next, with online mailing lists collated, shared and expanded. An anonymous plan was posted as to how GoldBlue could be effectively boycotted in response to their continued pollution of the Niger Delta.

The first regrets were registered on Tuesday evening, and by eleven the Foundation realised the swell of entries had surpassed their ability to read them. As they awoke on Wednesday, the website's counter read 61,000. They spent their day dipping in randomly; a montage of a nation's melancholy, each entry a piece in a mosaic of unfulfilled dreams.

By Wednesday evening over a million had added their regret. 24 hours later this figure was up to 4 million. By Saturday, the website's seven-digit counter stopped at 9,999,999.

It was described as the most collaborative public art piece in history. It was undoubtedly the largest piece ever commissioned by terrorists.

In later years it would be painstakingly reorganised into areas of regret: travel, family, friends, love, time and career. But for now, it read as an infinite scroll:

> I regret not asking more questions of how my grandparents fell in love
>
> I regret never having taken up an outdoor activity
>
> I regret not telling the people I love how special they are more often
>
> I regret not having the confidence to strike up conversations with strangers
>
> I regret not buying spontaneous presents
>
> I regret not looking after my parents in their old age in the way that I would like to be looked after by my children when I get old
>
> I regret never opening the four language packs I bought
>
> I regret nothing
>
> I regret using emails and text messages as a substitute for phone calls when congratulating my friends
>
> I regret not saying thank you to my mum before she died
>
> I regret hiding behind the idea of being tired as an excuse for not maximising my weekends

I regret, in 1964, never asking Sarah Brannell to marry me

I regret having let my dad convince me to study to become an engineer

I regret staying with my ex-husband ten years longer than I should have

I regret not remaining close to the people who knew me when I was young

I regret not taking advantage of my body when it was healthy

I regret not taking greater interest in things I didn't know

I regret not changing my career before I had children and got a mortgage

I regret holding people to standards higher than those I hold myself to

'Who are they all confessing to?' said Miller on Saturday afternoon. 'No one's going to read it.'

'People feel the need to leave their mark regardless of whether they're being read or not,' said Liam. 'Look at all the blogs and tweets forced upon the world for no other reason than to shout "I'm here" into the digital void.'

The men nodded, but noticed Jalila lightly shaking her head. They focused with Aiya in trying to read her thoughts.

'We've always been storytellers,' translated Aiya. 'Stories of our hopes, self-justifications, ways of comparing our experiences with those of others. But it's declining.'

'Yeah, that's what I thought she said as well,' said Jordie.

'You're telling me that Twitter exists because no one tells stories any more,' said Richard. They stared back at Jalila.

'More that no one's got the patience to listen,' said Aiya. 'So we've lost the patience to bother explaining. All the regrets are people wishing they'd formed better relationships with people or the planet, and the majority were caused by poor communication.'

Jordie shuffled. In the last decade, before arriving in Cairo, the only conversations he'd had about his own emotions were under the guise of complaining about work to his colleagues.

'It seems what we're talking about, gentlemen,' said Aiya, 'is extending the spirit of a week's kidnap in this basement. A bit of violently enforced peace can go a long way.'

On Monday afternoon the following statement was released.

Dear Britain,

We were heartened by your overwhelming response to the Museum of Regret. We thought the demand should build on this.

All day long the hostages talk about their pasts: the happy memories, the amends they would make. They have the time to talk and the patience to listen. What better way to save their lives than for you to do the same?

This week we ask you to write three handwritten letters, and post them through the Royal Mail. The first letter must be posted by Wednesday, the second by Saturday, and the third by next Monday.

The first letter you write must be a thank you letter. It can be to anyone about anything. We would encourage you to think hard about events you may have overlooked.

The Royal Mail must publish the figures of how many letters are posted each day so we can compare them against the average post.

Yours in service,

The Serendipity Foundation

Royal Mail released the figures for post collected on Monday evening. The demand had huge potential benefits for their ailing business.

'The lost art of letter writing' became a stock phrase over the next two days. Most people didn't really believe it was a lost art, but a redundant medium. Sure, everyone enjoyed receiving a handwritten letter; but there was a feeling the terrorists had become overly sentimental.

It is hard to say when this opinion started changing. Maybe when people began to select their recipient. They had been asked to consider what they might have overlooked, and so people delved into their pasts: the sacrifices that had been made for them, the sense of entitlement that had blinded them to the support from others, the taking for granted of love and friendship.

Or maybe opinions changed as they sat down to write. The words they effortlessly typed on phones and computers no longer stood up to the scrutiny of a communiqué that demanded its author imagine its reader sitting across the table. They had to leave a part of themselves on the paper. Their only hope would be to create a sanctuary free from modern distractions.

How strange the pens felt between their fingers. The smudges, the changing style as tentative fingers remembered old habits, the crossing out of letters as the writer sought to perfect the presentation of their thoughts, the patience bred from a desire to do justice to a belated thanksgiving.

The difficulty in finding addresses reflected how intangible location had become.

The taste of stamps and envelopes, the smell of ink on hands, the rubbing of middle fingers against the pen's grip, the sound of the folded page. The subtle arousal of the writers' senses gave a unique attachment to their creation.

As they posted the letter they might have felt a sense of excitement imagining how the letter would be received, a pride that the recipient would know how much time had been spent thinking about them.

On Wednesday morning a Michael Rayburn, residing at 10 Downing Street, received a letter. This was rare: his staff rarely deemed deliveries worthy of his time. He traced the black ink of his name with his finger, looking at the postmark for clues as to the sender. He didn't recognise the handwriting; only his wife and children had that honour. The envelope had been opened by his secretaries, but sealed back up, as a sign of respect for its contents. He pulled out a single sheet, filled on both sides with voluptuous letters and extravagant tails on the 'g's.

Dear Michael,

Even under such circumstances it feels strange writing your name and remembering how you were all those years ago. Like many others before and after you, you gave me such hope. Is that not why I chose this path? The faith that your life can be judged by the value you add to the young, who in turn will help better the world after you have gone.

My wife died years ago, I am retired and spend my days in a house that is too big, surrounded by belongings that reflect my misplaced optimism. Sometimes I hear of my old students, and how they have disgraced themselves, or lost themselves to families, depression, or paperwork. I see no traces of my life's dedication influencing a better future. It strikes me now how incredibly foolish my goal was.

So I want to say thank you. I doubt you remember much of

what I taught you. But I hold on to the hope that my guidance, no matter how far removed, had some distant bearing on the way you have led the country over the last few weeks. You have vindicated the life of an old man.

Your old Politics professor,

Mark Constance

In Edinburgh, eighty-five-year-old Edith McNally received a letter from her ex-husband of 60 years. Because of their acrimonious divorce, he had never had the opportunity to thank her for putting his future ahead of hers.

Café waitress Chloe Armitage received a letter from a customer, seventy-eight-year-old June Malford, thanking her for remembering her name and talking to her. June's trip for afternoon tea was the only time she left the solitude of her flat.

Thousands of parents received letters from their children.

Thousands of children received letters from their parents.

Mark Constance, a retired politics professor, received a letter from one of his former pupils, Michael Rayburn, thanking him for instilling in him a sense of morality that transcended the political spectrum.

'What an unexpected surprise,' said Michael.

Rawlins instinctively straightened his back and brought his feet together whenever he entered a room in preparation to salute if the audience warranted it. In this case, it did not; he held his pose for a few seconds, as if at the end of a catwalk, before taking a seat.

'And what can I do you for?' asked Michael once Rawlins had arranged his jacket and medals.

'This feels wrong.'

'This?'

'The nature of the ransoms.'

'I delivered PM's Questions in haiku a month ago. Pleased you've caught up.'

Rawlins fought his instinct to retaliate. 'We're now writing each other thank you letters.'

'And what?' said Michael. 'Would you be more comfortable with an old-fashioned demand to release or destroy something?'

'It's not about what *I* feel comfortable with.'

'I think it has everything to do with what *you're* comfortable with.'

Rawlins was concentrating so hard on what he wanted to say that Michael's wordplay passed over his head. He pressed his fingers to his temples.

'Prime Minister. Terrorism can largely be placed in two categories. The first is fuelled by perceived injustice and inequality; the demands are their dream of what a better world looks like. At the moment these demands are hardly a cohesive vision for crushing the new world order.'

'So what would you ask for?' Michael sat back, crossed his legs and raised his eyebrows.

'Well, if I was them, I'd . . . well . . . hmm.' Rawlins had spent most of his time criticising what others were asking for. 'I'd probably want to break the shackles of a foreign power.'

Michael smiled. 'Death to America! That sort of thing?'

Rawlins nodded lightly; he accepted he had gone too big too early. 'OK then . . . the cancellation of national debt.'

'And who exactly is going to forgive billions of dollars for four lives?'

Rawlins spent a lot of time weighing the cost of a life against national security, but had little idea of the hard cash equivalent. Judging by a report he had recently read on human trafficking, he felt confident it was not billions. He coughed to signal a change of tack.

'The second category of terrorism is simple, it's about making money. Let me repeat: these demands don't fit together. It's as if they were made up by four different people.'

Michael leaned back and smiled. 'Maybe you're presuming a vision of a better world has to be about ends rather than means.'

But Rawlins had stopped paying attention. His last comment had taken his thoughts somewhere quite unexpected.

It's as if they were made up by four different people.

Figures by the Royal Mail on Wednesday night indicated over 17 million extra letters had been posted in the last three days, although not all had been delivered due to the extra workload placed on the postal system. The kidnappers put back the deadlines by a day to ease the pressure on Royal Mail employees.

Included within the 17 million were responses to thank you letters, as old friendships became rekindled. It was hard to decide which one person was most deserving of a thank you; many people must have sent multiple letters. Maybe 17 million people sent one letter. Maybe one million sent 17.

On Thursday evening a statement was released.

> Dear Britain,
>
> Your next letter should be an apology. What sorry did you overlook?
>
> Lots of love,
>
> The Foundation

'Ex-lover you wronged or boy at school you bullied?' said Charlie as he entered the office to find Michael pen in hand.

Panic rose from Michael's stomach. He hadn't considered the bullying angle. 'I discounted the wronged ex-lover approach. The two I behaved badly towards look younger and happier than me. I was a slippery stepping stone on the path to their future happiness.'

'I'm sorry to hear that.'

'Yeah, I wish I'd ruined their future just a little bit.'

'Indeed, my selfless leader. So who are you apologising to?' Charlie walked behind Michael, who quickly covered the letter with his hand.

'All right. I was just coming to see if you wanted to publicise what you're thankful and sorry for. I presume you're not interested, then?'

'Well, you know, not sure I want the wife finding out, do I?' said Michael with a grin, moving his eyebrows up and down. Which, in many ways, he didn't. Michael had composed two letters. The first one was to his sister, to whom he was apologising for having hidden behind work to avoid taking care of his dad during his final course of chemotherapy. The second letter was to a young lady by the name of Lucy Smalling, to whom he was apologising for not having yet sent the demand he had promised her, which he now belatedly enclosed.

Sometimes apologies are not made in time. In graveyards throughout Britain, envelopes lay on graves in zip lock bags. Some people wrote an apology letter to themselves; presumably they recognised the handwriting.

By Monday, the extra post in the system since Thursday had topped 25 million.

By Tuesday there was still no word from the kidnappers. An additional 4 million letters were posted before the kidnappers eventually released their next statement on Wednesday evening.

Dear Britain,

In the third letter you send you must tell a story. It can be fact or fiction, tragedy or comedy, history or fable, paragraph or novella. Our only request is that within its lines, you express something you believe to be true.

By tomorrow morning everyone who registered for the Museum of Regret will receive an email containing the home address of another contributor of regret, where you should send your story. For all the unregistered: flick through an address book, pick a page, close your eyes and select. Alternatively, use an online address book, guess a postcode, and let serendipity take its course. You have until Saturday.

The Foundation

Across the country, people awoke to receive the address of their private audience. Apologies were one thing, but parading your imagination to a stranger was a step too far. Many had not told a story for years.

Of course, not everybody struggled to tell a story. Many had just struggled to find an audience.

Something you know to be true.

In a short story, a ninety-year-old couple both died peacefully within a week of each other.

A riddle was sent that appeared to make no sense at all, presumably as a statement that there is no truth.

A science fiction novella detailed the apocalyptic battle between the Wherearetheys, a race who appeared to be nowhere, and the Theyareheres, a race who appeared to be everywhere.

A fictional story of the rise and fall of a vaudevillian singer in 1920s Louisiana spoke of the fleeting nature of success and time.

Thousands of original fairy tales were sent, with countless castles, princesses, evil stepmothers and physically (yet humorously) deformed humans.

Countless myths outlined the debatable truth of there being a good and an evil.

People took the opportunity to recount stories of their lives: of their parents, of their memories of youth, of their siblings, of meeting their partners, of their first home, holidays, children, illnesses and retirement.

Role-plays, sonnets and haikus were test-driven, violated and folded inside envelopes.

But most of all, people wrote about love: celebrating it, lamenting it, questioning and vilifying it, immortalising and memorialising it, pledging allegiance and renouncing it, swimming and drowning in it, making myth or science of it; people wrote about love.

Heather Bassett awoke on Saturday to find a letter on the doormat of her waterfront cottage in Salcombe. She had been expecting a correspondence, but as she picked up the envelope she noticed a stamp on the back that read 'Number 10 Downing Street'. Her mind flooded with possible explanations and she sat down excitedly with a cup of tea before opening it.

The Parable of Small Beginnings

There once were two men called Ted and Tom. They lived on opposite sides of a village and owned the belt of land that surrounded it. Imagine a Polo mint with a village in the middle. Each man owned an exact half of the mint. They were the richest, most important men in town.

Unfortunately, Ted and Tom disagreed about everything. The first quarrel was over where the boundary lay between their lands. They argued without resolution, and returned home bitter and righteous.

The conflict soon spiralled out of control. Ted liked white bread, so Tom liked brown. Marmalade or strawberry jam, lager or ale, latte or cappuccino: they were divided on everything. Their personal feud started to affect the locals: Tom sacked anyone he saw drinking a coffee with equal proportions of hot milk to foam.

Eventually, an elder visited them both and told them the village was going into exile. They could no longer tolerate being pawns in Ted and Tom's personal battles. The two of them were shocked by the threat and pleaded with the elder to mediate a solution over dinner.

After arguments about its location, time and furniture (would the table be round or rectangular?), they got on to the menu. It proved impossible to find a dish or beverage they could agree on. The village packed their bags.

'Do you like peanuts?' the elder asked as a last resort.

Of course they did. They were so small and social. It was the first thing they had agreed on in years. It would be a dinner of nuts.

They arrived and greeted each other frostily, sat down in silence and obliviously munched on the salted peanuts. They soon became thirsty. After finishing the bowl they became positively parched. But they had not agreed on a beverage. Panic ensued as their tongues withered in their mouths. What were they to do?

Ted came up with the idea of water. Tom found no fault. So they drank some together. The relief was tangible, and in the following moments before they put their guards back up, they admitted they had been diagnosed with liver trouble and were off lager and ale. As their bodies rehydrated, they basked in the unique sensation of problem solving.

They soon felt hungry, and the nuts were finished. Ted remembered he had white bread in the car. Tom remembered he had strawberry jam in his. They agreed to put the two together and see what would happen. Strawberry jam on white toast happened. They were shocked by the complementary nature of the flavours. They soon discovered that neither liked coffee and only drank it to look cosmopolitan.

Strange habits emerged: when one spoke, the other listened. They sometimes took turns. Tom confessed to encroaching on one side of the Polo-mint-shaped land belt, and Ted encroaching on the other. The villagers unpacked their bags.

And it all started with a peanut.

By Sunday, over 30 million extra letters had been sent since Wednesday.

Pragmatism with a Heart of Gold

Monday, June 29th

Lucy was sitting at her dining table staring at the post that had just arrived. In her hands was an envelope, her address handwritten in lush black ink. She was surprised to receive such a letter as she had lived her life without feeling overtly wronged by anyone; she was owed no obvious apology.

Dear Miss Smalling,

I am very sorry for my belated response. I have been unseasonably busy, and although I have often thought about your request, I never got round to putting it to paper. When we met, you asked me if I could send you what I would demand if I were the kidnappers. So . . .

'It's not the sexiest fucker, is it?' said Jordie after Miller read out Lucy's text, detailing the Prime Minister's demand. 'My ransom took people through the full emotional kama sutra, whereas this is a dose of dry missionary with your haggard partner.'

The expressions of the others seconded the sentiment if not the image.

'The thing is,' said Miller, 'this isn't really a ransom, it's more like a . . .'

'Policy,' said Richard. 'And it's not like a policy. It *is* a policy.' The others looked at him to elaborate. 'Look, as CEO I used to pay a lot of people for information, especially on government energy policy. A few months ago an aide at Number 10 said the PM had been pushing for a pilot like this for a while. I guess none of the Cabinet got behind it.'

'Maybe we should release it as part of the Foundation's manifesto,' said Miller.

Jordie laughed. 'Why not? Let's form a party. We'll make pledges detailing how we're going to ransom people over the next five years.'

Everyone except Liam laughed along.

'Are we actually planning to do something with this power?' said Liam. The others stared at him, confused by his proactive tone. 'How many of us believe climate change exists?' They all nodded. 'And who here had given up on stopping it?' The nodding continued.

'So . . . ?' said Liam in an annoyed voice. 'Are we going to pass up an opportunity to actually do something just because it's not sexy enough for Jordie?'

'How much?' said Miller.

'50 grand,' said Lucy.

Miller called Lucy to explain the week's plan, and in return found out that Lucy had just received a sizeable offer to pose in a men's magazine.

'I personally think it would aid our release. Rarely do you get such an opportunity to combine grief and soft porn so tastefully.'

'I'm pleased my A-list boyfriend is so protective.'

'You can be the Daisy to my Gatsby.'

There was silence on Lucy's end as she struggled with Miller's analogy. 'I kind of hope you've never read that book.'

'Ends badly, does it? So . . . sure you're OK with it? The PM will know you're in on it.'

Lucy took a moment to imply she was thinking, but had in reality made her decision long ago. 'Why not? I don't think he'll advertise the fact he sent a request to kidnappers through the girlfriend of a hostage.'

There was a brief silence.

'We release the statement on Wednesday morning. If you have second thoughts, let me know.'

Dear Britain,

The word community comes from the Latin 'cum' meaning together, and 'munos' meaning gift: together in gift. The best gift you can give your fellow man is a solution.

Michael's hands trembled as he read the page. He closed his eyes and went back over his meeting with Lucy Smalling. Stories once more were to blame: her literary analogies had disarmed him. He thought she was a fellow traveller, yet she was just another with vested interests. But why else would he have sent her the ransom unless he had some closeted hope of it being used?

For the next month we call upon the town of Royal Tunbridge Wells to provide such a gift that will inspire a nation.

He had chosen Tunbridge Wells – a wealthy spa town in Kent – as he loathed its MP, George Shadwell, who also happened to be a leading climate change sceptic. But he felt bad. It was viewed as a bastion of conservative 'Middle England': the stereotype of a place partial to a gripe and grumble, and, as such, an easy target.

To guarantee the safety of the three hostages, Tunbridge Wells must design, finance and implement an energy plan to become 100 per cent renewable. The first two stages must be completed in four weeks, with a clear timeline and safeguards for completion.

Our gift to you is a gift you will give the nation, which will be a gift to the world.

The Foundation

Michael ignored the list of missed calls, and turned his phone to silent as he curled into a protective ball.

'Of course we won't stand for it. There has to be a point where we draw a line and say we don't negotiate with terrorists,' came Shadwell's voice as he walked from house to car past the TV cameras. His tone made a global terrorist threat sound parochial, as if he had been asked to ban fruitcake from the fête. His tweed jacket seemed an attempt to incite the wrath of his critics further. Michael was struck by how unfeasibly square his head looked. He was in his mid-fifties, had tumbleweed eyebrows and cheek pigments that had jammed on light pink.

The idea of Shadwell, all bluster and self-righteousness, railing against the world, originally made Michael smile. However, the demand could only be met with his support, and Michael doubted Shadwell had the makings of a hero. Maybe it was best that Shadwell and Tunbridge Wells refused, ending events before they became even more dangerous for him.

Rawlins prided himself as a man with a nose for fishy things. He was not a climate sceptic per se, but had a healthy respect for those who demanded irrefutable proof. Hints of renewable energy were scattered around the kidnapping landscape and he felt that he was the only one willing to join the dots together.

He wrote on a pad the cast of the farce. The conspiracy undressed itself in front of his eyes.

For two days Michael failed to comment on the demand. This void was quickly filled. The pros and antis traded increasingly hysterical arguments. The world's press descended to observe the harsh realities of suburban terrorism, as once peaceful communities became splintered over parking spaces. Camps to house the busloads of incoming activists were relocated by residents determined to protect the pristine town parks.

Shadwell rallied to protect Tunbridge's and, as he saw it, England's way of life. 'The terrorists don't like our freedom,' he said, to the bemusement of activists who had been angrily kicked off the grass. The oil lobby decided Shadwell was doing a better job than they ever could and put their PR teams behind him.

Michael himself felt under siege. Energy lobbyists lurked everywhere: Michael drily asked security to do a sweep of his sock drawer. His office fielded call after call from people unused to losing, powerful figures who could see how a successful pilot in Tunbridge could change the game: *you don't understand the consequences*; Ted Monroe called asking him to *think about national security*.

If industry was anxious, Michael was more so. He had lost his nerve, growing paranoid that his every move was being watched. When Charlie had commented how uncannily similar the demand was to his own ignored policy, he suspected Charlie had an inkling, but now was no time for confessions. Charlie was loyal, but he couldn't risk being the champion. Someone else would have to rein in the chaos.

'I'm here to tell them,' came Shadwell's voice from the TV,

'that we're not dependent on you. This country will wean itself off your demands. The price you're asking us to pay is too high.'

For a moment, Michael was uncertain if Shadwell was talking about the terrorists or the oil industry. And with the momentary confusion came an idea.

Rawlins marched down the corridor, a sense of purpose rising with each footstep. He nodded to the suited man, who adjusted his earpiece as he opened the door. The room was windowless and lit by a phosphorescent light.

'What . . . what is this place?' said the young man, sitting at the small table in the middle of the room.

Rawlins looked at his notes as he took the seat opposite. 'I'm sorry about the ambience. It was the only available room. So, tell me more about your dealings with Mr Pounder.'

Si looked like a man who felt that whatever answer he gave would be the wrong one.

'He . . . he came to me. It was arranged through a friend of his I'd dealt with before.'

'And what did he say he wanted to get out of your meeting?' Rawlins struggled to hide from his voice the sinister destination he hoped the answers would lead to.

'I think . . . yeah . . . he said he wanted to get into *Time*, that he wanted a stage again. Like he loved the power and wanted to get it back.'

Rawlins nodded and smiled in an attempt to put Si at ease. 'Yes. Yes. How interesting. And can you tell me why he decided on a solar energy project in Cairo?'

'Er . . .' Si looked at the ceiling to buy some time as he chose his words carefully: he didn't want to incriminate himself in an investigation with such sinister lighting. 'I believe he said something along the lines of screwing over the oil industry as much as possible.'

'So to get this straight, Richard Pounder went to Cairo to deliver a project that would screw over the oil industry and give him publicity and power.'

Rawlins stared intensely at Si, who slowly nodded his head.

'Don't think you can just waltz in here and dictate to us,' said Shadwell after Michael and Charlie had taken seats in a conference room in Tunbridge Wells Council Office. 'My people won't be ordered about by London.' It all came out a little William Wallace: Michael hid his smile at the thought of this being the opportunity Tunbridge Wells had always craved for secession.

'George,' said Michael, 'I have nothing to sell, and your electorate aren't consumers, but citizens.' Shadwell continued to stride nervously in front of the long elliptical table. Three local councillors took seats in the bright third-floor room, but looked overwhelmed at sharing the room with the Prime Minister. Silent secessionists.

'Then why are you here?' said Shadwell.

'Apparently I'm the leader of the country.' He said it more with resignation than irony. 'Look, I'm sorry you and your town have been picked on. I am. But here we are. So why don't we try to make the best of it.'

Shadwell stopped pacing and stared at Michael. 'The best of it?' he said, exasperated. 'I don't think you've understood our position. We refuse to be blackmailed!'

'Of course. Of course,' said Michael thoughtfully. 'You know, I had the same predicament not that long ago. I hated it. But then I thought, do I really want to be responsible for the death of innocent people simply because of a principle?'

Michael locked Shadwell's gaze. 'Do you want to be responsible for killing three people?'

Shadwell looked at Michael. 'I won't be. The kidnappers will. I'm not doing the killing. I'm sticking to a principle on behalf of my constituents.'

Michael smiled. 'Well . . . I mean . . . you could be held personally responsible.'

Shadwell pulled out a seat opposite Michael and leaned forward. 'Don't threaten me.'

'I would do no such thing. All I would say is that your principle is your own, and a large number of your constituents won't feel the same way. If the hostages do get killed they won't think twice about blaming it all on you. It's the unfortunate plight of the politician.'

Shadwell eyed him up.

'So do you want to be a murderer, or a hero?' said Michael.

Shadwell mumbled a response, embarrassed at the choice offered.

'Of course, you're a man of principle. So we have to find a way of you becoming a hero while maintaining them.'

'I . . . I'm not sure I understand, Prime Minister.'

Michael stood up and found a marker pen. 'I'm saying maybe we should be blackmailed in the name of something more inclusive.'

Shadwell stared back at him, speechless.

'The trick with leading is you have to tell stories everyone can see themselves in.' Michael scrubbed the whiteboard at the front of the conference room clean of acronyms and numbers, and wrote the words *exposition*, *rising action*, *climax*, *resolution* along the top of the board. 'At the moment you won't take up the challenge because you disagree with climate change?' He looked back at Shadwell, who nodded slowly. 'So maybe we can find a way to fulfil the demand without talking about it.' He turned back to his writing on the board.

Underneath 'exposition' he wrote: *terrorists demand town radically changes*; under 'rising action' he wrote: *population rise up against demand and idea of change*; he left the space under 'climax' blank; under the final column 'resolution' he wrote: *town becomes most progressive in world, cheap reliable energy, secures national energy independence, helps end majority of global war*.

'You against the ending?' Michael said as he turned around to Shadwell, who pursed his lips. 'So . . .' Michael said, looking at the board. 'Looks like we need a climax that will get us to our resolution. Any ideas?' He looked at Shadwell and the councillors, who stared at him in astonishment.

'How about this?' said Michael, who wrote under 'resolution': *local councillors and MP save the day by telling a different story*, and then in big letters with a circle around it, he wrote the word *heroes*.

They walked out of the council building together and were greeted by the hordes of national and international media who were gathered outside. They stopped at the top of the four steps. Shadwell stepped forward to the microphone.

'Last year thousands of elderly froze to death, not because of climate change, but because they couldn't afford heating. The prices are hiked by cartels, oligopolies and despots in countries ruled by chaos and uncertainty. How have we let our civilisation become dependent on something we have no control of? Why do we remain addicted to something so finite and short-term?

'So today I told the Prime Minister that I want my country's independence back. I believe that if we are able to secure cheap, safe, reliable, infinite energy, it is our duty to do so. And while we might feel picked on, we must try to see it as an opportunity to lead the world. It could have been anywhere, but it has to start somewhere.'

'We're living in a basement while Britain is jacking off to these guys. Where's the justice in that?' said Jordie.

'You've blackmailed a country for two months, you're sipping fresh mango juice and eating chicken shashlik. Anne Frank you are not,' said Richard.

'All I'm saying is we're not going to be down here for ever. Maybe Lucy should enquire about vacant ministerial posts or give details for our Swiss bank accounts. We could get our own show, say a hostage sitcom. But we can't pretend this is a viable retirement option.'

The population of Tunbridge Wells took their time adjusting to their MP's new role as visionary. Secession had been swapped for partnership – right-wing hardliners one day, icons for global progress the next. Now they were overrun by renewable energy companies fighting for a place in the greatest shop window on the planet.

'John,' said Rawlins as he looked up from his notes. 'I can call you John, right?'

Fairweather nodded. Interrogation rooms are no place for bow ties.

'Please. Excuse our surroundings. There was a mix-up with our room booking.' Rawlins rested his hands on the table to symbolise honesty. 'I just have a few questions. You can leave whenever you want.'

Fairweather nodded gravely.

'So I'm just wondering where all the funding for the projects Mr Carey and Mr Macpherson were working on came from?'

'You know the trip to Cairo was paid for by Pounder,' said Fairweather, who continued to eye the room with suspicion.

Rawlins attempted a smile. 'Of course. But I heard it was part of some wider funding.'

Fairweather looked at Rawlins, unsure what he was getting at. 'We've been working with a rich Norwegian foundation called Nynorsk Solar. They took a liking to Miller and Jordie's work. They have a vision of being the world leaders in local renewable energy grids.'

'And if these projects in Cairo and India went well it could involve some big contracts for you?'

'I beg your pardon?'

'I'm merely pointing out that the Norwegians planned to be the world leaders in the field, you were to be their sidekicks, and we currently have a ransom involving some of your employees that could see such systems being in great demand.'

Fairweather's eyes narrowed in a way he usually reserved for IMF staff. 'I've worked my whole life to eradicate poverty, quite often in places where this government's foreign policy has exacerbated it. We work with people who can't read or pay electricity bills. We have an office of 55 people. Taking over a country's energy is slightly beyond our means.'

Rawlins laughed with his imaginary interrogation partner. 'You sound a little defensive, John.'

'And I've decided I want to leave,' said Fairweather, getting up from his seat.

Anxieties about wind turbines didn't evaporate overnight. Evidence of their adverse effects on health, panoramas and house prices were held up in town halls like a bill of rights. Shadwell had had a reputation for taking a Shakespearean turn whenever he quoted low-frequency decibel levels statistics for 17-metre turbines.

But that was the old Shadwell.

Opponents found it harder to work themselves up when it was no longer a liberal or environmentalist on the other side. Shadwell didn't plead on behalf of Mother Nature, or the future of their grandchildren, or make an appeal to ethics. There was no scale in which one side was more moral than the other.

Instead he spoke of national security, of foreign policy, of energy independence, of training, of jobs. No one could argue with his concern for growth and low inflation, even if it was clear he had no real idea what these abstract concepts meant; no one else did either.

'But wind turbines spoil the natural landscape,' came a final complaint.

'You don't seem to argue too much about the completely "natural" man-made farmland, or hedges, or coppice woodland. I hear no complaints about the roads, or church spires, electricity pylons, or telegraph wires. It's the new you have a problem with, not the unnatural.'

'I'm sorry,' Rawlins said as he sat down, 'the room I'd originally booked is being painted.'

Barrett forced a smile without humour. 'I have to compliment your subtlety. Someone more sceptical might think you're trying to intimidate me.'

Rawlins smiled. 'I can't imagine why you'd think I want to intimidate you.' He tickled the wings of his moustache. 'So why did the kidnappers come to you first?'

Barrett had barely slept in three weeks. 'What do you mean "why?". I'm Liam's boss. I presume they thought I'd have a greater incentive to keep him alive.'

Rawlins pouted his lips. 'Hmm. Maybe.'

'I'm sorry,' said Barrett incredulously, 'maybe?'

Rawlins shrugged. 'Four Brits kidnapped. I'm pretty sure every newspaper would publish that on the front page, don't you think?' He picked up his notes in a way that made the question rhetorical. 'I also notice you used the phrase "I'm Liam's boss." A pretty strange present tense given the circumstances.'

Barrett looked at Rawlins with disgust. 'You absolute shit. Do you know what I've been through the last two weeks? Do you have any fucking idea? And here you are using semantics as your line of questioning.'

Rawlins shrugged as if taking the notes of an experiment. 'You were also the first, and only, newspaper to pick up on the fact that Miller had a girlfriend.'

'So give me the Pulitzer.'

'I just find it interesting. A man more sceptical than me might get the impression you're the kidnappers' mouthpiece.' Rawlins sat back.

Barrett closed her eyes and held her silence.

'It seems a little strange to send a journalist who through your newspaper had recently been threatened by a terrorist organisation, on his own, to a place he doesn't know, to track down another group of terrorists. It seems like you must have had an . . . um, how do I say it? Ulterior motive?'

'Fuck you.'

Rawlins smiled. 'So why did you send him?'

The anger on Barrett's face subsided to a look of pained tenderness. 'I . . . I'm not sure any more.'

'Can I put that down as an "I don't know"?'

Barrett gave him a look of pure hatred.

'I'll take that as a "yes". So finally: you're the editor of a liberal paper that educates its readers heavily on climate change, am I right?'

Barrett stared back, saying nothing.

'Would it be fair to say you'd be heavily supportive of a policy that showed Britain could free itself of fossil fuels?'

Barrett shrugged.

'My question is, quite how far would you go to make it happen?'

It was the start of week three of the ransom. Since Michael's visit to Tunbridge Wells, Shadwell had taken over the initiative and claimed it as his own.

And things were going well. Such dissent as remained was soon swept away by a wave of irresistible inducements as companies donated their highest efficiency appliances in a once-in-a-generation marketing campaign. This was even before residents had been made aware of the slashed energy bills they could expect in the future.

Since Jordie had drawn attention to the unsustainable nature of the foursome's current living arrangements, the future had begun to weigh heavily on their minds.

They took it in turns to leave the basement for walks around Cairo in disguise. Their disillusion with humanity seemed to have eased. Their walks lengthened. Jordie spent hours walking through the Old City, Miller walked to Giza, Richard explored downtown, and Liam went to Tahrir Square. The embers of their old interests in the world were starting to glow again.

Foreign groups started to call for their own benevolent terrorists. 'We demand that you demand what we would demand of ourselves,' cried a protest in the US. Copycat terrorists emerged. In Spain a group called for a higher tax rate for the wealthy, in the Czech Republic there were demands for a renewal in traditional arts, and in Canada a spoof group demanded something interesting happen.

'I am no hero,' said Shadwell. 'However, sometimes it takes someone to tell a more inclusive story, where everyone has a stake in the future.'

The masterplan had been agreed ahead of the deadline. While the financing wasn't fully complete, bid documents had been lodged and the hope was that this would satisfy the terrorists. The estimated completion date was June the following year.

No one had mentioned climate change in three weeks.

Up and down the country, MPs at their weekly clinics faced angry constituents demanding similar initiatives: why should Tunbridge Wells, already rich, get all the benefits?

Rawlins felt he was on the brink of uncovering a great conspiracy. He could taste immortality.

Five ransoms: the first four soften everybody up, the fifth the pay-off: the commercial motive that brought the unlikely cast together.

He flicked through a file of tender documents for the solar component at Tunbridge. A star was scribbled on top of one of the pages, signalling the committee's preferred option. It was Nynorsk Solar: a Norwegian foundation with a wealth of experience in Europe, North Africa and India.

Rawlins rocked back in his chair with the satisfaction of a man who had successfully filled in the last number on a Sudoku grid.

Acts of Guerrilla Kindness

Monday, July 27th

The Foundation released a statement applauding Tunbridge Wells, and Richard decided he needed some air. Disguised, he left the building to spend his walk daydreaming about a return to Britain, the opportunity of a new life, free of the corporate world he once inhabited. He looked up, exhilarated by the sun on his face, failing to notice a cart pull out in front of him. Richard fell forward, his weight tipping up the cart on two wheels and emptying its cargo of mangoes on to the road, knocking his sunglasses off as he landed.

As he got up, the mango seller approached, yelling and pointing his finger at him. A crowd started to gather, intrigued by his appearance. 'I'm sorry, I don't speak . . .' Richard instinctively blurted out. He stopped too late – his English had been overheard. In panic, he turned, pushed his way through the crowd and ran off.

On Tuesday, Michael met with Greenham to explore a way of gaining cross-party support for new banking reforms. They made a pact: they would work together in private without distractions and see what was possible. There would be no public announcements, attacks or politicking against each other.

Michael suspected this wouldn't last long.

By night he played through scenarios where his involvement might be exposed. But that would require catching the kidnappers, and no one had much motivation to do that.

Richard sat on the sofa holding an ice pack against his knee.

'I've seen eunuchs with larger swellings,' said Jordie.

Richard responded by throwing an ice cube in his direction.

'All I'm saying is, after your show of physical frailty out there, it might be best to accentuate the bruising. Cover up the pampering in case we get caught. I'm happy to help out,' said Jordie, punching his palm.

Richard had got back an hour earlier. After fleeing the mangoes, he had walked around the quiet back streets with his head down, checking he wasn't being followed, then returned from the opposite direction. The others had laughed it off, but all privately calculated the damage. Their faces had been broadcast around the world, and they doubted a beard and robes would protect his anonymity under scrutiny from a crowd.

'If anything,' said Aiya, 'this should provide a little urgency to the brainstorm.'

On Monday afternoon, Lucy received a call from a tabloid journalist.

'Miss Smalling, I was hoping to get a comment from you on a story we're running tomorrow. A number of sources are saying that you and Miller Carey have never been lovers.'

Lucy's hand started shaking as she held the phone to her ear. 'Wh . . . why are you doing this?'

'Miss Smalling, the kidnapping of Mr Carey has transfixed the country. I'm interested in why a friend of Mr Carey is pretending to be his devastated girlfriend.'

'How dare you. Do you journalists have no shame?' said Lucy.

'Can I ask you a question, Miss Smalling? Does Mr Carey have any distinguishing marks on his body? Marks, say, that only a lover would know about?'

The Foundation cheered as Miller stood up to receive the acclaim.

'I've actually given this a bit of thought.'

Boos rang out around the room. Richard and Liam threw the remaining ice cubes at him. 'Being prepared is against everything this foundation stands for,' said Richard.

'People have been kidnapped for less,' said Aiya.

'Throw him to a gaggle of English teenage girls,' said Liam.

'Sell his organs,' said Jordie. 'Seriously, how much could we get on eBay for his heart? Or his sperm? Shit, that business model's sustainable. I've got a good seller's history and everything. We could sell it as the semen equivalent of veal: young, locked in a room, never seen sunlight.'

'As opposed to all the other sperm out there. Any chance we could return to Miller saving the day?' said Richard.

Miller smiled and sat back down on the sofa. 'At uni I never gave to charity or volunteered because I was studying development and reasoned I'd be dedicating my life to helping others. I always said I'd do more when I had more time, or I made more money, but, well . . . The only good things I do for people are things I'm contracted for, and even those are abstract and confused. Then I look at the majority of good turns people do for each other. From presents, to charity events, or sponsored fun runs – there's always some type of affirmation that your good deeds are being recognised by someone else.'

'Nothing wrong with a thank you. I read this story about a terrorist organisation that ransomed a whole nation to say thank you,' said Richard.

Miller smiled back. 'I don't mean it's a bad thing, but we compartmentalise the times we allow ourselves to do good things for each other. You know that fuzzy feeling when you give up your seat on the Tube for someone more in need of it?'

'Never done it,' said Liam.

'I tried once, but the pregnant woman thought I needed it more,' said Jordie.

Miller smiled and shook his head. 'Well, apart from the rest of those sitting hating you, it feels pretty good. My point is that people's minds aren't switched on to do randomly nice things for each other.'

'And I thought mine was a bit soft,' said Jordie. 'Maybe we should ask everyone to give a stranger a really fucking good cuddle.'

As had become routine, they looked towards Jalila to summarise their conversations silently and point to a path forward.

'Mum thinks it's brilliant.' The other three men looked a little shocked. 'The world's full of wonder, yet we no longer recognise the magic that surrounds us.'

'Uh, yeah . . . exactly,' said Miller.

Lucy couldn't sleep. At five she walked to the newsagent, and waited for the papers to be delivered. To her relief she wasn't on the front page. Her hopes were dashed on page five, where under the headline THE MYSTERY OF MILLER'S FAKE GIRLFRIEND was a photo of her arriving at Downing Street.

The text was less robust than the headline, which in truth

was no more than unsubstantiated speculation. The comments below the online version of the article were less uncertain. 'Whore', 'Insensitive fame-crazed bitch' and a variety of shocking threats were posted by mid-morning.

And then the conspiracies started to appear.

'Have you seen the story today about the hostage's girlfriend?' said Charlie as he walked into Michael's office. 'It's saying they were never together.'

Michael looked up with alarmed interest. 'What do you mean never together?'

'As in she was pretending.'

'Why would she do that?' said Michael.

Charlie looked at Michael gravely. 'Some comments online are saying she's just the middle woman between you and the terrorists. Apparently you're the mastermind behind it all.'

Michael forced a smile. 'Imagine that.'

On Wednesday morning a story broke surrounding a postman who claimed that during the period of enforced letter writing he had delivered a letter to Miss Smalling bearing the stamp of 10 Downing Street.

It was Wednesday afternoon and Michael entered the COBRA meeting Rawlins had requested. He took a seat and invited Rawlins to speak.

'We've just received some promising intelligence from the Egyptians. On Monday there was a possible sighting of one of the hostages, Richard Pounder. Strangely, he was spotted in a market, disguised in Arabic dress. This has been confirmed by ten individuals, all of whom claim they heard the man speak English.'

'But that's ridiculous,' said Michael. 'Why would a hostage

be allowed to walk around?' Although he instinctively felt the rumour was true.

'Well, I know it sounds unlikely,' said Rawlins, 'but everything about this kidnap is strange.'

'That's your technical opinion. "Things are strange."'

'Yes,' said Rawlins with a hint of annoyance in his voice. 'The recent demand brought to my attention a host of irregularities that made me think our hostages might well be haggling for mangoes. In addition, there was the invitation to Downing Street of a hostage's girlfriend, who is now alleged to be a fake. Further to which, there are rumours that you sent her a letter . . .' Rawlins checked himself from following the insinuation through. 'Whatever the rights and wrongs of this, it's rumours that damage you, and if we don't sort this out quickly, well . . . That's my technical opinion. Sir.'

'So what? Someone thinks they've seen him, how does that help us?'

Rawlins had regained his composure. 'The sighting was in the same area where they first went missing. The police have since questioned people there, many of whom have confirmed seeing men dressed in white robes and sunglasses – 'like a disguise' – over the last few weeks.

'Now, if you look at the map . . .' Rawlins put a map of the Cairo neighbourhood on to the large screens. 'You will see the locations of the sightings.' There was a clear nucleus of dots in the streets surrounding where the hostages' driver had dropped them.

Michael struggled to keep up with events as he tried to work out the implications. 'So what are the police going to do now?'

'They've been joined by the army, and they've got eyes every-where: on the ground, on the roofs. They've set a perimeter cordon of five blocks around this area' – Rawlins showed its extent on the map – 'and they're stopping all vehicles going in and out.'

'And what if that doesn't work?' asked Michael.

'The army will flush them out.'

Michael got back to his office and paced around the room. His fate was now interwoven with that of the terrorists and hostages, if there was a difference any more. He called for Charlie.

'You rang?'

'I need a favour, but you need to keep it between you and me.'

'Is the body in the boot?' said Charlie.

'Oh no, I buried it myself. No, I need you to get me Miss Smalling's mobile number.'

'As someone who's paid to protect you from yourself, I wouldn't recommend that.'

'I just wanted to apologise for getting her involved in all this.'

'In all what?' said Charlie. 'Michael, no one believes in you as much as me, but I beg you to step back from the edge.'

Michael rubbed his face with his hands before looking at Charlie. His eyes spoke of deepening trouble. 'That's exactly what I'm trying to do.'

'Hello.'

'Miss Smalling?'

'Yes.'

'It's Michael.'

'Michael . . . Oh, right. Michael.'

'I was hoping you could come in for a chat.'

'I'm not sure that's a great idea.'

'Nor am I. But it's a better idea than you not coming in.'

Silence.

'Miss Smalling?'

'Look, I'm not sure I want to set myself up for more attention.'

'I repeat, it's a better idea than you not coming in.'

There was a pause. 'When?'

'Immediately.'

The Foundation had put the finishing touches to what they thought would be their final demand. They were currently arguing about whose ransom was best.

'Jog on, buddy. Mine was dynamite. If you're so confident, when we get back we organise a national poll,' said Jordie.

'If we're finished here, I'm going to head out for half an hour or so,' said Liam.

The others nodded distractedly as he left, while they continued to argue among themselves.

Miller's phone rang. He got up and walked over to the table where he had left it. 'Hey . . . what . . . yeah, Liam, why? . . . Oh shit.' Miller hung up.

'Aiya, you've to get Liam back in now.'

'Why not you?'

'Go and get him NOW.'

Aiya read Miller's panic and ran out the door. She came out on to the side lane and saw Liam at the end of it, deciding which way to turn down the main street. Aiya shouted his name three times. He turned around, motioning that he couldn't hear. She gestured frantically for him to come back. 'Run,' she shouted. 'Run.' He caught the urgency in her voice and sprinted towards the door, which Aiya quickly closed behind them.

A few seconds later, a man arrived at the junction of the lane, surveyed its emptiness, and reasoned that the suspicious figure he saw there must have continued further down the crowded street.

'He's safe.' Both Lucy and Michael sat back in their seats and let out a deep sigh of relief at the news of Liam's safe return.

'Well,' said Michael, 'I've never dug myself a hole *this* big before.'

They let Lucy's information sink in. With news that the Egyptian army would soon try to flush them out, waiting was no longer an option.

Jalila and Aiya were all too aware of Egypt's use of capital punishment. Miller was angry with himself for involving Lucy. Dreams of homecoming had turned to escape. The conceit of it all having been a game had disappeared.

Aiya would spend the next day on reconnaissance. They would need to know where the policemen were, and how thoroughly vehicles were being searched.

In the meantime, the show must go on.

Dear Britain,

We realise things cannot continue like this. We all have lives to lead. The next demand is simple.

Each week, starting on Monday, we ask you to commit one act of guerrilla kindness. Everyone in Britain must anonymously perform an act of generosity for a stranger, friend, or family member.

If you think you have been the recipient of such a gift, you must register the magic at www.guerrillaactsofkindness.org.

Be creative. Be subtle.

The Foundation

Even in battle, Rawlins had never felt responsibility weigh so heavily on his shoulders. An informant of his at Number 10 had just let him know the hostage's fake girlfriend had come in to see Michael immediately following the COBRA meeting. The PM's communication team denied the visit, while his informant had heard no reason for it. Rawlins could only think of one: and it was bigger than Watergate.

Aiya spent the following day walking the area. Some plain-clothes policemen were easier to spot than others: some leaned against walls smoking for hours, others found seats outside cafés. Some were on the rooftops. All vehicles with potential hiding places were searched at the roadblocks. Booths had been set up on the perimeter allowing female officers to check that those wearing a veil were indeed women.

They toyed with the idea of coming out on to the street claiming they had been released, but the police presence was such that it was impossible to get far enough away from the building without betraying the head office's location.

'So there's no way out?' said Richard.

'Well, gentlemen,' said Aiya, 'there was one type of vehicle that wasn't being checked properly.'

Thursday and Friday saw Britain getting acquainted with the premise of a guerrilla act of kindness.

Monday morning would see all those who had secretly dreamed of leaving gifts on people's doorsteps, or of paying the toll for the car behind, pushed into overtly living out their feel-good fantasies.

Others, however, drew attention to the fact that the kidnappers had urged subtlety. This school of covert generosity stressed the subliminal: declining the last loaf of bread at the bakery, having toast instead of cereal so housemates could enjoy the last of the milk, cleaning your friend's toilet floor during the house party. The goal of these acts was to protect others from knowing that a situation for kindness had even arisen.

In future years, the debate between the Overt and Covert Schools of guerrilla kindness developed. The Overt School happily conceded they had lost the debate, while the Covert School pretended there was never a divide in the first place.

After Friday's breakfast the Foundation took down the bunk beds, leaving an assortment of metal rods and bolts. Spare clothes were bundled into bin liners with bed linen, toiletries, phones and towels. The white robes were torn up and divided between the bags. Later that day, Aiya dumped the evidence by the large piles of rubbish that hung around the street outside.

Michael felt terrible. Despite visiting through Number 10's side entrance, rumours were circulating in the press of Lucy's most recent visit. He had only ever trusted Charlie in his office: it would be no surprise if one of his own aides were reporting to Rawlins. There was little he could do to help her now. The only relief either of them would get was with the safe return of the hostages.

He dreaded every phone call in case it was Rawlins announcing updates from Cairo.

On Saturday afternoon there was news.

'OK, I think we'll start,' said Rawlins after Michael had taken his place in the COBRA meeting room. 'When we spoke on Wednesday, the Egyptian authorities had eyes everywhere in this neighbourhood in Cairo.' A map came up on screen with the same red dots representing the possible sightings. 'Since then there's been one sighting of a person dressed in clothing that matches our description.' Rawlins pointed to a spot at the junction of the main street and a small lane blighted with piles of rubbish. 'However, they disappeared. That was the last lead, which indicates the kidnappers have caught wind of the search: probably a mole within the police.' Rawlins studied Michael's reaction.

'This intelligence is pushing credibility to its limit,' said Michael.

'It's almost as if you don't want to find them,' said Rawlins with a sly smile. 'From midnight tonight the neighbourhood will be shut down, no one in or out. Three thousand troops will search every building within the perimeter, top to bottom.' He looked at Michael. 'And no one's getting out.'

It was five thirty.

Jalila and Aiya had left to prepare food. The four men stared at the bare room. It was unrecognisable without the bunks. They were to make their bid for freedom the following day, and were searching the walls for any final lessons their captivity might offer.

Their sentimentality was dwarfed by their anxiety at what they were about to undertake. It was hard to believe that things would work out.

'On the plus side,' said Liam, 'most hostages planning an escape worry most about their captors.'

'On the downside, most aren't hunted by their rescuers,' said Richard.

Miller's phone rang. They exchanged glances; it was an unknown number.

'Hello,' Miller said. He listened to the caller silently for 15 seconds. 'OK . . . Thanks.' Miller looked at the other three.

'You better go get Jalila and Aiya.'

It was five past eleven. Jalila had disappeared to resolve a delay. At best they had an hour left, at worst – and this was where their minds were wandering – the army could have locked down the area already.

Jalila came back into the room and held up five fingers.

'Time to get your hands dirty, gentlemen,' said Aiya with a smile.

During the evening they had stapled bin liners and sacking to their clothes together with assorted rubbish. They were walking displays of crisp packets, fruit skins and water bottles. Their faces had been dirtied.

The four men lined up and looked at Aiya and Jalila. They broke into smiles.

'A life of legitimacy awaits,' said Richard.

'We've all got to come clean eventually,' said Aiya.

Richard nodded. 'Some more so than others.'

They fell into a comfortable silence.

Jordie looked at both of them. 'Thank you.'

Jalila returned his smile, nodded, and in a silky voice, weak with idle years, finally spoke. 'I have yet to tell you my regret.'

They looked at her with respect at the parting gift.

'I regret for years thinking the apocalypse would happen out there,' Jalila said, gesturing to the world outside, 'when actually it happens in here.' She pointed to her chest and gave a final smile before motioning them towards the door.

Aiya opened the front door and peered out into the darkness, the piles of rubbish gently illuminated by the light from the main street. A pair of headlights rounded the corner and a low-geared rumble echoed down the lane. Three figures slipped down from the cab, and started shovelling the loose rubbish into the back of the flat bed. Crates and bags were thrown on top as they worked their way towards the Foundation's entrance. Aiya checked on progress through a crack in the door.

The truck approached the main refuse pile outside the door. 'Ready?' said Aiya. She opened the door and gave a final glance up and down the lane. Just as she opened the door wide, a figure appeared at the end of the lane silhouetted against the main street. 'Stop,' she said, putting her arm across the doorway. The workmen met her anxious glances. The figure remained staring at the truck.

'What's wrong?' whispered Richard.

Jalila nodded at Aiya.

'Good luck, gentlemen,' said Aiya as she walked on to the street. She approached the watching figure. They remained in view for ten seconds before walking out of sight. Jalila gestured for the men to go. They ran to the truck. Miller and Liam helped Jordie pull up his own weight, then the other three joined him lying down in the back of the truck, to be covered by the bin bags of clothes and bed linen thrown on top of them. A workman winked at them as he distributed the bags evenly over their bodies. For the next ten minutes they felt the steady increase in weight bearing down on them from above. The smell was overpowering as bin juices soaked into their clothes.

They felt the truck drive off, turn a corner and change gear. They estimated the distance they had travelled, hoping they might have already been waved through the checkpoint. But after two minutes they felt the truck slow to a halt. Outside they could hear raised voices. Next, they felt an extra weight on top of them and the sound of forks being thrust into the rubbish above. They braced themselves against discovery, or, worse, impalement. But then, suddenly, the weight was gone. A couple of voices called, 'Yalla, Yalla,' and the truck pulled away.

*

Michael tried sleeping, but at 2am rose gently so as not to disturb his wife and made for the sitting room, where he switched on a news channel, watching distractedly.

His phone rang. 'Yes?'

'It's Rawlins,' came a voice heavy with disappointment. 'I've just had word from the Egyptians. They found nothing.'

Michael closed his eyes and breathed out heavily. His hand shook as he held the phone to his ear. 'Oh well,' he managed eventually.

'This is not the end. We will find them.'

'Let's hope so,' said Michael. 'Goodnight.'

The garbage truck continued its journey. It merged into Cairo's midnight traffic as it made its way south through the city limits. The engine noise made communication impossible. The intense, stinking claustrophobia filled them with panic and nausea in equal measure.

But they had escaped, and their minds drifted to the unknowns that awaited them. They had no idea how long they had been driving. At some point the truck turned off the highway and on to a road riddled with potholes. After a further five minutes, it juddered to a halt.

Spades worked noiselessly above them. The weight eased until the bin bags were lifted away to reveal a familiar face against a background of a starry night sky. The driver who had dropped them in a traffic jam three months earlier put a finger to his lips as he helped them up, smiled and shook their hands. 'Effect without cause,' he whispered.

They were led silently down a path that led to the banks of the Nile, where a sailing boat lay moored, bathed in moonlight. A figure approached them: a stooped elderly man, wearing a grin that each remembered from their pasts.

*

On Monday morning, all over the country, thousands of front doors were opened to reveal presents left on doorsteps.

Takeaway coffees were drunk that had been paid for by someone ahead in the queue.

Gifts were found on work desks: tickets to plays and football matches.

Buskers found £20 notes in their hats. Workers from stores, cafés and hotels invited the homeless to decide how they wished to spend the credit that had been left on their behalf.

Charity shops received donations that people wanted. Soup kitchens received boxes of supplies. TVs, guitars and laptops were left on the steps of youth centres.

Guerrilla acts were big and small. Struggling community centres, hospices, libraries and charities found their financial holes filled by unnamed philanthropists. Playground equipment was mended or replaced.

But the demand did not ask for a record of what was given, but what was received.

Silence filled the felucca's bows. The old man sat at the front, his back to his fellow passengers. The three workmen opened a bag with fresh clothes and threw a rope off the back of the felucca. They handed out soap and gestured for them to take turns being pulled in the boat's wake. Jordie took off his top, smiled at the others, and took an ungainly running jump that shook the boat as he entered the water. He seized the rope and leaned back, looking up at the clear night sky, the river in his ears. This brief idyll was broken as the other three impatiently jumped into the water, and huddled around him to find a space on the rope.

'Strange old day,' whispered Richard.

*

It was 3am and Lucy was at home, sitting on a sofa with her knees pulled up to her chin. She had tried watching TV, but for the last hour had settled on staring at the minute hand working its way around the clock on the mantelpiece, her mobile phone in her hand. The phone vibrated to signal the arrival of a text message.

'*I'm very sorry to inform you that the operation was unsuccessful in finding the hostages.*'

She closed her eyes, tears slowly running down her face.

They climbed back on to the boat, some more independently than others; two workmen grabbed Jordie under each armpit; Miller provided leverage from the water. 'You managed to smuggle four wanted men from under the noses of the army, but you didn't bring a ladder for the boat,' said Jordie in mock outrage. The workmen smiled, and handed them all long traditional shirts that fell to their ankles.

After a couple of hours, with the first hint of dawn, the boat docked at the riverbank. The old man finally left his place at the boat's bow.

'We are here,' the old man said.

'I'm sorry . . . where are we?' asked Liam.

The old man stayed silent as he walked past them.

Maybe the weekend allowed more time to plan and execute guerrilla acts. Maybe it granted a greater freedom to notice them. People started to appreciate the responsibility that lay upon them. The failure to recognise an act of generosity felt like a greater crime than not performing one.

On Monday morning the kidnappers applauded the effort, and hoped the following week would prove even more successful.

Week two saw a notable absence of cash injections into

bank accounts. Expensive gifts became scarce. In many ways, money was the easy way out.

Like Valentine's Day, anonymous cards, letters, Post-it notes and texts were received. But these did not speak of flames that burned in hearts and loins, but of the need to let the receiver know they were appreciated, loved, that they were inspiring, or beautiful, or brave. They wrote to let them know that everything was going to be OK.

Vicars arrived at churches to find flowers placed on every grave. Bouquets found their way on to the bedsides of sleeping hospital patients. Comedians and musicians were hired to perform at nursing homes.

Teachers found messages and chocolates on their desks.

Children posted artwork through random doors, signing off with the message: 'I made this for you.'

By midweek, a movement arose of people who wanted to present their gifts in person. They decided upon a code of ridiculous disguises to shield their identity. In workbags and purses lay fake beards, moustaches, wigs, glasses, eyeballs on springs, crazy hats, masks of every type, that would be put on at opportune moments throughout the day.

A million doors were held open.

Some realised they weren't living up to the example they would like to set. In week two, some smiled at everybody they met; others made pacts to say good morning to at least 25 people before the start of the working day.

They walked up a path that led through vegetation towards the edge of a small village. In the centre was a clearing, where an acacia towered over a fire's dying embers.

'First,' said the old man, 'you must sleep.'

*

By week three, uncertainties arose over what was an act of guerrilla kindness, and what was the world they had known before. How could they be sure? Smiles from pedestrians, jokes and conversations with strangers, buskers, street performers: they all started to feel like gifts, but were they? Car parking spaces and empty tables at restaurants all felt like potential acts of kindness.

People started noticing flowering plants in their front gardens. Had they always been there, or had they been planted or nurtured by someone else? Little details drew attention to themselves. People didn't know if they had previously taken them for granted, or whether they were newly delivered gifts: the clean streets, the trees rising from pavements, the flower boxes. They couldn't have just appeared, but how else could people explain them?

In week four, people questioned whether they could really have been this unobservant. How could they have become so blind to all these displays of beauty and happiness that surrounded them? Couples stared at each other, in awe of being loved for who they were. Friends marvelled at each other's capacities for empathy. Children thought about their indebtedness to parents and grandparents.

By week five the website had transcended the debate between overt and covert acts of guerrilla kindness, and instead saw lists of everything worthy of thanks. The source of the gift was no longer as important as its recognition. People gave thanks for their health and education. They looked at their homes and realised that despite their desire to better themselves, their position was still enviable in the eyes of billions around the world. They gave thanks for their ability to make themselves, and others, happy. They gave thanks for the people and things that gave their life meaning. They gave thanks for their skills, interests and potential.

They gave thanks for being able to see the best in everything if they chose to do so. They gave thanks for the fact that it was never too late to take advantage of everything they had been given.

The Serendipity Foundation made no further statements or demands.

PART FIVE

The Release

The Kingdom of How the World Should Be

The guests awoke around midday, and were given time to wash, eat and regain a little mental clarity. There was no rush: the best time to take a reputable walking tour was in the late afternoon. They started at the north of the village. They were shown inside stables, granaries and storerooms. They were invited in to see the work of carpenters and metal smiths; they witnessed strange instruments being strung, and drum skins being stretched; puppets were carved, clothed and animated. As they headed south down the only road, they entered huts where groups of children were being taught the various components of delivering a story that might just save the world.

They took a short break before being shown into more modern classrooms teaching IT, business, foreign languages, politics and law.

The sun started to set, and they entered a circular clearing, where a giant acacia stood over the embers of a fire that would soon be reignited. A middle-aged man invited them to take a seat and relax: Al-Shā'ir would join them shortly. The man read the confusion on their faces. 'The Poet,' he said with a smile, as if the translation solved the misunderstanding.

Which it did: without knowing it, they had been awaiting his arrival for years.

'I have a story to tell you that is, and is not so,' said Al-Shā'ir, his face gently lit by the fire. Jordie, Miller, Liam and Richard sat on rugs beside him.

'Once upon a time there was a land devoid of purpose. Things neither declined nor improved. Failure was unknown as no one could remember the last time anyone tried to do anything new. Sullen communities remained so without protest: things had always been so, and how could they change?

'However, in this land there was a king who dared to dream. His realm was known as the Kingdom of How the World Should Be. There were rumours this kingdom sought not only to tell stories about the world but also to imagine change within it.

'The king had a wife who was the most beautiful, intelligent and empathetic woman . . .' Al-Shā'ir paused and took a deep breath; a look of sorrow crossed his face before he smiled at his audience. 'When the king looked into her eyes he encountered something no man had ever experienced: in her eyes he saw possibilities. With her love he had the potential not just to be himself, but to be better.

'They had a daughter who took on the best attributes of both her parents.'

Jordie smiled at Al-Shā'ir from across the flames.

'At first the king's idea that things could improve confused his population: they had no reference to what this meant. So one day, he spent the kingdom's savings to provide food to his hungry population for a week. The population started to believe.

'The invention of the possible would change the world for ever.

'The myth of the kingdom held magical sway over the minds of the world's dreamers and visionaries. Among them arrived journalists, businessmen and development practitioners.'

The five men around the fire smiled at each other, before their gazes returned to the fire.

'It was a remarkable time. Harvests grew bigger; houses became more comfortable; a health system emerged.

'The king built an army, which struck terror into the hearts of other tyrannical kings; for this was not an army that marched visibly to your city's walls, with uniforms, banners and bugles. They arrived, one by one, dressed as citizens, armed only with an alternative to how things had always been. On street corners, cafés, taverns and inns, in squares and in hiding, the soldiers spoke of incredulous worlds where things – and thus, everything – could change for the better.

'As you can imagine, the despot kings were not best pleased. It was time to fight back. When fighting a change for the better, the obvious response was to change things for the worse. Crops were destroyed, houses burned: a reign of torture began. Secret police targeted those who harboured dreams of progress. The dungeons were filled with screams of hope that refused to die.'

Al-Shā'ir turned around to find a log and placed it carefully in the embers.

'But the tyrants became frustrated. While their torture apparatus kept them in power, what they craved was the absence of change, rather than opposing versions of it.

'One day, an adviser sought the ear of one of the tyrant kings. "Dear King," he said, "we have fought the wrong enemy."

'The tyrant king looked bemused. "What do you mean?" he said.

'"We thought our enemy was the idea of change. It is in my opinion, however, that our true enemy is that of the possible. It is this idea we need to destroy."

'"And how do you propose we do that?" said the tyrant king.

'The adviser laughed. "It is my greatest achievement yet. I have created the idea of the *impossible*."'

The four-man audience smiled.

'Before long the tyrant king's plan wrought its damage. The Army of How the World Should Be still inspired thousands to dream, but it took only a few years until they started to believe their dreams were unattainable. The tentacles of scepticism proved the greatest form of suppression the tyrant king had ever known.'

Al-Shā'ir gestured to a boy to refill their tea glasses.

Al-Shā'ir stared at the fire for a few moments. 'But this is not a story about the tyrant king, but about the King of How the World Should Be, and his daughter. The impossible affected him more than most. The more he tried to change, the more his visions were criticised. His court focused on abstract utopias rather than real change. The king slowly withdrew from the world, believing good could only survive if it was heavily fortified.

'Soon after, his wife died . . .' – Al-Shā'ir paused and took a couple of deep breaths – 'and with her his ability to imagine possibilities. The world no longer seemed worthy of his faith in it. The possible no longer contained any magic.

'The daughter, too, tragically lost her husband before her own daughter was born. This princess grew up to be the most precocious child the court had ever seen. If she had arrived a decade earlier, her grandfather would have celebrated her as a saviour. But now the king could see in her only futility.

'The king had been blind to how his disillusionment had

affected his own daughter. She had retained her belief in the world, but hidden it to appease her grieving father. Now she too had a child, she could no longer accept such denial. One day she found her father in the palace, looked into his eyes, and said, "I still believe in the world."

'The next day, she left the palace with her daughter. They left behind the luxury of the court, and departed through the gates dressed as peasants. They arrived in the City of Cynicism, a city whose people endured unceasing loneliness. They found a small building in a run-down part of town that had two rooms: one on the first floor, and one in the basement.

'The king retreated even further into his utopias. He would receive letters from his daughter inviting him to visit, but with each year his fear of the world that had robbed him of his wife and of his hope increased.

'The city disintegrated further. The acceptance of failure hardened hearts and silenced tongues. The Cult of the Impossible had destroyed every last sign of confidence. The last optimistic voice had been ridiculed into silence with the taunt that it did not understand the real world, that it was sentimental and naïve.

'The king asked what she hoped to achieve.

'"It has never been about the destination, Father. Only the journey is important."'

Al-Shā'ir took a sip of tea and stared at the fire as if it were a portal to his past.

His audience thought it was a momentary pause, but a minute passed and it appeared his story had finished. Jordie and Liam looked at each other, confused.

'And?' said Liam. 'What happened next?'

Al-Shā'ir looked up at Liam, gave a light smile, and shrugged. 'The greatest battle in the world is not between good and evil, but between the idealist and the cynic, the optimist and the pessimist. For too long the king fought for good against evil. It was only as he grew old he realised that was never the battle. It was the princesses who fought alone in the battle to save the world.'

Crackles from the fire merged into the soundtrack of river and cicada.

'How did they do?' said Liam.

Al-Shā'ir once more lost himself in the flames. 'Sometimes the one who listens knows more of the story than the one who narrates.' He looked up and smiled. 'But I believe even the king, hidden in his palace as he was, heard of their courage, his heart overflowing with pride and regret.'

Smiles broke out over the faces of audience and storyteller alike: each of them was the king.

'Do you think the king will be with his princesses again?' asked Miller.

Al-Shā'ir nodded slowly. 'If they can forgive an old fool,' he said in a wavering voice.

Miller smiled as he looked at Al-Shā'ir. 'I think they'd like that.'

Open Returns

'Hello.'

'Larry, it's me.'

'Larry it's me who?'

'Wow, this phone call hasn't quite hit the emotional climax I imagined.'

'Is that . . . is that you, Richard?'

'Am I not sounding so recognisably narcissistic as before?'

'Man . . . Jesus. Where are you? How are you? What's happening?' Larry said with urgency.

'Calm down. Seriously, I'm fine. Being held captive for three months was more bearable than your haiku CD.'

'I hoped it might've helped you find God in 88 ways. Fear can keep you prisoner; haiku can set you free. Where are you? Tell me what I can do.'

'I'm fine. If this was the end of a bad drama, I'd say something like, "For the first time in my whole life, I'm truly free."'

'People say that stuff as they're about to die. It's the type of freedom only imminent death provides.'

'I hope it's not imminent.'

'Thank Christ. What can I do? Who can I get hold of?'

'Larry, you know I only come to you for special types of advice.'

'And what type of advice do you need now?'

'Nautical.'

'Nautical?'

'I thought it might be nice to sail on the ocean rather than destroy it. I heard from someone you were close to finishing a boat.'

'You have reliable sources.'

'I was wondering if you still needed a first mate.'

'Not so much. But I could do with a best mate.'

There was a brief pause.

'The boat's done. I was kind of hanging around in case I had to go to my friend's funeral.'

'That's nice of you.'

'I wasn't sure if anyone else would show up. We can leave when you get back.'

'I was hoping you might come pick me up.'

For five weeks, the male members of the Serendipity Foundation immersed themselves in the daily routine of the madrasa. By day they attended classes on delivery and repertoire. They learned how to turn a silence into poignancy, excitement and comedy; they found ways of accessing the stories that had lain within, and were given the confidence to showcase their vulnerability to an audience.

On the second evening they sat with Al-Shā'ir by the fire.

'It is said that hidden among us, a secret order lies in wait.' He smiled at his audience. 'It is entirely possible that one of them might have sought out your company for pleasure. They could be masquerading as your colleague, friend, or lover . . .'

Over the duration of the next five weeks, Al-Shā'ir initiated them into The Order. It seemed a purely fantastical tale: talk of Persian assassins, Arabian nights and sleeper storytellers spoke to their Orientalism, not to their experiences within the Serendipity Foundation. By the end of their fifth week, they were still unsure what they had to do with storytelling.

Al-Shā'ir nodded. 'Before you leave the madrasa, I have one final story to tell.

'Once upon a time there was the Kingdom of What Could Have Been. The kingdom lay in torment: its people lived a life haunted by their dreams. As they awaited sleep, their younger selves returned to berate them for having given up on their ambitions. Their young idealism felt betrayed by how their older selves had settled for mediocrity.

'Then one day, a coach carrying four of the kingdom's most noble minds got held up by a group of bandits. "We don't want your money, but your life," they told the travellers.

'The next day the kingdom received a statement by the bandits. "In return for the four men we have kidnapped, we demand that the younger selves who haunt each and every one of us at night, write what they demand of their older selves . . ."'

Al-Shā'ir remained silent for a few moments.

'In life, you can either tell a story worth telling, or you can be a story worth telling.'

They had agreed with Jalila and Aiya to stay in the madrasa for five weeks to let the final ransom run its course, but with those weeks at an end, the four of them focused on their return.

'I think for the first couple of months,' said Jordie as they sat around the fire late one evening, 'I'm just going to sleep around. Put it about a bit.'

The others burst out laughing.

'What? I don't think you guys understand how women love the whole damaged genius thing, even if you're 80 pounds overweight. They'll see straight through the fat and get stuck into the pain. "Who hurt you, Jordie, my love? Who hurt you?"' he said in a high-pitched voice as he stroked his face.

'You're not going back a superstar,' said Miller, 'but a hostage, who over three months in captivity managed to put on an extra ten pounds.'

Liam and Richard laughed.

'Richard,' said Jordie. 'You're with me on this one, right?'

Richard shrugged. 'I don't think I'm going straight back.'

Miller and Jordie looked at him, confused.

'I'm being picked up by a sailing boat in two weeks' time in Alexandria.'

Jordie shook his head. 'I mean like . . . fuck, Richard. You were going to be my wingman. You were also going to pick up my bar tab. Well, with Miller filling his boots with lusty teenagers, it looks like it's down to me and you,' he said, looking at Liam, 'to give the mature women what they want.'

Liam remained silent as he poked the end of a twig into the embers.

'Not you as well? Women love a second coming.'

Liam looked up and smiled. 'I was thinking of hanging around a bit longer here.'

'To do what?'

Liam shrugged, slightly embarrassed. 'I feel that my last book needs a bit of a rewrite, based on some first-hand experiences. This seems as good a place as any to write it. See whether I can rebrand myself as a writer of relevance.'

The others nodded.

Liam smiled, but quickly reverted to an introspective look. 'I suppose in some ways what we've done shows how it's possible to achieve the change you'd dreamed of. But what about the others who are fighting callous regimes? Are we saying they should do a bit of street performance, big picnics and an injection of good manners? In places that are massacring women and children, it seems ridiculous, and in many ways offensive. But then again, I look at all these people who've put their faith in international law and politics and been repeatedly let down. I'm not convinced that forcing enemies to share a communal meal is any less futile than a UN resolution. I guess I want a few weeks out here to work out where I stand.'

Jordie smiled. 'Modern futility does seem to be defined by a room of 10,000 bureaucrats all staring at screens and wearing headsets.'

'Thank God they hold the meetings in places I like holidaying in or else the lobbying would've been a nightmare,' said Richard. 'Copenhagen, Lisbon, Cancun, Durban. It's like a bucket list.'

'If the UN were serious about a climate change agreement,' continued Jordie, 'they'd hold the conference in Aberdeen and say no fucking off until an agreement has been reached. A threat of winter in Aberdeenshire focuses the mind like no other.'

They descended into a brief silence.

'What about you?' said Miller to Richard. 'What are you planning to do after your boat trip?'

'I'm a rich man who wants to do some good in the world. I should probably get involved in some philanthropy, right? You?'

'Development practitioner,' said Miller. 'I think I was doing the right thing in the wrong way. But before I forget, can you do me a favour?'

'Potentially.'

'I was hoping you might offer a large amount of money to

my organisation to convince them never to send me back to an Indian village.'

Richard shrugged. 'Sure. Not the first time I've had to pay to secure your future.'

There was a brief silence.

'You know what?' said Jordie. 'After a few months of debauchery, I was thinking about heading out to a poor neighbourhood in a poor city, and using renewable energy to transform the lives of people who live without cheap, reliable energy sources.'

The other three smiled.

'To do this,' he continued, 'I'll need an experienced development practitioner, a donor with a large pool of resources, some international coverage to help boost the visibility of the programme, and some local partners.'

They looked at each other as the improbable band of brothers they had become.

'I know a foundation in Cairo that may be interested in working with us,' said Miller.

At 2.30pm the next day, two men dressed in beige galabeyas entered the British Embassy in Cairo. They were dropped off by a taxi driver who had picked them up near a service station an hour south of Cairo. The two men would tell embassy employees how they had been blindfolded and driven around for two hours, before being thrown out of the back of the vehicle. Their two fellow hostages (including one whose execution had in fact been faked) had been released the day before, but had spoken of a desire to 'reflect on their experiences' before returning home. Their captors had treated them well.

The news that all the hostages had been released alive, and

that two were arriving imminently on British soil, received a mixed reception. No one outwardly expressed their disappointment at the end of the hostage crisis, yet there was sadness that the journey had come to an end. People were nervous how these characters giving interviews would influence their own memories of what they had experienced.

Michael heard the news through Charlie, who stormed into his office.

'The press are going to want a statement.'

Michael flicked a pen around his thumb with a newfound casualness. 'I don't think it's for me to say anything about it now.'

'Whether you like it or not, you're a major protagonist in this story. You have a responsibility not to let its ending slide.'

Michael smiled. 'Getting back to our narrative roots, I see.'

He went down on to the steps of Number 10 and gave a brief statement on his relief at the hostages' release.

'Prime Minister,' came a voice from the press. 'Do you feel sad that the ransoms are over? With an approval rating of over 70 per cent, you must be nervous how you'll fare without the kidnappers' support.'

The press laughed, and for the first time in office, Michael laughed along with them. 'I guess there comes a time,' said Michael, 'when you've got to stop relying on others demanding the best from you, and start demanding it from yourself.'

Two members of the Foreign Office escorted Miller and Jordie off the plane. Before going home, they would have a debrief with figures from the Foreign Office, MI6 and the police, followed by a visit to Downing Street to meet the Prime Minister.

A room had been arranged at the airport where friends and family gathered to welcome them. Miller's parents ran towards him, and suffocated him with hugs and tears. Jordie's two sisters, whom he had not spoken to in years, approached him more calmly, but with an expression suggesting they would not allow such a hiatus to arise again.

As the initial excitement calmed, Miller saw Lucy hovering at the back of the room. He walked towards her, big grins fixed upon both their faces. 'Thank you,' said Miller, before holding Lucy in his arms. They rested their foreheads against each other.

'I suppose we're going to have to break the news,' said Lucy. 'You know . . . that we've decided to spend some time apart to see where our relationship stands.'

Miller smiled. 'I was thinking you could be the Hermione to my Ron.'

Lucy's smile spread, like a woman whose lover had returned from danger. Tears joined her laughter. 'You've finally nailed one.'

From across the room, Rawlins stared at Miller and Lucy's embrace. He was no expert in intimacy, but he struggled to convince himself such emotion could be faked. He felt guilty at doubting the motives of individuals who must have suffered greatly, but reasoned there was a fine line between a conspiracy and a coincidence.

The car entered Downing Street. A sea of flashes went off as Miller and Jordie made their way into Number 10. The Prime Minister's press secretary greeted them.

'We're scheduled to have a ten-minute meet and greet with various government figures in the Cabinet Office followed by a quick photo session. However, the Prime Minister has requested a quick private chat before then. If you'd follow me.' Charlie led them down the corridor to Michael's office and closed the door on his way out.

Michael stood up and walked towards them, hugging them both before he took a step back, smiling and nodding in silence.

'So . . .' Michael said. 'Your girlfriend seemed lovely.'

Miller smiled.

'I'm hoping I'll have less need to send her late night texts now you're back.'

Miller nodded, before fixing eye contact with Michael. 'Thank you.'

'What can I say? I'm a sucker for a request. Out of interest, where are the other two?'

'They've taken a little R and R,' said Jordie. 'We've endured a terrifying experience, don't you know?'

There was a knock at the door. 'One minute,' Charlie shouted through the door.

'Ah, before I forget,' said Michael, 'as requests between the three of us go, this seems quite reasonable.' He went to his desk, where he picked up an A4 picture of Miller with his shirt off on holiday: it looked as if it had been torn out of a magazine.

'You see, my daughter is fifteen, and has become slightly besotted with you. When she found out I was meeting you she begged me for your signature.' Michael's embarrassment was heightened by Jordie's fits of laughter.

Miller wore an awkward smile. 'I . . . er . . . can't see why not.' He followed Michael over to the desk.

'Do you have a pen?' said Miller.

'Oh . . . yes, of course,' said Michael as he reached into his shirt pocket and handed it to Miller.

Miller turned the pen around between his fingers, and as he did so, noticed a marking that twisted around its base. His expression gave away his mental calculations.

'What is it?' said Jordie, as Miller brought the pen closer to his eyes and turned it once more between his fingers.

Miller looked up at Jordie, before looking at Michael.

'It looks to me as if,' Miller said slowly, smiling at Michael, 'it's the insignia of a rababah.'

A Street Performance

It is ten in the morning on a street in Old Cairo. The sound of car horns fills the air. Traffic works have appeared without warning, and the workmen are struggling to provide a reasonable explanation.

A small crowd witnesses the spectacle at the blocked intersection, but they soon drift away. They remember the last time the street closed down, and decide instead to contact their friends and tell them the news.

A football match takes over the street, and cafés bring their tables outside for spectators. Toys magically appear and the screams of excited children fill the air.

At around two, a truck appears by the barrier and delivers a load of giant umbrellas, tables and chairs, which are set up on the street without any idea who ordered them. Food vendors appear with their grills and pans at four. At five, a band of musicians arrive and set up their instruments; an anonymous client has paid them in advance. By six, the sun is setting and there is electricity in the air.

By the time the musicians have stopped, the street is filled with hundreds of residents. Whole families are sitting enjoying refreshment; home-cooked delicacies are shared among strangers; groups of men have brought their board games on to the street. At seven, attention is drawn to a small platform, where a black screen stands four feet high. Two makeshift spotlights turn towards the stage.

An old man, a woman and a girl get up on stage. The females position themselves behind the black screen, and spend a moment organising some hidden objects. When they are ready, they nod at the elderly man, who is standing to the side. The smile he directs at them stretches from his forehead to his collarbone, and it is impossible to ignore the love etched into their faces as they smile back at him.

The man turns to face the audience.

'I have a story to tell that is and is not so.'

Thank yous

To Dad: collaborator, counsel, editor and mate. I would have given up on this book long ago without you.

To Mum: for being Home, and the endless support, belief and friendship that Home offers.

The Smit gang: Bruv, Schmitty, Dwards, Vic, Gran, Nic, Will, Lowen, Binky, Daisy, Opa and Gina for putting up with a #failednovelist.

To Grandpa for surrounding me with books, and then entrusting me with his.

To my Maldivian clan: Ibrahim, Jeedu and Hussein – this would not have been possible without you, nor would it have been possible without the wider family welcoming me so warmly into it.

And to all the Maldivians fighting for what I only have the bravery to allude to on the page.

This book ran over time and over budget: to all the hosts in all the countries who put me up as things turned desperate – in particular chez Eva, Ramsey, Pips, Alex, Saralee, Oli,Elen.

Thank you to all my extraordinary friends who offered distractions, encouragement and perspective.

Who said mates don't make great editors? Huge thank yous to those who endured the cringey first drafts: Furrukh, Elen, Pips, Oli, Sal, Siad, Aunt Jo, Gran, Eva, Ramsey, Nic, Barbz, Ellie.

To Joseph Dwyer, the original guerilla of kindness.

To Mike Petty for providing confidence where there was none.

To Marcus Brigstocke for blindly lending his credibility and substantial talents.

To those whose ideas have shaped this book, but should not be held responsible for it: in particular Richard Sandbrook, Tony Kendle, Nabs Hamdi and my dad.

To the Unbound team – in particular John Mitchinson for pulling my manuscript out of the slush, and Isobel Frankish for scrubbing it into shape.

A huge thank you to all of my Unbound pledgers and those who helped spread the word. As pledges arrived amidst the endless refreshes, your names appeared as gifts – which they will remain.

Supporters

Unbound is a new kind of publishing house. Our books are funded directly by readers. This was a very popular idea during the late eighteenth and early nineteenth centuries. Now we have revived it for the internet age. It allows authors to write the books they really want to write and readers to support the writing they would most like to see published.

The names listed below are of readers who have pledged their support and made this book happen. If you'd like to join them, visit: www.unbound.co.uk.

Tamara A
Ehab Abdulla
Andrea Abrahams
Gloria Abramoff
Arbi Ben Achour
Eva Adulla
Hussain Afeef
Aishath Hudha Ahmed
Fazna Ahmed
Khadeeja Ahmed

Nazee Ahmed
Isra Akhthar
Shahla Ali
Abdul Rahman Ali (Ralle)
Kath Allen
Yoosuf Anna
Paul Arman
Tim Arnaudy
Kannan Arunasalam
Michael Atkins
Amie Atkinson
Charles Attlee
James Aylett
Shruti Aythora
Jason Ballinger
Ant Barrett
Jenny Bates
Adam Beaumont
Sinclair Beecham
Julie Ben-Achour
Ramsey Ben-Achour
Sophia Ben-Achour
Edward Benthall
Heddie Bienstman
Hiske Bienstman
Rose Biggin
Roger Blunden

Daniel Bosley
Richard W H Bray
Sherry Brennan
Emma Bridgewater
Glenn & Aisky Briggs
Suzanne Brindley
Oliver Broadhead
Ramon Olaf Broers
Simone Brooke
Jason Brooks
Liam Brosnan
Nick Buckland
James Bulley
Jonathan Bullock
Kate Bulpitt
Joseph Burne
Ali Burns
Michelle Burton
Andrew Campling
Sofia Casas
Harriet Cavanagh
Kumud Chandra
Robert Chatwin
Amanda Chesterfield
Lowen Chesterfield
Will Chesterfield
Bill Cole

Dominic Cole
Will Coleman
Martin Colledge
Victoria Collins
Keir Cooper
Isabel Costello
Amber Cotgreave
Jess Curtis
Charlie Dawson
Sally de Courcy
Sarah de Courcy
Michelle de Villiers
Elin de Zoete
John Dean
Ryan Dehmer
Daisy Demirag
Les Dennis
Peter Desmond
Sidath Dharmapala
Ali Didi
Farah Didi
Mie Ali Didi
Sarah Dilnot
Ashley Dobbs
Rosemary Dolman
Judith Donovan
Adam & Tania Dorrien-Smith

Marina & Tristan Dorrien-Smith
Robert & Lucy Dorrien-Smith
Michael Dorrien-Smith & Issy Monson
Conor Doyle
Mareta Doyle
Tom Doyle
Robert Eardley
David Edmondson
Mark Edwards
George Elworthy
Phoebe Emond
Jakob Engel
Nae English
Elen Evans
Eyan & ND
Ishva Fairooz
Umar Fairooz
Ushva Fairooz
Sarin Family
Neville Farrington
Peter Faulkner
George Ferguson
Colin Forrest-Charde
Tom Ngui Min Fui
Jo Gale
Hilary Gallo
Guy Garfit

Shahi Ghani
Kathy Gilfillan
Ed Gillespie
Kush Goonetilleke
Clare Gordon
Gus Grand
Granny and Grandpa
Heather Grant
Rebecca Gregson
Viv Guinness
William Hackett-Jones
Faathina Abdul Hakeem
Nabeel Hamdi
Parasto Hamed
Ronald Hampel
Chad Hamre
Robin Hanbury-Tenison
David Harland
Daniel Harris
Emma Harrison CBE
Jesse Hartigan
Graham Harvey
Andrew Hearse
Marieke Heijnen
Will Henley
Chlöe Herington
Melinda Herron & Gurleen Hans

Alex Hill
Hamish Hill
Jo Hill
Sue Hill
Chris Hines
Paul Holmes
Ibrahim Hood
Phil Houston
Saralee Howard
Raoul Humphreys
Jeff Hutner
Lewis 'Like a Boss' Ibrahim
Sarah Ibrahim
Yaman Ibrahim
Hanna Caroline Imig
Mo Imms
Sioban Imms
Johari Ismail
Munira Ismail
J.S.M
Caroline Jackson
Yasra Jaleel
Yusry Jaleel
Anna James
Daphne Jayasinghe and Chris Crowe
Pippa Johnson
The Johnson Family

Morag Jones
Ellen Joyce
Kaafa
Janine Kelk
Hilary Kemp
Val Kemp
Peter Kirby
John Kjellberg
Knut Landsverk
Mike Large
Jimmy Leach
Sonia Leach
Geoffrey Lean
Nicholas Lee
Susan Leech
Brian Leonard
Grant Leslie
Charlotte Linne
Amal Lockwood
Zahira Lough
Alistair Love
Rob Love
Francesca Luke
Brian Lunn
Maama
Guy Macpherson-Grant
Keith Mantell

Sally Anne March
Nathalie Margi and Joseph Dwyer
The Mathews Family
Malcolm McIntosh
Alex McKinlay
Stewart McKinlay
Bridget McNamara
Tim and Sue McPugh
Anna Meneer
Neil Merrett
Eva Meyer
Margrit Meyer
Michael and Anna
Colin Micklewright
Rebecca Mitchell-Tomkins
Takaaki Miura
Ahmed Mohamed
Aishath Mohamed
Hykal Mohamed
Iffy Mohamed
Mayan Mohamed
Rugiyya Mohamed
Thoyyib Mohamed
William Molesworth-St.Aubyn
Michael Moonesinghe
Hamza Moosa
Dashiel Munding

Aishath Rubeena Naseem
Edam Naseem
Emon Naseem
Ena Naseem
Hajja Naseem
Mohamed Naseem
Mohamed Nasheed
Meekail Nasym
Carlo Navato
Saf Nazeer
Ahmed Nazal Nazim
Billy Neal
Emma Newman
Chris Nicolson
Lindsay Noble
Aishath Noordeen
Hussein Noordeen
Ibrahim Noordeen
Sabra Noordeen
Umi noordeen
Aiminath Nuzuhath
John O'Brien
Ruth O'Brien
Mike O'Connor
Rodney O'Connor
Bart O'Donnell
Julia Ogilvy

Richard Oliphant of that Ilk
Helen Owers
Maria Padget
Aminath Panabokke
Nathalie Panabokke
Shenali Panabokke
James Craig Paterson
Tom Pearson
Alex Penfold
Adam Penman
Abigail Perrow
Dan Peters
John Petrie
Mike Petty
William Pickwell
Ben Pinsent
Chris and Mary Pinsent
Olga Polizzi
Michael Pollock
Max Potter
Lubu Rahman
Ricza Abdul Rahman
Rena Ramiez
Ahmed Rasheed
June Rasheed
Jess Ratty
Nico Raubenheimer

Nicholas Rees
Barbara Reichwein and Patrick Reyburn
Warren Reyburn
Furrukh Riaz
Anne Richards
Asher Rickayzen
Conor Riffle
Kylie Rixon
Andrew Roberts
Paul Roberts
Victoria Robinson
Sally Rogers
Chloe Rowley-Morris
Linda Rutenberg
Matthew Sabin
Mira Saidi
Louvain Sanders
Wendy Sandford
Nashida Sattar
Christian Savage
Ellie Mendez Sayer
Arthur Schiller
Bryher Scudamore
Karen Sellwood
Oliver Sellwood
Shamau Shareef
Shauna & Thoriq

Tara Elena Shifah
Eva Shivdasani
Sonashah Shivdasani
Ali Shiyam
Lara Ali Shiyam
Mahjoob Shujau
Rohan Silva
Jim and Jo Simpson
Andrew Singer
Anthea Smit
Bellamí Sennen Smit
Candy Smit
Daisy Smit
Edward Smit
Jan and Gina Smit
Nicole & Alex Smit
Vicky Smit
Michael Snaith
Ibrahim Mohamed Solih
Heather Speight
Martin Spencer-Whitton
Justin & Frances Spink
Peter Stafford
Martin Stead
Jason Stevens
Samuel Stocker
Aishath Suha

Maryam Suha & Jordy Ibrahim
Jessica Taplin
Jerry Tate
Matthew Thomson
Ryan Thoyyib
Bernard Toal
Jack Todd
Christopher Tomlinson
Stuart Trotter
Louise Tucker
Charlotte Turner
Paul Turner
Petia Tzanova
Karin Ulin
Afra van ‘t Land
Maarten van Doornmalen
Elizabeth Van Pelt
Nikki Vane + Mike Cornfield
Mark Vent
Janet Voyce
Akhthar Waheed
Rizma Waleed
Sue Walker
Ben Walton
Paul Warren
Joanna Webb
Deborah Weber

Charlie Webster
Ravin Weerawardena
Hannah Whelan
Ben Whitehouse
Russell Wickens
Sion Williams
Sally Wilson
Louise Wood
Tonya Wood
Emily Wootton
Colin and Rachel Wright
Glen Wright
Jenna Marie Wright
Weh Yeoh